A WARRIOR'S HEART

Christina Rich

Published by Forget Me Not Romances, a division of Winged Publications, previously published by Heartsong Presents as The Warrior's Vow

Copyright © 2019 by Christina Rich

All rights reserved. No part of this publication may be resold, reproduced, stored in a retrieval system, or transmitted in any form or by any means, electronic, mechanical, recording, or otherwise, without the prior written permission of the author. Piracy is illegal. Thank you for respecting the hard work of this author.

This is a work of fiction. All characters, names, dialogue, incidents, and places either are the product of the author's imagination or are used fictitiously. Any resemblance to actual events, locales, or people, living or dead, is entirely coincidental.

ISBN: 979-8-8689-8432-7

Chapter One

Judah
Circa 835 BC

The sound of horses' hooves thundered into camp. Abigail's pulse hammered in her chest at the commotion outside her tent. She tucked her hands into her sleeves and paced. Had the warrior priests who had attacked the palace and killed her mother found them?

"What is happening, Bilhah?"

Her cousin sat on a pile of furs, her knees drawn to her chest. Black kohl trailed down her cheeks. Abigail knelt in front of her and tried to imitate the strength she had seen her mother exude. "Bilhah, now is not the time for weakness. What if we must make haste?"

Soulless amber eyes stared at her. "There will be no mercy."

A chorused bellow startled Abigail, sending a tremor racing through her blood, until she realized what she'd heard had been a cheer of victory among her men. Uncertain of her new role as future queen, she forced a smile and rose. "Of course, there will be none. Jehoiada and the usurpers will pay for killing my mother." She inhaled a shaky breath. "And my brothers all those years ago."

Bilhah's brow furrowed as if she was confused. Many such looks had tainted her cousin's beautiful face since their flight from the palace and Jerusalem. She tilted her head and scanned Abigail from head to toe. "You misunderstand me, Abigail. The God of the priests, the God of our forefathers

Abraham, Isaac and Jacob, will not grant us mercy, not if we continue in our rebellion."

The hot desert wind rippled the canvas around them. Gooseflesh rose on Abigail's arms and she hugged herself to ward off the omen. She'd heard the servants speak of a god greater than the ones her mother had worshipped, but she'd yet to see him with her own eyes, as she'd seen the wooden and bronze statues in the courtyard outside the palace. "You've had a great shock, Bilhah. You do not know what you speak."

"If they did not spare your mother, the Queen of Judah, they will not spare us, Abigail." Bilhah's shoulders sagged as she pressed her face into her hands. Abigail swallowed her fear as the memory of the frantic cries of the servants assaulted her. It was the one time she had willingly crawled into the wooden chest in order to hide from the warrior priests.

It was no wonder the confident, alluring woman who prowled the palace at will crumpled into another round of sobs. The change in her cousin's behavior since the priests and temple guards had stormed the palace was disconcerting. Abigail was having a difficult time being cast from her home, too. However, if she hadn't been forced to abide by Captain Suph's demands, Abigail thought she might actually enjoy her freedom from the palace.

A dark shadow passed outside their tent and then pressed against the fabric. "Princess," Micah called from outside. "The captain requests your presence."

As if her nerves weren't already taut, now the captain requested her presence. He'd not been kind since their flight from Jerusalem and he'd always made her feel less than human, as if she were a stray dog begging for scraps. How could she make him understand she was his rightful queen, would be his queen once her throne was restored in Jerusalem, and as such deserved his respect?

Abigail dried her palms and pulled back the flap. "In a moment, Micah."

The young servant nodded and crossed his arms over his linen tunic; although no more than a child, he'd been one of her only constant companions for the past few years. One of the only people her mother had allowed to attend her. Abigail faced her cousin. "Once you've rested and I've taken my position as Queen of Judah, all will be well. You'll see." She took two steps, bent at the waist and started to press her lips against Bilhah's smooth head before halting. If she was to go on as her mother had, if she was to succeed as Queen of Judah, such comforting gestures would no longer be allowed. "Rest, while I see what Suph requires of me. And dry your eyes, Bilhah. Our people need you. You cannot perform in your current state."

She shook out her tunic and brushed a hand over the dust-infested tunic. With a trembling hand, she patted down her hair before slipping between the folds of her tent. She scanned the desert encampment, pleased that many of her mother's subjects had followed their exodus during the priests' attempt to take over Jerusalem. Soon, with Suph's help, she'd see them returned to their beloved city, where she would reward their faithfulness with a banquet to rival her great ancestor King Solomon. Of course, she'd have to gain Bilhah's help since she'd no idea how kings and queens dined.

"Come, Micah, let us see what Suph wants, shall we?" She smiled at the boy. His black orbs sparkled before his lashes dipped against his tanned cheekbones. She followed behind him, twisting and turning through the maze of tents that had been hastily erected after their flight from Jerusalem. The people lowered their heads as she passed as if she were already queen. Their actions humbled her. And disheartened her. Until a few days ago many knew not of her existence. Those who did had slighted her, not even treating her with the acknowledgment a servant receives.

Now they looked to her to lead them, to give them back Jerusalem, a task that seemed near impossible given she'd rarely been allowed outside her chambers.

Micah halted and Abigail stumbled into his back because she'd been preoccupied with how she was to lead these people as those who had done so before her.

Captain Suph turned toward her, the lines around his mouth firmed. His eyes remained cold, filled with hatred. She stopped herself from taking a step back, from fleeing to her tent, and allowed a smile to curve her lips. She would show him courage, lest he find her weak and incapable of ruling Judah.

"I have a gift for you, Abigail."

She tilted her chin and waited. Suph stepped aside, revealing a rather muscular man in nothing but a loincloth and a gem the color of amber hanging from a leather cord around his neck. She drew in a shallow breath and forced calm into her limbs. Her practiced reserve kept her from blushing at the man's near nakedness, kept her from flinching at the grotesque swelling of his face and the open cuts decorating the rest of his body. She knew her mother had been cruel at times, but had she been this vicious? Would the captain expect the same from her? Abigail hoped not.

"This is the brother of Ari, former Commander of the Temple Guard. This man's brother is responsible for placing that imposter on the throne, and I've no doubt our prisoner took part in the rebellion as well. He'll fetch a handsome price. Perhaps even the return of your throne, Abigail."

She stepped forward and bent closer. The scent of his wounds hung in the air. The whites of his eyes glowed from the bloodied mess of his face. "Is this true?"

The man's nostrils flared. His jaw clamped tight. Suph yanked his sword from his sheath and swung wide.

Anger surged through her blood, thundered in her heart. How dare the captain threaten a man who couldn't even stand on his own? "Enough."

Spears of fire sparked in Suph's gaze. "You cannot think—"

"You will not dictate the thoughts of your future queen. Is that understood?"

Suph's chest expanded as he squinted his eyes to mere slits. The lines creasing the corners of his eyes twitched in tandem with the tick of his jaw. "Yes, Your Majesty."

"Good. Now, clean his wounds. We cannot negotiate using a dead man."

She twisted on the balls of her feet. Holding her shoulders straight and head high like she'd seen her mother do, she walked toward her tent. She ducked inside, fell to her knees and retched into an earthen jug. A gentle hand smoothed back her hair. Bilhah knelt beside her.

"What is it, child?" She pressed a cup into her hand.

Abigail swiped the back of her hand over her mouth and gave a nervous laugh. "You call me 'child,' yet we are the same age, you and I."

Bilhah scooted back to the furs and sank against a mound of decorated pillows, her eyes downcast. "We are. Come, what has upset you?"

Abigail curled beside her. "Was my mother so cruel?"

Sadly, Abigail had witnessed a few floggings, and from the way the servants spoke, her mother took pleasure in the beatings. Abigail had also heard them speak of others losing their heads. A part of Abigail had believed it was only to cause her fear so that perhaps she'd behave.

Bilhah's fingers stopped toying with the furs. "You've been sheltered."

Abigail sat up and looked into Bilhah's eyes. "You did not answer my question."

"I do not wish to speak ill of the dead, even your mother."

Abigail laid her palm against Bilhah's cheek. "I've always known she was cruel to you." She ran her hand over Bilhah's shiny head. "Forcing you to serve her gods when you should have married well."

Bilhah shook her head. "I was your father's niece—with my father dead I was nothing more than a servant. At the time it seemed a high honor. Or so your mother convinced me."

Abigail laid her head against Bilhah's chest. "Thanks to Jehoiada we are all that's left. I would see him pay."

Her words sounded hollow as the image of the bloodied prisoner invaded her mind. Her stomach churned. If treating a man like a mangy dog was what it would take, she did not know if she'd have it in her.

"Perhaps, not all has been as it seems, Abigail."

She ruminated on that for a few moments. She was about to ask Bilhah what she meant, but the rhythm of her heartbeat against Abigail's ear slowed. Rising up on her elbow, Abigail gazed at her cousin, so young yet hardened by the life chosen for her. She sat up and tucked her knees beneath her chin.

Had she truly been sheltered, or had she been forgotten? Bilhah was not the only one who'd experienced her mother's cruelty. Although she would miss her mother, Abigail would not miss the viperous tongue reminding her she was weak like her father and not the beauty her mother had hoped for. Her arms were too long, her hips too thin. She was lanky and awkward. With her limp hair, her lack of golden hues, her green eyes, a curse from the gods....she hadn't needed to see the disgust in her mother's eyes to know her she was a disappointment. Aye, she may miss her mother a little, but she would not miss the way she flogged the servants for their inability to make Abigail presentable.

A breeze blew from beneath the tent, carrying with it Suph's raised voice. Abigail rubbed her arms and rose. She pulled back the flap and peered at the group of men surrounding the prisoner. They had moved the man near the center of camp. To do her bidding and cleanse his wounds, she supposed. She had been unable to tell what sort of man he was. A warrior, if his sculpted chest and arms were any indication. He was taller than the captain, even slouched beneath the burden of the yoke around his neck. The captain tossed water into the man's face, causing him to straighten somewhat. The captain, a handsome man when he genuinely smiled, paled in comparison even with the cuts and bruises marring the prisoner's body. Especially knowing the man had been cruelly treated by Suph.

It had been a rare moment when she stood up to Suph. She'd never spoken with such boldness in her life, but something about the beaten man called to her sense of compassion. She would not allow Suph to kill him.

And how was she to stop him? She glanced down and dug the toe of her sandal into the ground. Her mother's beauty had commanded respect when she walked into a room. People near fell at her feet and begged to do her bidding, especially Suph. And though he'd shown her some tolerance since their flight from the palace, Abigail was certain it was a ruse. He held no great affection for her.

She was not so naive to believe she'd rule Suph, with or without great beauty, which meant she'd have to take care around him lest she found herself in a worse position than being locked in her chambers.

~

Cold water splashed against Jesse's face. His muscles refused to move away from the offensive attack. His arms were wrapped over a yoke, bound with leather straps. It seemed, by the grace of God, his captors intended to keep him alive. The least he could do was open his eyes and face the traitors.

His uncle Elam hovered before him. "Aye, nephew, you would do well to end your torment and join the captain's pursuit to recapture the throne."

"I am not a coward, Uncle. Nor will I betray God as you have done." Jesse still had difficulty believing his uncle had betrayed his family. If he'd not witnessed his uncle's insanity he would not have believed it.

Elam let out a low, harsh laugh. "You cannot think that the child you and your brother helped Jehoiada place on the throne is the rightful heir to the throne?"

"How can you believe otherwise, Uncle?" There were no doubts in Jesse's mind. Joash was the son of Ahaziah, descendant of King David. Grandchild to the deceased wicked Queen Athaliah. The Queen, in a jealous rage, had killed all her husband's descendants seven years before. All except the infant Joash, who had been rescued by his aunt.

"It is like Jehoiada to deceive the people to gain their cooperation. He's hungry for power."

Jesse drew in a breath and clenched his teeth against the pain throbbing in his head. "Is that what you believe? Jehoiada is a man of God, chosen to be God's high priest to intercede on behalf of God's people. He does not need to deceive the people, Uncle. He has the approval of God, unlike you and that queen you were loyal to."

A low growl emanated from his right. The captain shoved Elam aside and pressed the tip of the dagger beneath Jesse's chin. Eyes, red from too much wine and hatred, glared at him. "It is with great providence our future queen has a soft heart, else I'd leave little of you for the birds."

Queen?

Certainly the young woman with the pointy chin and high forehead wasn't a product of Athaliah. Although pretty with her waist-length chestnut hair and her strange green eyes, she wasn't the stunning beauty her mother had been; nor did she seem to carry the same abhorrent character. Her pale complexion at the sight of him said as much. No, the guard toyed with him. But if Suph thought to play games with the people of Judah, at least he could have chosen a more prominent woman, not one frightened of her own shadow.

Jesse straightened his shoulders, removing his flesh from the man's blade. "I killed your queen. And I'll kill her too, if need be."

The guard's fist slammed into Jesse's jaw. A flash of white light exploded in his head a moment before his feet were swept from beneath him. He landed on his back. Air stole from his lungs as the wooden yoke jammed against his shoulders.

The sun captured and glinted off the dagger held above his attacker's head. The captain's chest heaved with each breath. He meant to kill him.

Just as well. Although he did not relish passing from this earth, he hated being a pawn even more. With his eyes set on the captain, Jesse arched his neck. "Go on."

The captain inhaled as his blade rose higher.

"Enough!"

Jesse pressed his lips together at the sound of his uncle's voice. The old man's sanity returned at the oddest times. If Elam hadn't kidnapped Mira, Jesse's brother's betrothed, Jesse wouldn't have been taking him back to Jerusalem to face the elders, and he certainly wouldn't be facing death at the hands of a coward. Who killed a man when he was half-beaten and bound?

"Killing him will not achieve our goal, Suph."

The captain rolled his shoulders, leaned over Jesse and cut the leather strap holding the carbuncle from his neck before sheathing his dagger. "Stretch him out near the altar, but keep him alive."

Suph kicked Jesse before stalking away, his helmet tucked beneath his arm and Jesse's tribal identity loose in his fingers. Jesse narrowed his eyes. When he was free from his bindings, he wouldn't show such mercy. When he was done with the traitor, the captain would beg for the sun's hottest kiss.

Elam knelt beside him and smoothed a cool cloth to Jesse's lips. "You should not provoke his anger."

Jesse narrowed his eyes. "You should have let him kill me."

A nervous laugh rumbled through Elam's chest, trembling his fingers. "Your father would have my head if anything happened to you."

"Your loyalties confuse me, Uncle."

Elam tilted his head, his brows furrowed. "I've always been loyal to my family. Have done what I thought best."

"And God?"

"Has abandoned us in our greatest time of need." Elam braced his arms beneath Jesse's shoulders and helped him to sit. "We must fend for ourselves, stand with those who are strong and bound to rule like Suph's pawn, Queen Athaliah's disgraceful daughter. Whether we agree with their beliefs or not."

Elam motioned for two soldiers to approach. "Stretch him between the postings erected, and then have a servant clean his wounds and feed him. My nephew needs his strength for what he is about to endure."

The soldiers lifted Jesse to his feet. He looked at his uncle. "I do not know how, or when, but God will reign. He did not restore Joash to the throne only to fail, of that I have no doubt."

They began to move forward, but Elam's hand held him still. He leaned close and whispered, "You've great potential, nephew. You are strong and with a bit of discipline you could be self-controlled. If you would only see to reason you could become what your brother Ari rejected. You'd make a much better captain of the guard than Suph. A much better husband to Judah's rightful queen. If you would only choose, I could make it happen. You could be King of Judah and I the high priest."

An image of unique green eyes, the color of olive leaves, flickered through his mind.

"So be it, Uncle, but I would not serve a god imagined in the mind of a fallible man. And you can be sure I would never marry a spawn of Athaliah."

Chapter Two

Heat infused Abigail's cheeks as she slipped between the folds of her tent and stepped in front of Suph. His jaw hardened. His chest rose and fell in harsh, rapid movements. She laid a hand on his shoulder. A gesture she'd often spied her mother do from the balcony outside her chamber.

His gaze flicked to her hand before settling on her. He shifted his stance, dislodging her hand, and propped a fist on his hip. "What is it I can do for you, Abigail?"

She straightened her shoulders, standing a few inches above him, and tilted her head. "My apologies if I wounded your pride, Suph. However, I believe you can see the wisdom of keeping the prisoner alive."

He firmed his lips. "Alive, yes. Being left capable of killing what few men we have to protect you, no."

Her gaze sought out the man carried by her soldiers. His wide shoulders sagged, his arms limp. He couldn't even walk on his own.

"Do not allow his condition to fool you, Abigail."

"Even hale I doubt he could do as much harm."

A harsh chuckle burst from Suph. His eyes bore a mocking yet dangerous glint. "Do not think to underestimate him, dearest. He's an elite soldier trained in ways I can only imagine, as much as it wounds me to admit. Given the chance, he'll kill me, kill my men." He gripped her chin, the scent of blood heavy on his hands. "And he'll kill you if only to save that child he claims is your brother's. The child he helped set on the throne. Are you willing to risk as much?"

She thought of the child and the varied stories that had whispered off the palace walls. She'd seen only twelve summers that awful year when word of her brother's death reached them. At first, she'd heard her mother had gone mad and had had all of Abigail's male cousins and nephews killed, but then her mother told her otherwise. It had been that priest Jehoiada who had infiltrated the princes' chambers and annihilated them all.

But then, only weeks ago, rumors of a surviving child began anew. Many said he had the look of her brother. Could it be he'd been spared Jehoiada's wrath? Why would the priest spare him when he'd killed all the others? To instill the beliefs of their so-called god? Certainly the boy was not her nephew. "Of course not, Suph. However, my stance remains, do not cause the prisoner further harm."

His lips twitched as if he were about to defy her. "As you wish, but I will do nothing to ease his wounds." Suph spit at the ground. "His wounds can fester until he dies. I care not. There will be other ways to remove the child from the throne."

She reached into her soul for courage. "Your grief over my mother credits you, but do not allow it to own you, Suph. You serve me now and will do as I bid. Even if it means cleaning the prisoner's wounds."

"You surprise me, Abigail. Your mother claimed you were weak. However, your commands reveal your mother's courage. Although, she never would have begged for a prisoner's life such as you have."

"I do not beg, Suph. I demand his life be spared as I demand his wounds be treated."

Hatred fired from his eyes, burning through her. His nostrils flared. She halted the shiver of fear snaking through her limbs. She reminded herself that he would not kill her. He needed her. She recognized the moment when he must have realized the truth of the matter, for he rolled his shoulders and began to move around her, but she stayed him with her hand. His gaze dropped to her upturned palm. "What is it you wish, Abigail?"

"The prisoner's gem." She arched her eyebrows, daring him to deny her request.

A muscle ticked in his jaw. Fear increased her pulse. One thing she had learned from her mother was that trust should be held tightly within one's own breast. Her trust did not belong to Suph. His lack of respect for her position proved as much, but if not him, then who?

The sound of a hammer beating bronze caught her attention. She glanced to the temporary altar where workers had erected an image of her mother's god. A soldier struck the back of the prisoner's knees, forcing him to kneel before the statue. Another guard yanked his head back by his shoulder-length hair. Even from her position she could see the rebellion shining through white eyes. Working his throat and lips, he spit.

Red-tinged spittle splattered over the man-made idol. The guard holding on to his hair forced his head back further and uttered a few words Abigail could not hear. The corners of the prisoner's mouth tensed in obvious pain and then he smiled in satisfaction.

"Do you not see his actions?"

Abigail shifted her gaze to Suph's, and then to her empty hand. "The gem, Suph."

He held the jewel up to the light of the sun. It sparkled. The once dull brown caught fire before her eyes. She sucked in a sharp breath as Suph dropped it into her palm.

"Mind my words, Abigail, and tread with care. I see the way you watch the prisoner with curious eyes. He's not to be trusted."

Suph pushed past her, and her gaze followed his retreat. "Neither are you," she whispered to his back.

She squeezed her fingers around the stone. It warmed the palm of her hand. Her gaze settled on the man being stretched out before the bronze idol. His life's blood flowed freely from his many wounds. Strange how he seemed more alive in his beaten body than Suph did in his able one.

Even the bronze statue, meant to be worshipped and obeyed, held more life than Suph. Odd, it did not breathe. It did not move of its own accord. It was not like the wind to come and go at will, yet her people bowed at its feet. Was there something to what Bilhah had said? Was there a living, breathing God? Was the God of her forefathers real?

The stone heated further, and she unclenched her fingers; orange fire glowed and ebbed, taking on a life of its own. Her lips parted; her eyes once again sought the prisoner. Could she trust him to tell her the truth about this God of his?

She took a step forward.

"Where are you going?"

Abigail glanced over her shoulder. Her cousin gripped one of the folds of the tent in her hand, but she remained hidden in the shadows. "To speak with the prisoner."

"Do you think that wise?" Bilhah moved from the protection of their shelter and out into the sunlight, her arms wrapped around her midsection. Although the kohl had been wiped from her cheeks and repainted around her eyes, she still seemed shaken from their recent ordeal.

"I do not see why not. I have questions about his cause."

Bilhah laid a hand on her arm. "The sun is waning. It is near time for the nightly worship. Trust me, Abigail, you do not wish to bear witness to such festivities."

Abigail scanned the camp. She hadn't noticed the leather tables laid out on the ground overflowing with bread and wine. Her attention had been on the hammering of bronze, Suph's words and the actions of the prisoner. She'd not realized couples strode toward the altar. Heat filled her cheeks.

"They cannot think to...to dance, not in front of the prisoner, Bilhah. He's not used to our ways." Not that Abigail was used to their ways, either. She'd been kept from the ceremonies. Not because her mother thought to protect her, rather because her mother was ashamed of her lack of curves and spindly arms and legs. Too ashamed of her pale complexion, and even more ashamed of Abigail's green eyes.

Bilhah's gaze flicked toward the beaten man tied between the posts. Her lips curved upward. "You're not much like your mother, you know?"

Her shoulders sagged. No, Abigail was weak like her father had been. She'd heard that often enough.

"Do not fret, Abigail. That is not such a bad thing." Bilhah grasped Abigail's fingers. "Come, let us go rescue your prisoner."

"And how do you propose we do that? Suph would not be happy."

Bilhah laughed. "You are a princess, his future queen, are you not?"

The corners of Abigail's lips curved upward even as she choked on the knot forming in her throat. She nodded.

"Then behave as such. Come, I'll walk beside you. Your people will not deny your request, not with a shrine priestess at your side."

"If you will give me but a moment." Abigail ducked into the tent and placed the prisoner's gem and the leather strap tied around it into an ornately carved wooden box. She wiped her palms down the front of her tunic, straightened her spine and then stepped beside Bilhah. "I am ready."

They wove through the throngs of people preparing for worship. This time they dropped to a bow as Bilhah glided past them in her purple robes. Her earlier sullenness was gone. "I see your rest has done you well," Abigail whispered.

Bilhah inclined her head. "Very much so. However, for reasons even I do not understand." She halted her steps, bringing Abigail beside her. "When this—" she waved her hand about them "—is done. When you are on the throne I intend to leave my position."

Air caught in Abigail's lungs. The thought of losing the last of her family, her only real friend in this uncertain world, churned her stomach.

"Head high, Abigail. You are being watched. We will discuss this matter later, but be certain I weary of performing for the masses. I weary of worshipping false gods made of bronze."

Abigail glanced at the bronze statue and then back to her cousin. "I do understand." Abigail had often witnessed the sadness in Bilhah's eyes when she sought refuge in Abigail's chambers.

"Princess," Micah's voice sounded ragged, as if he'd run a great distance. His eyes downcast, he shifted from one foot to the other. "You should not be here."

She smiled and patted him on the head. No more than ten summers, his concern warmed her. Would he remain faithful to her no matter what fate directed for her future? "I am well, Micah. Please fetch Dara the Healer and bring her to my tent."

His eyes shifted to hers, his mouth agape. "Abigail—"

"Go, Micah."

The child dipped his chin and left to do her bidding.

"Nicely done." Bilhah's purple tunic swirled around her feet. She clapped her hands above her head. "What is this," she screeched, like the commanding priestess Abigail knew her to be. "You dare risk our god's wrath with the presence of this heathen?"

Bilhah spit toward the man, missing his stomach by inches. The people swarmed around, begging apologies, even the soldiers tying the knots at the prisoner's hands and feet. Her beauty had nothing to do with their fear of her. No, they feared her because they believed she held sway with their bronze statue and if they angered her they'd be cursed.

"Untie him." Abigail motioned at the soldiers. "Take him to my tent."

They glanced at Bilhah. "Go on. Do as your princess commands."

Their fingers fumbled over the knots as they worked to loosen them. The prisoner's body seemed to relax. His hard eyes settled on her. A sneer curled his bloodied, swollen lip. The desert wind pushed against her, forcing her to take a step back.

Perhaps she should have listened to Suph.

~

Jesse's muscles tensed when the soldiers jerked him from the ground. A groan rumbled from his chest. The woman who would call herself queen tossed a look over her shoulder. Her waist-length hair danced at her hips. The slip of concern in her eyes soured his stomach.

What game was this woman about? The princess's cohort was no more than a prostitute, even if she was considered a shrine goddess and held in high regard by those who worshipped the bronze statue. Jesse had no doubt she wouldn't have considered his presence a defilement to her dead god. He was quite certain the priestess would have relished forcing their rituals upon him. So why would the princess and her priestess move him when their captain demanded otherwise? The tops of his toes dragged over the pebbled desert, biting into his already raw flesh. He'd seen what happened to men pulled behind a horse, but he never imagined the incessant burning of his nerves or the way his bones seemed to detach from his muscles.

His eyes caught hold of the gentle, purposeful sway of the princess's slender hips. Although she lacked the voluptuous curves of the former queen, she had a regal bearing about her. Of course, that alone did not prove she was royalty. Certainly he would have heard if Athaliah had a daughter.

She halted before a large tent and pulled back the flaps. "You may lay him on the furs in the corner."

One of the soldiers snorted. "You wish him to bleed on your bedding?"

The lack of respect for the woman, queen or not, did not sit well with Jesse. He pulled against the soldiers' grips and tried righting himself. He was met with an elbow to the back of his head.

"I requested this man receive no more harm. Would you seek my wrath?" The attempted bravado in her tone eased some of the tension from his muscles. "Those furs belong to my dogs. I'm sure the prisoner will be placed elsewhere before they are returned to me."

"As you wish." One of the soldiers pulled Jesse through the tent and dumped him to the bedding. He was thankful for the soft blow to his chest and battered face.

"You may stand guard outside if you'd like, or return to the festivities. My servant will be here shortly with a healer."

"The captain will have our heads if this man escapes."

Jesse didn't need to look to know which of the two guards spoke; nor did he need his eyes to see the way she tilted her pointed chin and looked down upon them from her impressive height. "I assure you he is in no condition to escape. He can barely hold up his head."

"As you wish." He heard them duck outside the tent. "We will stand guard until the healer arrives."

He rolled to his back, closed his eyes and concentrated on sucking in air. He no doubt had a few broken ribs among the dagger cuts. Jasmine swirled around him as she moved closer and knelt beside him. The warmth of her hand settled on his brow. He grabbed her wrist as he snapped his eyes open.

Fear glittered in her olive-green eyes.

"You play with fire, lady." He gritted his teeth with the effort to keep her from pulling away.

"That may be so, but I have questions and you have answers."

Her eyes shifted back and forth, searching his. He released her, dropping his hand to his side. She reached across him and dipped a cloth into a bowl of water before bathing his face. Her gentle caress bit into his flesh yet warmed his heart.

"You are bold for one who trembles with fear."

Pulling away, she curled her legs beneath her. "I've rarely had cause to step foot outside my chambers, let alone leave Jerusalem's gates. All this is new and a bit fearful."

"Your honesty does you justice."

"As I hope will yours."

She wrung the cloth out into the basin and then ran it over a deep gash on his bicep. He pulled in a sharp breath. "You should not trust me. I will kill you if need be."

"So I have been warned." Her lips curved upward; the brilliance of her wide smile lit up the darkened tent. Perhaps he was wrong about her. She was more than pretty, she was an exotic beauty; not like her mother had been, but a beautiful creature nonetheless.

"What is it they call you?"

"Jesse. And you?"

"Abigail."

"A father's joy."

She furrowed her brow.

"Your name, it means a father's joy."

Her gaze dropped to her lap, and a deep sadness crinkled the corners of her eyes. Before he could ask her the source of her sadness, a small boy entered with an elderly woman.

"Ach, I've heard the rumors of your madness, but now mine eyes have seen the truth." A buxom gray-haired woman peered over Abigail's shoulder. "Your captain will not like this, not one bit. I will not risk his wrath. I will not." The woman planted her fists on her hips.

Abigail jumped to her feet, towering over the woman, hands clenched at her side. "Yet you'd risk mine, Dara." She glanced at the boy. "Micah, remove her from my presence and fetch a willing healer."

"Yes, Princess." His dark head bowed. Jesse rolled his eyes and stared at the billowing tent. Even this child believed her to be a princess. Their future queen if Suph had his way. "Come, Dara. I will take you back."

"May the gods allow you a restful sleep, Dara." Abigail's tone held a hint of sarcasm. It was not lost on the old woman, either, for she twisted her lips as if to consider Abigail's wishes.

"Allow me to retrieve my herbs." The woman slipped between the opening.

"Micah, I do not trust Dara to keep from mumbling." Abigail twisted her hands together. "You know how she is when agitated. Make sure she speaks to no one. If she does, you'll tell me?"

"Of course." The child left.

"You risk death to save me. If Suph does not kill you in a fit of rage, I might."

She stared down her slender nose at him. A manicured eyebrow arched upward. "You are a man of honor, Jesse."

He tried to prop himself up on his elbow but ended flat on his back with air whooshing from his lungs.

Abigail bent over him. "Are you all right?"

"Yes, of course. Considering your captain used me as target practice while my hands were tied behind my back."

Her lips parted. Her hand pressed against her heart. "A coward?"

Jesse blinked.

"Here." She grabbed hold of his shoulders. Jasmine filled his nostrils. She propped pillows behind his back until he was sitting and then fetched him a goblet of water. "Better."

"Yes." He considered her a moment as she pressed the rim of a cup to his lips. Cool liquid flowed over his tongue and down his throat. He pulled back. "What makes you think I'm a man of honor?"

She set the cup aside and swayed across the room. Her long tapered fingers reached for a small wooden box. She opened the lid and pulled out a leather strap. His signet dangled from her fingers. She lifted it to the light and then glanced at him. "You are a Levite, no?"

He forced air in and out through his nose and forced calm into his limbs as he recalled Suph cutting it from his neck.

She held it above her head. The firebrands caught the gem, shooting little sparks of light upon the fabric walls. "A priest, a man of this so-called living God? A man of honor?"

He'd known many a Levite, many a priest, with no honor, his uncle Elam included. "What is it you want, Abigail?"

She wrapped her fingers around the stone and knelt beside him. Her gaze bored into his a moment before she pressed her curled fist against his chest, and then she flattened her palm. The stone was the only barrier between them.

"The truth about this living God of yours, Jesse."

Chapter Three

The stone warmed against her palm. Jesse's eyes blazed with fire. Lines of pain etched his jaw as he grimaced. She inhaled a sharp breath and sat back on her heels. "I am sorry. I should not have done that. You have wounds, which need tending."

The beat of a drum pounded in tandem with her heart. A lyre struck up a chord. The nightly ritual of chanting sounded much more eerie this close to the revelry. She began to scoot away from Jesse, but he grasped hold of her wrist. His hold, gentle, unlike his earlier attempt at holding her still, sent an awareness of him straight to her toes. He slid his fingers down the leather thong and wrapped them around the gem.

"It is nothing more than a rock, Abigail. A sign of my tribe. It does not mean I know the truth of God." He coughed, his body propelled upward until he doubled over in a harsh moan. He settled back against the pillows, his eyes closed. "You may keep it if you wish."

Her lips parted in disbelief. She knew from Shema, her old nurse, the signets were of great import, especially to a man of a Levite tribe. Why would Jesse give up his treasure?

Perhaps, he was not to be trusted after all. She studied the lines formed across his brow and the discolored swollen cheeks above his black beard. Thick, dark curls rested against his bare shoulders. She wondered what he looked like when not so badly beaten. Even now, with his eyes closed, he was nothing more than a man. A giant of a man to be sure, but not the trained warrior Suph had cautioned her about.

She slipped from the edge of the bedding and replaced the jewel in her box. She would have Micah fix it for her later and wear it around her neck for safekeeping. Sitting on the far side of the tent, she watched Jesse for a moment. The palm resting on his chest rose in small jerky movements as if each breath was difficult.

"Does it hurt?"

He squinted one eye open. The coldness of his glare froze the blood in her veins.

The chanting of the worshippers grew louder. The richness of the roasting wild fowl permeated the air, churning her stomach. Abigail picked up one of the pillows and buried her nose into it.

Dara pushed into the tent, carrying a linen bag of supplies. Abigail dropped her pillow and composed herself as a princess should.

"They're more riled than usual. I'd say—" Dara's gaze darted toward the prisoner and she clamped her lips together. "Are you sure you want to save him? He looks to be at death's door. A bit of this," she said, pulling a tiny earthen jar from her bag and holding it up. "He'll be out of misery if it's mercy you wish to give."

Abigail folded her hands together. Would Dara understand her need to keep this man alive? Her gaze settled on Jesse, uncertain if he would understand Abigail's true motives and not the lie she was about to speak. "Suph needs him to restore Jerusalem back to my hands. He'll not die, Dara. Not if you wish to continue on in your position."

The skin around the old woman's eyes crinkled. Dara had been a constant in Abigail's life, ever since that day when Shema had abandoned her to the cold isolation of her chambers.

Air caught in Abigail's throat as unshed tears burned at the memory of Shema. Her old nurse had been like a real mother to her, one who kissed her scraped knees and comforted her after night terrors. Now all she had left was Bilhah, a child servant, and Dara, a rancorous old woman. For which she was thankful, even if the old woman wasn't Shema.

Guilt cloaked Abigail's shoulders, for she had never threatened Dara. Doing so now did not settle well in Abigail's stomach, but what choice did she have?

None if she were to discover the truth. Not only about Jesse's God, but she hoped he would also tell her the truth about this high priest and whether he had ordered the deaths of so many of her family.

One corner of Dara's mouth curved upward. "Ach, I'd heard you were crazed. Turned into your mother." Dara settled beside Jesse and dug through her bag before looking at him, and then Abigail. "I see I've heard wrong. You always were one to mend a wing. Perhaps, you'll do Judah some good after all. I had my doubts, I tell you. Call your boy in, I'll need light if my eyes are to see. And I'll need you. My hands are too old to be closing his wounds."

Abigail felt the blood drain from her face and she stood frozen. It was one thing to clean his wounds, which she'd failed to do. Quite another to force more pain upon him.

"Come along, girl. I've not got all night"

Abigail's eyes flickered to his, catching his anger. He nodded. It was a slight movement, one that Dara missed. However, it gave Abigail the courage she needed. She moved toward the opening of her tent. "Micah, bring a firebrand and come here."

The boy pulled back the flaps as he entered, giving Abigail a glimpse of the rituals of her people dancing around the fire. Embarrassment knotted in her stomach. She glanced down at her own form swathed in fine linen and knew her lack of beauty had been a blessing.

"Would you rather me leave him to die?" Dara's sharp tone broke through her musings.

She jerked her chin up. "Of course, not. I told you he is needed."

After she knelt beside Dara, the old woman handed her a thin bone needle threaded with sinew. Abigail's hands shook as she swallowed back the bile forming in her throat.

"Now's not the time for weakness, child. Pay attention." Dara poured olive oil over a long gash on Jesse's midriff and then pinched the gaping wound together. Jesse sucked air, whistling between his teeth. "You ready, boy?"

His jaw clenched as he nodded. Dara poked the needle near the edge of the flesh and into the second piece. "You must leave a finger's length of the sinew hanging, else it'll pull through."

Smoothing her hair over her shoulder, Abigail leaned closer, paying attention to where Dara stuck the needle. The old woman worked fast with gnarled fingers, creating a clean pattern like that of a ladder. Engrossed as she was in Dara's work, she'd forgotten about the man until he flinched when Dara cut the sinew with her dagger.

Abigail sought out his gaze. "Are you well?"

Deep brown eyes the color of polished cedar stole her breath. "I am well, Abigail."

She expected his hatred, his anger. She did not expect the gentle soothing in his tone as if he sought to comfort her in the midst of his pain.

"We've no time for this." Dara's bleary eyes roamed from Jesse's legs to his chest, and then his arms. The wealth of blood made it difficult to tell which wounds were the worst. "We'll allow those on his chest to bleed. Give his body time to purge the poisons. You start on the deeper wounds on his arms. I'll tend the wounds on his legs."

Abigail's cheeks warmed.

Dara cleared her throat. "Not proper for a princess, but we've no choice, have we? Now watch and learn quickly. The sooner we get him stitched, the sooner I can return to my bed."

The old woman poured wine and then more olive oil over one of the cuts. Jesse hissed through gritted teeth. Abigail held her breath as Dara once again pierced the bone needle through his flesh.

"When the sutures are complete, we'll dip cloths into a honey bath and bind his wounds." Dara's thick, gnarled fingers fumbled with the sinewy strand. After long, agonizing moments, she raised her gaze to Abigail's. "Well, what are you waiting for?"

The white bone needle gleamed beneath the firebrand as Dara pushed it through Jesse's torn skin. The process looked painful, but minus the first sharp intake of breath, Jesse hadn't reacted. Abigail drew in a steadying breath. Pricks of anxiety welled in her throat, threatening to spill from her eyes.

"All is well, Abigail." Jesse's whispered encouragement tugged at her heart. She stared at the needle in her fingers. Her heart slammed against her chest. Her shoulders sagged and she started to drop the needle to her side. Warm fingers wrapped around her ankle and squeezed. She dropped her gaze to Jesse's. The hardness in his eyes softened. His silent encouragement gave her the backbone she needed.

With trembling fingers, she gripped the neck of the jug. The liquid spilled, pouring over the myriad of gashes on Jesse's biceps. The sweet scent of fresh grapes mixed with the olive oil and the bright splotches of blood left a metallic taste in her mouth. She drew in a slow breath and once again flicked her gaze to his. Brown eyes held hers.

His swollen lips curved upward. "You should take care not to drench your dogs' bedding. I'm sure they would appreciate a dry place to sleep."

She nodded and blinked her lashes in thanks. "I have no dogs."

Holding the wound together, she poked the bone needle through the flesh. Jesse's chest hitched, halting. She glanced at him. He nodded as he exhaled. She pulled the sinew through both sides, leaving a finger's length just as Dara had shown her.

Whipping the sinew around in tiny strokes, she pulled the open flesh closed as she worked her way along the length. The wound was deep, cutting into his muscle. She wondered if he'd lose the use of his arm. She had no doubt that had been Suph's intentions.

She tied off the knot and turned his arm to inspect the smaller cuts before turning her attention to the x gashed into his shoulder. "You'll have quite the scar."

"Ach, he's many already," Dara snarled. "Men fight and die. You obviously did not heed your training, boy."

A deep chuckle rumbled from Jesse's chest. "Not so. My scars are no more than love pats from my older brothers."

The needle halted near the edge of his wound. Laughter danced in his eyes. Admiration and affection colored each of his words. He must love his brothers deeply.

She bit down on her lip and wondered what it would have been like if Jehoiada had not ordered her brothers' and cousins' deaths seven years ago. This man followed the same God the high priest did. Had he killed one of her brothers with his own hands? Anger fired in her chest. Swallowing past the knot in her throat, she jabbed the needle through Jesse's flesh.

He rose off the furs with a roar.

~

"Woman, what are you about?"

She jerked back, eyes wide, hand over her mouth. Her chest rose and fell rapidly. The needle and sinew yanked through his arm. The old woman spilled wine over his stomach as Micah jostled her. The boy had jumped in front of Abigail. A dagger gleamed in one hand, the flickering firebrand in the other. Jesse thought the boy looked scared as he squinted his eyes and glared at him. Jesse emitted a low growl just to see if the boy would run, but Micah held his ground. His courage gave him much credit. He'd make a fine warrior one day and Jesse relished the thought of training such a courageous soul. A shame he would not be around to do so.

"I—am sorry." She leaned around the boy's wiry legs. Tears filled her eyes.

He scraped his palm over his face and settled back against the pillows. "It is I who should apologize. I was not prepared."

No, he'd been thinking about his brothers and their families. Thinking about how quickly life could be lost and what a shame it would be to never experience the kind of love his brothers shared with their wives. A love God had intended between a man and woman. A husband and wife.

Abigail crept forward and bent over him. Jasmine once again enveloped his senses. Her hesitant gaze flicked to his.

"Go on." He smiled. His mouth ached with the movement. "I'll behave."

She nodded at the child. The boy tucked his weapon into his belt and stepped back. Abigail lowered her head, and her fingers slid over the edge of his wound and closed the flesh together. The needle pierced more gently. She tugged and pulled the thin line of catgut through his wound.

Her movements, although shaky, were gentle and efficient.

This shy, yet courageous, curious woman drew him. He wanted to calm her, to soothe the wounds hidden in her green eyes, even as she sought to heal his. The care and gentle touch of her palm against his skin, even though it caused more pain, scared him as nothing ever had. Not even when he rushed into battle.

"Here, sip. It'll ease the pain." The old woman pressed a copper cup to his lips.

He curled his nose and moved his hand in front of his mouth. "I'd rather suffer."

"It is true what they say about your people." The woman's gray eyes pierced his.

"What is this, Dara?" Abigail tilted her chin. "What truth do you speak?"

The early eagerness in her request for truth lit her pale cheeks, illuminating her eyes like blades of grass in the morning dew.

"He does not drink wine." Micah's lips twisted in disgust.

The needle paused in Abigail's hand. She glanced over her shoulder and then back to Jesse. "Is this true?"

He nodded.

"What sort of man does not drink wine?"

"The kind who wishes to indulge in pain." Dara set the cup aside and replaced it with another. "Here, it's water with chamomile."

"You're not trying to kill me, are you, Dara?" he smiled.

The wrinkles lining her cheeks smoothed. "I could have done that with my knife, boy. I do not resort to poisons."

"I will remember that."

He sipped the offered water. The herb clung to his tongue.

Abigail and Dara resumed their stitching and plastering his skin with glutinous bandages. The discordant drums settled into a steady rhythm, matching his breathing as he relaxed. The lamps flickered and waned. His eyelids slid closed. The soft linen of Abigail's tunic whispered against his skin as she tended each wound. She leaned over him, her breath soft and warm against his cheek. She prodded a cut above his eye. Her tresses, a light caress on his chest, soothed him like his own mother's tenderness had done when he was but a child.

"Jesse." Her whispered song curled his toes. "Can you roll this way?"

He blinked his eyes open. Her green ones hovered above his. His mouth parched, he licked his lips and swallowed, wishing he could form the words to ask for a drink.

"We need to tend the wounds on your back."

He reached up to touch the wound above his brow. The flesh puckered between the sutures. How had she been so quick with her needle, he wondered as he tried to comprehend the situation.

"Jesse, we cannot roll…lie on your stomach…" He never willingly gave a man or a woman his back lest he find himself killed.

"No." He shook his head. Everything seemed to move in slow motion. What had the old woman done to him?

"Ach, boy. You're too big for us to move you. You've gashes on your back what needed stitching."

He pulled and twisted. Although the pain dulled, the movement stretched his skin in ways not common to man. He plopped on his chest, his cheek heavy against the pillows. Warm liquid poured over his back. A raging fire burned within the wounds, and he arched his neck.

"Ach, you need to hold still if I am to stitch you." Dara's tone, harsh as it was, held a hint of sympathy.

He tried to keep his eyes opened but he became mesmerized by the flickering lamplight and his lids grew heavy. No sooner had he lain on his chest than it seemed the insistent women were waking him. "Jesse, you need to roll back now."

He wished they would make up their crazed minds. All this moving about caused him great discomfort, especially with the pounding in his skull.

"Jesse." Hearing his name from Abigail's lips soothed a loneliness inside him he did not realize existed. He opened one eye and looked at her. "You need to roll back."

She touched her palm against his ribs. He squeezed his eyes shut and rolled onto his back. Pain cut deep, halting the movement until it could be held no more. He coughed and released the rebellious air before gripping his ribs. "Surely the cords of death have entangled me."

"You should not move." Abigail's gentle voice lulled him into a sense of peace.

Once he gained control over his breathing, he peeled his lids open. A soft golden hue bathed the chamber. With the glorious crown of silken tresses dancing about her shoulders she looked to be an otherworldly creature. "Beautiful."

He thought he saw the beautiful woman smile. However, it wasn't but a moment later, an aging brow and crooked nose appeared. Gnarled fingers pulled back his swollen bottom lip, probing his mouth, before pasting his mouth with a thick salve tasting of honey. "You've all your teeth. A good sign you will not perish from starvation."

Nightmares did not visit him often in his sleep, but he feared the old woman would stay with him for a time. "What is it you tainted my water with, old woman?"

A trickle of laughter danced in the room as a cloth touched his brow. His gaze flicked from the gray-haired woman to the beauty beside him. "Only chamomile to ease your pain and help heal your wounds." She bent close to his ear. "Dara will not harm you. She's a healer."

"I should trust her?"

The tilt of her chin was the only answer he received. The lady was mad if she thought he would trust any of them with his life. Perhaps he was the mad one, for he *had* put his life in their hands.

"Ow!" He bellowed when Dara poked at the wound near his temple.

"Your captain did not want this man to live long, did he? His wounds are making him crazed."

Green eyes turned sullen. She dipped her chin to her chest. "I fear the captain is angered by my mother's death."

Jesse thought to tell her it had nothing to do with the queen's death, but his vision began to blacken. Perspiration beaded on his chest. He shivered. His tongue grew heavy and cleaved to the roof of his mouth. He was parched, as if he'd spent weeks in the desert with no water. After a great struggle he swallowed, pulling his tongue from its mooring. "Thirsty."

Olive oil, honey and figs bathed the inside of his mouth. Certain he would die if he continued to lay still, he tried to push up onto his elbows.

A gentle touch prodded him back to the soft mat of his bedding. "Do not move."

"Thir—thirsty." He swallowed hard against the raw scratchiness.

"Here." She lifted his head and pressed a cup to his mouth.

He clamped his lips shut against the herbs lulling him out of his senses.

"It's only water."

He stared into her eyes, seeking deception.

"You can trust me. I will not allow harm to befall you this night." Her soft whisper broke through the pounding in his head. He parted his lips. Cool water glided over his tongue and down his throat. With the same gentleness his mother had used when he was but a boy, she laid his head back down and brushed her fingers across his brow, smoothing back a lock of hair. Her soft eyes bored into his. His last thought as the light began to dim and his eyes once again slid closed was that maybe he could trust her enough to pay her court.

Chapter Four

"What is this?"

Abigail jumped to her feet and faced Captain Suph. She'd feared he would arrive but hoped he'd been too caught up in his wine to care about the prisoner for the night. Micah once again puffed out his chest as if to protect her from the captain who had always left her feeling as if she should disappear. His black eyes were cold and soulless. What had her mother found pleasing in him?

"Dara is healing his wounds." Abigail stiffened her spine.

Suph pushed farther into the tent. He peered down at the sleeping prisoner and then at the bone needle between her fingers. "It looks as if you are tending his wounds, Abigail. It's not fitting for a queen to demean herself as such."

Abigail felt her eyes widen. "Until a few days ago nobody cared much about my activities as long as I remained in my chambers."

He reached out and grabbed a handful of hair. His fingers clung to her tresses. "That was before your mother was murdered, leaving you heir to the throne. Your mother never would have lowered herself to a servant's duties."

How was Abigail to know this? She rarely saw her mother. If the servants hadn't told her, Abigail never would have known who her mother was. The beautiful woman had rarely paid her any heed. "You are right, Suph. My mother would have been more likely to help you torture a man than help him."

Suph swung his arm back. Abigail squeezed her eyes closed and hunched in on herself, waiting for the blow. After several long moments she opened her eyes. Micah, as small as he was, stood in front of Abigail with his arms crossed in front of him.

Suph curled his lip. "You are brave for one so young. It's an admirable quality. However, I fear it will see you killed if you're not careful." He clouted Micah's shoulder, knocking him to the ground. With nobody standing between them, Suph's menacing eyes bored into hers.

The hammering in Abigail's chest picked up the pace. Tears stung the backs of her eyes. "I will ask you kindly to leave, Suph."

The captain growled; grabbing hold of her neck, he pressed his wine-soaked breath close to her ear. "I'll remind you, Abigail, your position as queen depends solely upon me. Without me, without my men, you are nothing. If this rebel regains his strength, he'll kill you." He pulled back. The lines at the corner of his eyes melded together as he clenched his jaw. "Do not doubt me in this, Abigail. He will kill you."

"Captain, would you be liking a drink? From the royal coffers, I'm certain."

Suph pulled his gaze from Abigail's and glanced at Dara. He tore the goblet from the healer's hand and gulped it down. Red liquid sloshed onto his beard and tunic.

"I forgive you for your lack of wisdom, Abigail, dear." He handed the cup back to Dara. "Do not cross me again and never speak ill of your mother. Ever"

Abigail stretched to her full height and looked down on Suph. "When I am queen—"

He grabbed hold of her arm, his fingers bruising her through her garments. "When you are queen, you'll be my wife and you'll learn to respect my wishes." His fingers bit deeper. "Is that understood?"

Abigail couldn't say a word. The smell of blood, Jesse's blood, mixed with Suph's drunkenness, which clung to his person, caused her stomach to churn and bile to rise.

Suph jerked her forward. "I demand an answer."

Why had he obeyed the earlier commands she'd given him in front of his men, when he now demanded his own of her in private? Did he not trust his men would allow him to treat her poorly?

"Captain, the princess has had a grueling time of it. Having lost the last of her family, being cast from her home and raced through the desert. Ach, my old bones are crying out in agony. How our delicate princess must feel. She'll be her more biddable self once she's had some rest, I'm certain."

Suph released her. His gaze bounced from Dara to Micah, and then to the prisoner before once again halting at Abigail. "Do not touch him. Do not attempt to heal him, or I'll kill him and things will not go well with you, my dear." He curled his lip and glanced at Micah. "Nor with you."

Micah held Suph's murderous gaze. Suph settled his hand on the hilt of his sword. His fingers clenched around the bound leather. Fear permeated Abigail's core, causing her knees to quake. She stilled the temptation to shield Micah from Suph's wrath. Doing so would only insure Micah met a wicked end.

Perhaps worse than Jesse's.

"Do not force my hand, Abigail. I will do what I must." He dropped his hand to his side, turned on his heel and ducked between the tent flaps.

She buried her face into her hands, her shoulders sagging. "What am I going to do? I cannot bow to his demands. He'll perceive it as weakness and use it against me."

A warm hand touched Abigail's forearm. She glanced down at the gnarled, papery hand and then into the warm, kind eyes of Dara. "We should go back to Jerusalem. The priest, Jehoiada, would offer you refuge."

Abigail sucked in a sharp breath. "He had my family killed."

Dara shrugged and then knelt beside the prisoner. "Only your mother, child."

"What do you mean by such words?" Silence echoed against the fabric of the tent. Abigail paced, uncertain of what she should do.

"Dara is correct, Abigail." Micah's soft, childlike voice whispered in the tent. "The captain means you no good. He needs you to rule Jerusalem."

Of course. Fool that she was, she somehow believed her position as queen would gain her respect. Even from the captain. She did not ask to be queen and had no desire to be as such. If only she could return to her chambers and be left alone…her gaze dropped to Jesse's sleeping form. He needed her help. No matter Suph's threats, she would not allow him to die or to remain within reach of the captain's cruel hands.

"Do you wonder why your mother did not marry him, child?"

The question knotted in Abigail's chest, twisting and turning. "I was kept in a chamber, Dara. I have little knowledge of my mother's activities." She sighed and dropped to her bedding. "I fear I have little knowledge of the city I grew up in. Perhaps, you're right and I should rest. The morrow will look much brighter."

Her words seemed hollow. As long as Suph controlled her and threatened the people within this tent, nothing would be bright.

"Child, there is no time for rest. You must decide to act now."

Abigail jerked her head up. The skin between her eyebrows knitted together. "What is it you are suggesting?"

"She's suggesting—" Jesse swallowed, his voice weak "—you choose your own fate, Abigail."

She shuddered. "How am I to do that?"

"I will help you." He pressed up on his elbows. Tremors raced through his body at the effort.

Abigail laughed. "You are half-dead, prisoner."

He smirked. A dark eyebrow arched under his black curly hair.

"I will help," Micah offered. "Suph's reputation is fierce. Cruel. He'll do as he says and kill us if we don't obey." The boy dropped his chin to his chest. "And most likely even if we do as he demands."

She shook her head. "I do not see how we will make it out of the camp. Alive."

Dara's raspy chuckle filled the tent. "I can help with that, and there are others who would help. Of course, you may never be Queen of Judah. However, you would be free to live as you please."

Abigail pressed her fingers to her forehead in an attempt to ease the beginning of a head pain. "I can't. That child the priest insists is the rightful king—"

"He *is* the rightful king. The son of your brother Ahaziah, your nephew, Abigail."

Butterflies danced along her skin. She'd wanted to know the truth but hadn't expected this. Could she trust this man? "How is it you believe this?"

"I do not just believe it, Abigail. I know it. I knew your brother." Dark shadows flickered in his eyes. "The child is his."

~

He had no idea how this was going to work. An old lady, a child, a timid woman and himself. Abigail was right, he was barely alive, but if he did not convince her to leave, no doubt he would soon be dead. As would she.

"I do not know who or what to trust." Abigail pulled her knees into her chest and rested her chin there.

"I will not ask you to trust me. We are strangers. However, you should trust your captain's words. He will not hesitate to kill Micah, nor you if he chooses." His strength began to wane and he dropped against the pillows.

"How can you be certain of Suph's character? How do you know he is not full of words?"

Her innocence reached somewhere deep inside. This was not only about his survival but hers, as well. After fighting the excruciating pain for so long he'd dozed off only to wake to an atmosphere so tense he wouldn't have been able to cut it with his sword. Suph's threatening manner had tempted Jesse to rise and dispatch the man. If he'd been able to he would have, too. But Jesse knew better than to interfere lest he meet his death then and there. If that had happened there would be no rescuing this lady and her young protector. He wouldn't be able to keep Judah, his beloved country, safe.

Jesse shifted his gaze toward her. "Suph left many villages in desolation. He burned their crops, slaughtered their animals." He paused, uncomfortable with his next words. He closed his eyes, recalling with clarity the devastation and the weeping mothers. "He cut down their children in the name of your mother, looking for a single child, your nephew, King Joash."

"This cannot be true. My mother—"

"Ordered the atrocities." He tore his gaze from hers. The horror etched on her face left him feeling like the worst kind of evil. Perhaps he shouldn't have told her, but she'd asked for the truth, and that was one truth she needed to hear, even if it wasn't the one she had meant.

"Ach, your mother was as cruel as any." Dara hid her dislike behind a goblet.

"It is true," Micah said. When Abigail glanced at him he shuffled his feet. "I heard some of the soldiers speaking about it."

Jesse found it odd that these people agreed with him. It was a mercy he was more than thankful for.

Abigail wrapped her arms around her waist and bent over. A soft keen echoed in the tent, intruding on the flickering firebrands. Piercing his heart. He wanted to reach out, take her in his arms and offer her comfort. However, it was not his place.

"If we are to sweep you away from the camp, child, we need to act now."

Her rocking motion came to a sudden halt. She sat up straight as she swiped at the tears on her cheeks. "How is it even possible?"

The corners of Dara's mouth slid upward. "You give the command. A little of this," she held up a small earthen jar no bigger than the palm of her hand, "in their wine and the entire camp will sleep until midday."

Abigail's gaze settled on Jesse. "And what of him?"

Her question formed a knot in the pit of his stomach. Not that he thought she'd leave him behind. The care she and Dara had taken with his wounds told him they were both compassionate, even if he was their enemy. No, the fact that she thought things through, when he had a tendency to act first and think later, caused him a bit of shame.

"I've chamomile and my sons. They were not pleased to be forced from their home. They do not like Suph."

Jesse did not like the way the tension left Abigail's face, nor the way her eyes lightened at the mention of Dara's sons. Had she affection for them? Not that it mattered. However, a part of him did envy whoever it was that caused such a reaction in her.

He glanced at the old woman and prayed her sons were able-bodied men and not frail. Given the size of their mother he doubted such mercy had found him. "You would be surprised what things a man can do when he has the will to live. I will have no more of your herbs, old woman." He couldn't risk having dulled senses.

Abigail considered him for a short time as she chewed on her bottom lip. Jesse smiled. The more time he spent in her presence the more beautiful she became. Not the magnificent beauty her mother had portrayed, but a beauty in her own right, with her high forehead and wide mouth. But what made her even more splendid was the gentleness of her soul. The pureness radiating from her.

Abigail glanced at Micah. The boy nodded and she seemed to sigh in relief. It was odd she took cues from the child. She looked back toward Jesse. "I do not trust you, Jesse. However, something tells me you will help me find the truth I seek."

The truth of the one true God. He only hoped he could offer her counsel. He was not his brother Ari, a man well versed in God's law. No, he was a warrior who spent much of his time praying, nothing more. She bowed her head. "It is obvious I am in danger if I stay here."

"I can make you no promises, Abigail. I have vowed to protect Judah. At all costs. As long as you and your people do not stand in the way of that goal I will bring no harm upon your heads. However, one hint that you betray the greater good of Judah and King Joash, and I will have no constraint. In that your captain is correct."

"You are loyal to your cause. I admire that strength. If only I knew what my cause was." She tilted her chin. The glow from the firebrands illuminated the innocence in her eyes.

"I am loyal to the one true God, Abigail, and Judah belongs to Him. Not the false idols your mother worshipped. Not the one your people shame themselves before tonight."

"Where would we go?"

Jesse twisted his lips. Where would they go? He couldn't take her to Manna. He would not risk the people and their secrets there, not even to protect this woman, though she might be innocent of her mother's crimes. He had no doubt Ari and Mira would welcome them, but he had no way of knowing if his brother and his love had returned safely to her father's village, which left him only one choice.

"I will take you to Jerusalem to see Jehoiada, the high priest."

Her lips parted as her eyes widened. She shook her head.

"Ach, our time is running short. What will it be, Abigail?"

"I do not know."

"If you stay here, Suph will force a marriage upon you. He said as much. And if he succeeds in ousting King Joash he will raise himself up as King of Judah. You have seen his cruelty, Abigail. Are you willing to chance how he will treat you as his wife? How he will treat the people Judah?"

The color in her cheeks drained, leaving her pale. She buried her face into her hands. She looked so small, no more than a child. The desire to protect her and those she cared for flowed in his blood. He glanced at Micah. The boy's fierce protectiveness caused pride to swell in Jesse's chest.

"What will it be, Abigail?"

Chapter Five

The turmoil of the past several days was enough to make her weep. How was she to decide which choice to make? One thing was for certain—Suph was a tormentor. One look at Jesse told her the truth of that. What kind of man tormented another man to near death, even if he was a prisoner?

And there was something about Jesse that urged her heart to trust him. What little she could see through his swollen lids beckoned her trust. Besides, if there was the slightest chance that this boy king was her nephew, she owed it to her brother to protect him, even if that meant coming face-to-face with the man responsible for murdering her family. She owed it to herself and to Judah to discover the truth.

She recalled little of her father other than his crazed rantings about a living God, a God her mother had called weak, else he would have rescued the royal family when Jehoiada had slaughtered them in their sleep. If what Jesse said was true and Joash was her brother's son, why would her mother seek to kill him? Wouldn't she want to embrace her only grandchild?

Ha, she had never embraced Abigail. She'd only loved Ahaziah. Her joy, and then he was murdered. Releasing the tension in her neck, Abigail exhaled. "I cannot leave Bilhah."

"You trust the priestess?"

Abigail crossed her arms over her waist as she bit down on her lower lip and then nodded. "I trust her more than anyone." She smiled at Micah. "Besides you, of course, my young friend."

Micah bobbed his head. "I understand. She is your cousin."

Jesse scrubbed his hand over his face and mumbled something unintelligible. "Your cousin? Another princess?"

"Yes. She was my father's niece. My mother honored her by making her the priestess."

He laughed, coughed and then moaned through battered lips. Her heart lurched at his discomfort. Pride kept her feet planted. Why would he laugh at such a thing?

"It is more likely she thought your cousin a threat and sought to remove her from the royal house by soiling her reputation."

Heat climbed up her neck and to her ears. She rose to her feet, fists clenched at her side. She glared down at him. "I should allow Suph to kill you for speaking such things about my mother. And my cousin. She is not soiled."

Jesse held her gaze. He didn't move a muscle for long moments. When he spoke it was clear to her he fought for control. "But you won't. You desire the truth. You need me to meet that end. Without me you get nothing but a marriage to Suph. I've no doubt he'll control your every move. That alone would be a slow death to a woman like you who is used to doing as she pleases."

She sucked in a sharp breath. Doing as she pleases? Ha, as long as she was locked in her room where nobody could lay their eyes on her. Her lack of beauty had brought her mother much shame. "You know nothing." She turned to Micah. "Find Bilhah, tell her to not drink the wine and to come to me as soon as the revelers begin to seek their beds."

Micah's eyes lit with excitement. An excitement Abigail wished she felt. "Dara, find your sons and do what you must. We will need donkeys. Gather a few days' worth of supplies."

"Donkeys will be no match to the captain's horses," Jesse said.

"Ach, I will see what can be done." Dara pierced Abigail with one eye. "I cannot leave you here with him."

Abigail raised her brow. "It's not as if he can move much."

"True, child." She turned a hard glare on Jesse. "Don't make me regret tending your wounds."

"You have no need to fear me, old woman."

"And Dara, I'll need a plain tunic. Two, one for Bilhah. We can't wander the desert in these." She gripped her intricately decorated tunic and held it out.

Dara's gaze climbed from her feet to her head. "I'll see what I can find." She tossed one last glance at Jesse. "S'pose I'll find something for him, as well."

Abigail's cheeks warmed. "Of course."

She watched as Dara left.

"Abigail, it is not my wish to upset you. I should not have spoken harshly about your mother."

She wrung her hands together and then sighed. "Rumors of her brutality were often whispered. However, I do not know what to believe. Was she kind and gentle? Or wicked as they say? Truth be told, I did not know my mother well. She rarely visited my chambers. Instead, I was cared for my nurse, Shema." Abigail wouldn't tell him why, for the shame and disappointment in her mother's eyes still haunted her. Nor did she mention that Shema had left her for the same reasons her mother didn't visit. Abigail was an oddity, a curse from the gods.

"It remains. I should not have spoken about her thusly. I would ask your forgiveness."

She shook her head. "What is this forgiveness?"

"It is where I apologize for my actions and you accept it, if you are willing."

"Then there is no need. It is obvious my mother was not kind, but I believe she adored Bilhah and for good reason—she's beautiful. More beautiful than my mother, even." The corner of her lip inched upward, even as pain sliced in her chest. She looked at her toes peeking from beneath her tunic. "My mother loved beautiful things."

"Then she must have loved you deeply."

Her head snapped up as if she'd been slapped. She blinked, disbelieving what it was she'd heard. There was no sign that he mocked her or played her false. Only sincerity. He'd said the word *beautiful* in the fit of pain, but she hadn't dared to believe he spoke of her. Abigail thought him harmless in his current condition, but given the way her knees wobbled at his compliment, she'd been wrong.

Thinking to take her mind from his words, she paced to the opening of the tent. She snaked her fingers between the slits and pulled back the fabric. The shadow of dancing bodies disappeared into the firelight. The music faded as Jesse's words echoed in her head.

The words tumbling from him had caused air to knot in her throat and the blood to beat faster in her veins. She glanced over her shoulder at the man who had no idea of the turmoil he'd caused between her heart and mind. His words pulled on her emotions, tempted her to trust him, even though he distinctly told her not to. She puffed out a sigh. As much as she wanted to believe his words, believe that she was beautiful, too, she knew he spoke lies, for she was not beautiful. Far from it.

How was she to discern when he did speak the truth? For she had no doubt he would kill her if she threatened Judah's new king. Moreover, how could she put her life in the hands of a man who lied to her?

Because she needed to know the truth. Needed to know if this Hebrew God her mother hated, the one her father had spoken of during his madness, the one Shema had loved, was real. And she needed the truth concerning the death of her brothers and cousins.

Abigail had no choice but to save this man from Suph's wrath and trust he wouldn't kill her. And hope he did not wound her heart.

~

The way Abigail continued to worry her lip told Jesse a battle waged within her. She did not trust him, but he could also tell by her reaction to Suph that she loathed him. With good reason.

He adjusted his position and groaned. She spun around, the tent flaps closing behind her.

"Are you well?" Her cheeks reddened in the lamplight. "It is obvious you are not. Would you like some more water?"

"It is not tainted with poison?" He smiled, his lips smarting with the movement.

A soft lyrical tone danced into the air and skidded along his limbs as she laughed. "Of course."

Her teasing turned his innards upside down and set a knot in his chest. He rubbed his fist against the uncomfortable ache. He'd often joked with his family. Not many outside their close-knit ties had understood his humor or dared to return his teasing. She was a rare gem to be held and cherished, much like the carbuncle he'd worn around his neck. "My throat is parched. I could use the sustenance."

She glided toward the earthen jug and poured water into a goblet before kneeling beside him. He allowed her to help him to a sitting position as he sipped. After he emptied the contents, she lowered him back to the pillows and then rocked back on her heels. Her gaze roamed over his arms and chest. "I fear our journey will not be easy for you."

He believed many of his wounds were superficial. The chamomile he'd drunk along with the honey slathered over his broken flesh had eased the pain and would bring swift healing. If it weren't for his ribs poking his innards, he'd have no trouble moving. However, he was not about to inform Abigail, lest she change her mind. "I will manage. As I told you before, you'd be surprised at what a man can endure when he wishes to live."

Her brow puckered, leaving a little crease above the arch of her nose. "Why is that?"

"I believe God gives man courage and strength."

She shook her head. Her tresses waved down her back. "Why do you wish to live?"

"That is an easy question to answer."

Her chin tilted at an angle, she leaned forward. "What is it?"

He smiled. "Someone must convince you of your beauty since it's obvious you do not believe it yourself."

Her lips parted and her eyes grew wide, and then she smiled. "You tease." She tapped him on the shoulder.

"Ouch!" He bellowed at the unexpected jab.

"Oh, oh, I am sorry." She leaned over. Her hair fell over her shoulder, brushing his skin. She gingerly pressed the tips of her fingers to his wound. He could not feel the tender probe for he was distracted by the way her hair cloaked him. The way cinnamon bathed his cheek as she breathed. Dare he wish for a kiss to his forehead as his mother had done? A kiss to the cheek? "It does not bleed."

He swallowed the stone in his throat. It tumbled to the pit of his stomach, like hard bread.

She pulled back, her soft green eyes peering into his. "Will you...how did you say it, forgive me?"

As he breathed air into his nose, his chest expanded, causing all the minor cuts Suph had inflicted onto his body to split apart. There was something about this woman, the daughter of one of his greatest enemies, the daughter of the woman he'd killed only days ago, that drew him. He trod on dangerous ground, and if he knew what was good for him, he'd leave her to Suph and walk away from this camp of his own accord. Without the help of this shy yet courageous teasing woman.

He raked a palm over his face and felt the swelling and bruising. He must look a beast, he knew, but in his heart he could never act one. He'd killed her mother for the good of Judah. It was a just cause, but he could not, would not leave Abigail to the hands of Suph's evil, for Jesse knew the wounds he sported were no more than child's play. If this woman did not do as Suph wished, he'd no doubt leave her scarred much worse.

"After the care you and Dara have given me, how could I not forgive you?"

The soft glow of the firebrands bathed the smoothness of her skin. Slices of light reflected in her eyes. "My thanks."

He reached for her hand, the hitch in her breathing tumbling in his gut. "I should be the one thanking you."

"Ach, I knew I should not leave you two alone." Dara bustled between the flaps, a linen bag hung down her side. "Your people are dropping off to their sleep. Soon my boys will gather the horses and we'll be on our way." She dug into the linen bag, pulled something out and thrust it at Abigail. "It's the best I could find. There aren't many women as tall as you are."

Twin roses painted Abigail's cheeks. Did her height embarrass her? It shouldn't. Jesse found it appealing, especially since he wouldn't have to hunch over too far to press his lips to hers. Aye, where had that thought come from? The old woman's herbs must have dulled more than his pain.

"I'm sure it will be fine."

"I'll cover his eyes while you change."

Abigail's gaze darted to him; her cheeks brightened further.

"You've no choice unless you decide to stay."

Abigail nodded. Dara dropped to her knees beside Jesse and draped a cloth over his eyes. Her gnarled fingers poked a cut. Jesse gritted his teeth. "The honey works. I'll be binding the rest of your wounds now." He felt her move closer, and the smell of decaying teeth permeated his air. "Do not think to peek at the princess, or I'll leave you to rot."

"You've my word, old woman." Jesse waited in anticipation as Abigail's soft movements filled the tent enclosure. He tried to tell himself that it had more to do with their need for haste; however, he knew otherwise. He wondered if her green eyes would dominate her face once her hair was veiled, making them even more luminous. Aye, he could not fathom such a thought. The woman already lured him to think upon things like marriage and children with her innocent glances. He was so distracted by his thoughts he barely noticed the old woman hovering over him, binding his wounds. If this was how his thoughts turned with only a short time spent in her presence, how was he going to endure their travels to Jerusalem without becoming completely enamored with the princess?

Chapter Six

Abigail dropped the tunic over her head. The scent of sandalwood cloaked her. Embarrassment stained her cheeks at the awkward intimacy of wearing a man's garment, but it was quickly replaced by curiosity and delight. She hadn't looked forward to her skin being chaffed by a rough-spun garment, especially traveling in the desert, but this…she raised her arms, the fabric falling to her ankles, and then wrapped her arms around her waist. The linen, a finer weave than that of the tunic she'd just discarded, was like being cloaked in fleece. She dropped her gaze to the hem pooled at her feet. Where had Dara found such a garment?

"What is this?" She held up a worn leather strap.

Dara looked over her shoulder. "A belt."

"Oh." Abigail inspected the wide material. A tanner had taken great care to pound out the designs. "What do these symbols mean, Dara?"

"Ach, how should I know? They belong to your prisoner."

Abigail's fingers trembled. The belt slipped to the ground. She bent and picked it up. She stood over the man whose belongings she now wore. "Jesse, what do these symbols mean?"

"Do you not know your father's language?"

She glanced at the belt. Her fingers traced the indentations. Some of the symbols looked familiar, but nothing she would have learned from her father.

Rather Shema. Abigail tried to recall the time she'd spent with her nurse. The woman had always smiled at Abigail whenever she entered her chambers. Had always embraced her. Those were the things she remembered most. Perhaps because Shema had made Abigail feel loved.

An image of Shema drawing her fingers through a box of sand forced its way into her thoughts. *"See this one here, Abigail. It is Ya."* It was no more than a curl of Shema's finger, much smaller than the other characters, much like the one carved into the leather. Abigail could not remember what it meant but knew Shema had thought it important.

"This one, what does it mean?" She pointed to the indented symbols as she held it before Jesse's face.

"Yahweh."

Dara clapped her hand over mouth and began muttering beneath her breath. The adoration in Jesse's voice as the word rolled off his tongue left a hunger in Abigail's stomach, a pang in her heart and a thirst for something she did not understand.

"But what does it mean?"

The healer turned a dark eye on her as she held a shaky hand toward Jesse. "It is well we rid our camp of him before Suph gets his hands on him again. We'll all perish of fire and brimstone if he dies. No more questions, child. Some things are best left unspoken." She turned to Jesse. "And you, you should not encourage her. Her life is precarious as it is."

"I want to know, Dara." She glanced at the belt in her hand before turning pleading eyes to Jesse. "I need to know."

His gaze danced between her and the healer. His lips parted as if he were about to say something, but they were interrupted asBilhah ducked into the tent.

Abigail turned toward her. "Are all asleep?"

Bilhah nodded. "Those that linger are too drunk to have their wits. Let's hope Suph will not chase after us for some time." Her eyes twinkled with mischief. Her cousin had never liked the captain. "Grab your things."

"What of my uncle Elam?"

"He is drunk." Bilhah picked up a bag and draped it over her shoulder.

"Here." Dara thrust a plain tunic at her. "You must change."

"Of course."

Once again, the healer covered Jesse's eyes. Abigail wrapped the belt around her waist and clipped it closed. She slipped the wooden box with Jesse's gem nestled inside into a bag. It was all she needed, nothing more. Bilhah tugged the veil from Abigail's head and wrapped her hair into a knot. She then tied a plain linen cloth around her head much like Dara's. A piece braided over the top of her head and tucked in the back.

"Come, Abigail. Micah is waiting." Bilhah parted the tent.

Shaking her head, Abigail rooted her feet. "Not without him."

Bilhah dropped her hands to her side. "We cannot take him with us. He'll slow us down."

"He has given his word to help me."

Bilhah assessed Jesse. "He cannot even lift his head from the pillows, how is he to help?"

"He'll guide us and he'll tell me the truth."

Bilhah's eyes widened. "I will tell you what you want to know, but we must go. Now."

"Not without him," she repeated.

Bilhah paced to her and grabbed hold of her hand. "Why is he important to you, Abigail?"

Abigail's lashes brushed against her cheeks. How could she explain to Bilhah, a woman who'd served her mother's false gods all this time, that this man could not only tell her the truth about her family, but about his God? She pressed her fingers against the indentations on the belt and bit down on her lip. She opened her eyes and looked at her cousin. They'd shared the same nurse. Perhaps Bilhah would remember Shema's words, as well. "Because he knows," she whispered as she eyed Dara.

"Knows what?"

"Yahweh."

Dara began another fit of muttering. Bilhah looked as if she did not believe her. She glanced at Jesse. Abigail willed her cousin to believe. To hope in the stories told them by a beloved nurse as she had tucked them into bed.

Bilhah shook her head. "The people believe this God of his is dead."

"It is not so." Jesse's voice cut through the silence.

"You are nothing but a rebel, willing to sacrifice Abigail's life to meet your end." She looked at Abigail and squeezed her hands. "When the temple guards stormed the palace, there was a moment when I thought..." Her gaze darted to Jesse. "I thought He might live, that his God might rescue us, but here we are cast from our home and at the mercy of a mad man if we do not leave now."

"Bilhah, you said earlier this God would show no mercy."

Her cousin gave her another reassuring squeeze. "You are correct. I did say such things, but now I have to wonder...."

"In time, you will see God has never left Judah." Jesse eased off the pillows.

"I cannot risk Abigail's life. If Suph discovers what we've done this night, he will kill her." Bilhah wrapped her arm around Abigail's shoulders.

"Ach, he'll kill all of us, no doubt."

Her cousin leaned away from her and peered into her eyes. "It is why we must leave now."

"Bilhah, I will not leave him."

Her cousin sucked in a breath. "He cannot even stand on his own. How is he supposed to travel across the rough terrain?"

"The old woman is quite the healer," Jesse said as he rose to his full height.

"You—you are well?" Abigail trembled. She wrapped her arms around her waist. The musky scent of sandalwood cloaked her. She felt protected in his tunic.

Hard lines formed on his brow and near the corners of his eyes. He swayed and she reached out to steady him but he waved her off.

"I am well enough to leave this place."

Bilhah nodded. "Fine, we will take him. However, if he falls he stays where he lands. We will not stop."

Sweat beaded on his face and he swayed once again. "I would not expect you to."

Abigail knew better than to argue, but if he fell, she'd stay with him, no matter what Bilhah thought.

~

Jesse sucked in a breath and girded his loins. He pressed his palm against the stabbing in his side. It took all his strength to stand, even more to speak without slurring his words. The pounding in his head roared with a vengeance and the pain in his ribs felt as if he were being severed in two. He was beginning to think the old woman's herbs hadn't dulled his senses and perhaps he'd been knocked in the head too hard.

"Ach, are you able to walk?"

Clenching his jaw, he nodded. The old woman must have seen the way he gripped his side for she dug into her bag and pulled several long strips of linen from its depths.

"Bilhah, hold on to him while I wrap this around his ribs."

"We do not have time."

The old woman's beady eyes pierced the shrine priestess. "He'll move quicker if I bind the breaks."

"Very well, be quick." Bilhah wrapped his arm around her shoulder to steady him.

"You were more charitable earlier."

Bilhah glanced at Abigail and then glared at him. "That was before I discovered you would have us killed."

"He cannot help his wounds. It is not Jesse's fault Suph captured him." Abigail twisted her hands together.

Jesse growled. It *was* his fault. He should have been alert to his surroundings and taken heed of the warnings that there was a faithful remnant to the deceased queen who would seek to harm King Joash and remove him from the throne. Jesse shouldn't have stopped for rest and fallen asleep before returning to Jerusalem. However, Jesse had not been wise to the threat. In his arrogance he believed all of Judah celebrated the new king and the removal of all idol worship. How wrong he had been. As each of his wounds testified.

"That does not mean we have to save him, Abigail. You always were one to rescue the weak."

Her taunt wounded his pride. He puffed out his chest and quickly deflated it when his ribs sliced at his innards.

"Hold still, boy," Dara said as she began wrapping the linen. "Suck in your air and hold it." She pulled the linen tight. After wrapping three layers and tying the ends, she held out a tunic to Bilhah. "Can you—"

"I'll do it." He grabbed the tunic from Dara's hands. "If I cannot dress myself, I might as well wait for your captain to sleep off his stupor and kill me."

He gathered the ends of the tunic to the neck and dipped his head, thankful Suph had not crushed his hands. He slipped the tunic over his head. Dara handed him a braided belt, which he tied around his waist with great effort. Every movement caused him discomfort, but the bindings around his ribs seemed to sturdy his midsection and lessen the pain. At least now he could breathe without too much difficulty.

Bilhah stuck her head out the tent flaps and then waved them forward. Abigail, seemingly anxious and excited, if the curve of her lips was any indication, rushed out behind her. Dara held the opening of the tent back and motioned for Jesse to exit. He ducked, the movement causing him to lean a little too far forward. Digging his feet into the ground, he rocked back to steady himself. Dara's aged palm flattened against his back. "Do not crush me, boy."

He smiled. "I will try not to."

They skirted along the edge of the tent and made their way out of the silent camp. The large crackling fire cast their shadows before them as if to lead their way. A horse whinnied, another snorted as they proceeded through the maze of tents with as much silence as possible. Warmth rushed into his cheeks; if they got caught escaping he knew it would be his fault, considering his gait was unsteady. How was he to protect this queen's daughter, a shrine priestess, and an old woman?

Sweat beaded on his forehead and he raised the back of his hand to wipe it away. Soon they'd take on Micah and Dara's two boys. If God had any mercy, they'd be of some help. However, he had a feeling the boys were no older than Micah.

After what seemed like half an hour's time but was mayhap only ten laborious minutes, Jesse spotted a lone tree. Shadows began to separate from the trunk, appearing now as if there were three trees. Jesse swiped at the sweat pouring into his eyes and tried to focus on the images. One tree, not three. He gritted his teeth. His brothers had given him beatings during training when he was a boy and he'd received many wounds in battle, but he'd never been sliced open so many times at once. The wounds must be taking their toll if he was imagining things.

His muscles began to shake more viciously with each step. His legs reminded him of honey outside an earthen jug, with no real substance to hold its shape. He was about to give up and lie down on the rocky desert when an odd noise pierced through the thundering ache in his head. He narrowed his eyes into the dark and fought for focus.

Bilhah and Abigail halted their steps. Dara ran into his back. He clapped his hand over her mouth before she could "ach" him and waited. Another low-pitched chatter skirted down his spine. The mimicked sound of a bird did not belong to an animal, but a human. He grabbed for his sword and met his hip before recalling Suph had taken his weapons when he'd captured him.

Biting back his foolishness for once again letting down his guard, he pulled Abigail and Bilhah behind him. It was one thing to be captured while in the presence of his traitorous uncle, quite another with harmless women. He motioned for them to crouch low and was surprised to find even Dara do his bidding. Two behemoth-sized apparitions separated from that tree. Swordlike shadows rose from their sides as they crept toward where Jesse and the women crouched. *God, I need Your help.*

Jesse moved forward. His gaze focused on the armed men. "Who goes there?" He mustered the strength to keep his voice steady. Blood pumped hard in his chest as he waited for their answer. How was he to take on two armed men in his condition?

"Nathan and Jonathan."

"Ach." Dara's whisper rippled through the tension. She rose and tried to rush past Jesse.

Jesse grabbed her arm. "Do you wish to meet your Maker?"

She swatted at his hand. "From my own sons? I think not."

Abigail's quiet laugh caused him to relax as she and Bilhah skipped behind Dara. He tried to keep his eyes on her proud shoulders, on the veil swaying across her back but his vision darkened. A tremor raced over his muscles and his legs quaked.

"The horses are beyond the rise. We did not think it wise to keep them within sight of the camp," one of Dara's boys said.

The display of wisdom by Dara's boys released some of the tension from his shoulders. Jesse breathed out a sigh of relief that Abigail seemed to be in capable hands. If only they knew how to get her out of the captain's reach, then he could give in to the nothingness beckoning him from the grave.

Jesse rocked back on his heels, his head snapping back. He looked up at the twilight sky and breathed deeply. He exhaled, closed his eyes and fell to the ground. Air stole from his lungs. His ribs jolted his innards at the impact. Rocks invaded the cuts and scrapes, pierced his flesh anew and jarred his already thundering head. "Lord, take me into Thy eternal sleep, if You will."

"Are you well?"

He didn't need a firebrand or the light of the moon to know Abigail leaned over him. He didn't need the thundering in his head to halt in order to hear her voice. He could smell the scent of her, feel the way her jasmine scent made the air seem lighter. A peace cloaked him. A peace that came from her genuine concern, for no woman outside of his family had ever cared to ask if he was well.

He reached his hand up and ran his fingers along the curve of her jaw. She shivered beneath his touch, and he smiled. If he died this moment, he'd go a happy man. For what more could a man ask for than to be cared for by such a beautiful and kind woman? "I am."

Chapter Seven

Abigail plopped down beside him and tucked his hand into hers. A warm sensation fluttered in her chest. "I am happy you are well."

The corner of his lip curved upward and she wondered what he looked like beneath the swelling and bruises. If fate shined on her, he would not be handsome. Not at all. For why would a handsome man wish to court her even if she was a princess...or a queen.

"You cannot stay here, Abigail."

"I will not leave you."

His eyes slid shut and for a moment she thought he might be sleeping. If it weren't for the warmth of his hand or the pulse in his palm, she'd weep.

"Abigail, listen to me. Go with Dara's sons. They will take you to Jerusalem."

"She cannot go to the City of David now." Bilhah stood near, her arms crossed over her stomach.

"You are right. Suph is sure to have spies. If she is found—" He coughed, his body jerking with each movement.

"Come, Abigail, we must not tarry." Bilhah reached down and grabbed her upper arm.

Abigail shook her head. "I told you I will not leave him."

"Just as well, if Suph found him he'd know you tried to help him escape instead of his kidnapping you." She waved her hand and Dara's sons approached. "Carry him to the horses. We must figure out how he'll stay seated."

Nathan and Jonathan knelt on either side of Jesse and hefted him to his feet. They carried him toward the tree.

Bilhah reached down and helped Abigail stand. They followed behind Dara's sons and Jesse. "I do not know what it is about this prisoner for you to act so."

"He is a Levite, Bilhah."

She shook her head. "What does that matter to you? Elam is a Levite"

"Ay, but Elam has wickedness burning in his eyes. Jesse does not." Not even when he was angry or in agonizing pain. "Do you not remember the stories Shema told? Do you not remember the God she spoke of?"

"Yes, of course, I do, but what does Shema have to do with Him?"

"Did you ever wonder why Shema left us?"

Bilhah halted, holding on to Abigail's hand. "Shema did not leave us, Abigail. She died."

"Died?" Abigail turned toward her cousin. "My mother told me she left."

Abigail wouldn't tell her cousin that Shema could no longer abide such a gangly child and thus abandoned them. Those reasons were too painful, especially since Shema had seemed to be kind and loving. Nothing at all like Abigail's mother.

"No. Shema died. She was killed. Somehow she had angered your father and he ordered her death."

Abigail jerked her hand from Bilhah's and walked away. She slowed once she was near Jesse. Bilhah grabbed her arm and swung her around. "Abigail, I am sorry."

Abigail swiped at her tears, disbelief washing over her even as guilt bore down upon her shoulders at hearing what she knew in her heart to be true. "Why? Why did he kill her?"

Bilhah hung her head and began to walk away, but Abigail caught her. "Tell me the truth, Bilhah. That is all I want. I have no notions that my father was good. I heard rumors that he killed his brothers, but why, why so much blood on his hands?"

Jesse shook from Nathan and Jonathan's hold. "Your father killed his brothers because he feared they'd take his kingdom."

Abigail believed he spoke the truth, but how was it this stranger knew the reasons when she did not? Because she'd been kept locked in a chamber away from all who might realize Athaliah had a plain daughter with big eyes—green eyes—and was too tall by far. She looked to Bilhah. "Why did he have Shema killed?

"Because he feared she would turn you against him."

Abigail's brow furrowed. "She never spoke of my father, good or ill."

"No. However, she did speak of God, the one your father forced from Judah."

Something in Abigail's heart lurched. She glanced between Jesse, who leaned heavily on one of Dara's sons, and Bilhah. For once her cousin spoke the truth. "Is that why he killed his brothers. Your father? Because they believed in the one true God?"

The sliver of moon illuminated the sadness flitting across Bilhah's face. "We must go before anyone realizes we are gone."

Abigail unwittingly looked toward the camp. Glimmers of white tents stood off the desert and reached into the sky. The glow of the fire continued to burn as her curiosity burned. She'd been hidden away, kept from so much; she wanted to know the truth and she wanted to know now. However, she did not know what Dara had tainted the wine with. The more time they remained close to camp, the less time they had to escape.

"Let us go, then. Soon you will give me the answers I seek, Bilhah." She looked at Jesse. "You too." Somehow she knew once he regained his strength she'd not be able to command him. He was not the type to obey orders but rather give them. She knew that in the way he spoke and the way he tried to carry himself as if he was used to commanding an army.

She would have the truth, even if it caused her great heartache. The thought that her own father had killed so many was like drinking poison. Why did he? And why kill Shema?

She thought back to the last moments. Shema had been bathing her and Bilhah, telling them a story of the burning bush and how God came down and spoke with a man. Later God had led the Hebrew people out of slavery from Egypt and they wandered in the desert for many years. At the time, Abigail couldn't imagine four days in the desert let alone forty years. When Abigail had asked her why they had to walk so long, Shema had told her that God needed to purge the Egyptian gods from their minds and reestablish Himself as their God and then He took a man to a mountain and gave them laws to follow.

Abigail had dreamed of burning bushes and talking mountains that night and she had waited anxiously for Shema to return. She never did. Until now she never knew why. To discover her father had had her killed burned in Abigail's stomach and all because Shema had told her a story.

~

Jesse lumbered between Dara's two boys. Two boys? Not likely. They were grown men, near the same height as he. From the way their muscles bunched and pulled with each step, they were fit. He recalled their raised swords and at the time had thought them to be soldiers in the queen's guard. However, now he was not positive. Their feet did not carry the surefootedness required of a successful man of war, but then neither did his at the moment. Still, he'd have to keep an eye on them. Certainly they were loyal to their mother, but was Dara loyal to Abigail or to Captain Suph?

He grunted. Perhaps he should not be so quick to think ill of the old woman. She had worked diligently beside Abigail tending his wounds. If she intended to see him dead she would not have wasted her time or her precious herbs.

"The horses are not that much farther," one of the men said.

"Will you be able to sit a horse?" the other one asked.

"I would like to tell you with great assurance yes." He drew in a breath. "But I find each step jarring to my innards."

"Aye, broken ribs will weaken a man." The man on his right adjusted Jesse higher onto his shoulder. "I fear no matter how you sit a horse the ride will jar you even more."

Of that Jesse was certain and did not look forward to long hours on a horse. And since they had decided not to go straight to Jerusalem it looked as if he'd spend more time than he'd like riding.

"Do we even know where we are going?"

Jesse had thought about it since Bilhah reminded them Jerusalem would not safe for Abigail, and he agreed.

However, that meant most of Judah would not be safe for the wayward princess. Those areas that would offer her sanctuary he could not take her to. He would not risk the safety of his people. "I need to get word to Jerusalem. There is a man who will help—"

"I will go. Give me direction."

Jesse shook his head. "My forgiveness, but I do not even know which of you is Nathan and which is Jonathan."

They laughed.

"I'm Jonathan."

"I'm Nathan."

Of course, their tandem chorus did Jesse no good in the dark. "The fact remains, I do not know if I can trust you."

The men halted. The one on his left looked at him. "Do you intend to go yourself, then?"

The one on the right said, "Either one of us goes and the other stays, or we both stay. You have no choice at the moment other than to trust us. Nathan is swift footed and can help protect the women. I can ride faster than most. It will take me no time to reach Jerusalem."

"How do I know you won't return to camp and alert Suph?"

They laughed once again. "If we wanted to hand you over, we would have done so before we stole the captain's horse and saved ourselves much trouble."

Jesse chuckled even as he heard the neighing of horses.

"We are there," Jonathan said before he let out a low rumbling chirp that rolled down Jesse's spine.

Jesse looked from one to the other. "We learned our ways from our father. He didn't trust anyone easily, either." Nathan leaned in closer. "And he despised those who worshipped the false gods."

Before he could respond they settled Jesse against a tree. Jesse slid down its base and sat. The two crouched beside him. Micah stepped from the horses and greeted Abigail.

"Who is this man in Jerusalem you wish me to find?" Jonathan asked.

"I do not even know where to find him, only that he is in the city. Perhaps if you seek counsel with Jehoiada…"

Nathan and Jonathan glanced at each other and then shook their heads. "With the uprisings it will be near impossible to get word to Jehoiada. Tell me his name. I will find him."

"Ianatos."

"The Philistine?" Jonathan raked a hand through his hair.

"Ye—yes." Having lived in Jerusalem much of the past seven years, Jesse was familiar with most of the people, but even being part of the temple guard he'd never before met Ianatos. It hadn't been until a week ago when Ianatos helped him and Ari defeat Suph and the palace guard when they'd sought to kill young Joash that he'd met the elusive warrior. So, how was it these two knew of him? Jesse narrowed his eyes. "How do you know of him?"

Their faces lit into identical smiles. Jesse couldn't be sure but he thought the two might be twins. "We know many people and many things. Things not privy to ordinary people."

Jesse furrowed his brow. "How is it you came to be in Suph's camp?"

"As my brother said, we know many things. The captain's plans for Abigail cannot be good, and our mother loves her like a daughter. She's loyal and would do anything for the princess." Jonathan lowered his voice. "As would Bilhah."

"Those who are here, except you, have Abigail's best interest. We do not wish to see her used as Suph would, even if she is the rightful leader of Judah." Nathan said.

"Brother, it could be the child who is in truth the rightful heir."

It seemed that even though the brothers agreed on protecting Abigail, they disagreed on her position as queen.

"Jonathan will take your message to Ianatos and I will stay. However, we cannot remain here so close to camp. Where is it we shall meet?"

"You are correct," Jesse said. "Tell him to meet us by the creek where we fought the queen's guards a few days ago."

Nathan placed his hands on his hips. "Out in the open?"

Jesse shook his head. "No, we will be close by and keep watch. Tell him Ari's brother Jesse needs his assistance in saving our king." He glanced from one to the other, daring them to say otherwise. "He will come."

"What makes you certain this Philistine will help your king? Only days ago he was loyal to Athaliah." Nathan jammed his hands on his hips.

Jesse considered the question. For some reason he felt the man's question was a test, but what sort of test Jesse did not know. It was obvious they knew of Ianatos, which meant they possibly knew what he was. Besides, their reaction to the truth would help him ascertain exactly where their loyalties laid. "Ianatos comes from a line of Philistines warriors who have vowed to protect the line of King David. He is a Carite and recognizes King Joash for who he is. The rightful heir to King David's throne."

Chapter Eight

His words penetrated every bit of her being. She had not believed the child was truly the king, not for certain. However, if this Philistine Jesse sought believed it enough to change his loyalties to protect the child, then perhaps it was true. She may have been sheltered but she had been taught much about the Carites, the Philistine guard and their ancient vows. The entire royal house knew of them, even her.

What was it was about the child that made everyone believe he was her nephew? She thought to ask but Nathan said his goodbyes to Jonathan. Soon Nathan was lifting her and then Bilhah onto a horse. A thick blanket draped over the horse's back cushioned her seat. Nathan handed her a thick braided rope that was attached to something in the horse's mouth. "Do not yank on this, Abigail, else you'll find yourself quickly on the ground. Stay relaxed. She'll follow us when it is time to leave."

"She is a beauty." Abigail patted the horse's neck. Muscles quivered beneath her fingertips.

Bilhah grabbed hold of her waist. "Whatever it is you are doing, please do not."

Abigail glanced over her shoulder. "Does the beast frighten you?"

Her cousin shuddered. "I have not had much chance to ride one."

Abigail laughed. "Neither have I, Bilhah, although I've often wondered what it would be like. They are majestic, proud beings. I loved watching them parade through the courtyard."

"Ach, but they always left a mess. Not so majestic if you ask me." Dara scratched at her head.

"Can you mount on your own?" Nathan held a hand out to Jesse, who leaned heavily against a tree.

"I believe so." Jesse grabbed his hand. With Nathan's palm beneath Jesse's elbow he helped him off the ground. A painful growl emanated from Jesse's throat. The horse danced around.

Bilhah squeezed her tighter. "Would you quit petting the beast?"

"I fear the horse will move whenever it wants."

"Then I'd prefer to walk."

"Ach, me too."

"I do not think so, Mother." Nathan said. "We must make haste and you walk slower than any snail shriveling in the sun." Her face paled. "No worries, Mother. I won't let anything happen to you."

Nathan assisted Jesse onto the horse and then lifted Micah behind him. "Her name is Papyrus because Suph believed her to be a rare creature in her beauty. And if tales be true, she was stolen out of Egypt. If we have cause to run fast you'll see why."

"My thanks," Jesse said, his jaw clenched in pain.

Nathan's hand rested on his hip. "You are certain you can ride?"

Jesse straightened his spine; the grimace deepened. "I have no choice in the matter unless I wish to die. Besides, God will give me the strength I need. And young Micah is strong. He will hold me steady."

Nathan smiled and then nodded. Abigail glanced at the night sky. Tiny lights flickered all across the horizon. Her nose tickled and tears pricked her eyes as her heart lightened. There was something about Jesse's hope in this unseen God that invaded her caution. Somehow it dispelled her fear of the unknown. She was unsure what it was, but it seemed as if all would be well as long as Jesse was near.

But what would happen when they parted ways? Where would he go? Where would she go?

Nathan hefted his mother onto a horse and climbed behind her. "Lead the way."

Jesse guided his horse toward the south. They rode in silence for some time. Abigail bit her lip to keep from asking the questions clinging to her tongue. She did not wish her voice to carry and she did not wish to tax Jesse's strength any more than what was being exerted from remaining seated on the horse.

She watched him for signs of weakness, but none showed. His hands weren't clenched around the braid. They were loose as if he were comfortable around horses. His shoulders were relaxed, not wrought with the pain he'd endured earlier. His swollen jaw, although cut and bruised, seemed to have lost the tenseness. Every so often he glanced at the stars and then guided them in a different direction. She tried to see what sign he was looking for, but she could not discern one star from another, although she'd heard of those who could.

So many questions itching to be asked ran through her thoughts. She maneuvered her horse beside his and glanced at him.

"We are safe enough to speak. What is it you wish?"

"How do you know where we are going?"

"The stars and landmarks guide me. You see that star there?" He pointed toward a bright one. "If you look at the stars around you'll see the pictures they make."

"I do not—"

"There, it's a ladle hanging upside down," Bilhah said.

"Yes, and by looking at the star at the end of the handle I know I need to go west until I meet up with that grove of trees there." He pointed toward the trees. "And once we get there we turn south and east until we reach the hills."

"Then where do we go?"

"We rest and wait for Jonathan to arrive with help."

She glanced toward the sky, then to the trees before looking to the sky again. "You make it sound easy."

His lips twisted. "I've had practice. A lot of it. My brothers and I were taught by our father to find our directions by the stars from the time we could walk."

Sadness swirled in her heart. Jesse's life had been different from hers. It was obvious in the way he spoke that he loved his family greatly. Her brothers had been kept from her as if she'd taint them in some way. Even if Ahaziah hadn't been groomed to be a king the difference in their ages would have kept them from bonding like Jesse and his brothers. "You love your family very much?"

The light of the moon caught his white teeth and glinted. He smiled. "I do."

Bilhah patted Abigail's thigh as if to comfort her, as if she understood the sorrow building in her eyes.

"And you spent a lot of time outdoors?"

A rumble bubbled from his throat. At her silence he glanced at her. "I did. What of you, Princess?"

She shook her head. Before she could say a word, Bilhah spoke up. "Abigail's mother feared the sun would taint her flawless complexion."

"I forget you were raised in the royal house, but certainly you were allowed to run and play in the courtyard."

Bilhah's arms tensed around Abigail's waist. "Future queens do not run and play. They learn how to comport themselves and serve their husbands."

He pressed his lips together. He looked up to the sky and then back ahead of him. He swayed on the back of the horse but straightened his shoulders.

"What was it like? Having your father teach you things?"

"Abigail, you should not torment yourself," Bilhah whispered in her ear.

"I have many fond memories of my childhood. My father was, still is, attentive to his children, even my brothers who were sent to Jerusalem to study. My father is wise and loving. He has sought to follow God's will and instill in his children the same values. He always made us feel as if we were important, not just to him, but to God. He also made us feel as if we were loved above all things, except my mother and God. More importantly he showed us how to worship the Creator of heaven and earth."

"Why would you do that?"

"Why would you worship an idol carved of wood or hammered from bronze by the hands of man?" His words snapped like a mangy dog fighting for a bone.

Although she had never partaken of such festivities, she felt the shame nonetheless.

He blinked his eyes closed. "My apologies. I should not have spoken with such harshness. I worship a God who created the heavens and the earth we live on. A God who loved me enough to knit me in my mother's womb. A God who is faithful, who will never leave me."

Bilhah laughed. "How can you say that? Where was your God when Suph captured you?"

"Right beside me. I cannot see the plans God has for me. All I can do is seek His guidance and trust that He is faithful in all things."

This intrigued her, but she wanted to know how he ended up in their camp. "Where were you going when Suph caught you?"

He remained silent for several long minutes and she thought he chose to ignore her. His chest rose and fell; his lashes blinked against his cheeks, the only sign he had not fallen asleep.

"I was taking my uncle Elam back to Jerusalem."

Bilhah mumbled something beneath her breath

Abigail glanced over her shoulder.

"Elam is the one who told your mother about this boy king. She promised to allow him access to the temple as the new high priest if he gave her the boy," Bilhah said.

"He is also my uncle. My father's brother."

Abigail sucked in a ragged breath at Jesse's revelation. Jesse's family wasn't without fault? "Why would he do such a thing? If you believe this child to be the rightful heir, why would your uncle betray you?" And why had her mother wanted the boy found? If he was an imposter then he was no threat to her position. However, if the boy was in truth the descendant of King David, then her mother would lose her throne. Would her mother have had the boy killed? A mere child? Her own grandchild?

"I would tell you my uncle thought he had Judah's best interest in mind, but I fear he was obsessed with selfish ambitions. It is fortunate for him Suph found us when he did else my uncle would have stood before the elders and would have been judged for his actions. The punishment would not have been easy on him. I must trust God will see justice served for the wrongs he committed against innocent people."

"You would see him die?"

Jesse pulled up on the braided rope, halting his horse. "Because of Elam's jealousies people died. Children have died. If that is not enough to convince you, he had my brother beaten and left for dead, worse than what Suph has done to me. If it were not for the bravery of a young girl, he would have perished in the desert and my family would never have known." He shifted. "He tried to have Joash killed. Even after Joash was set on the throne and your mother dead, he refused to acknowledge the will of God and kidnapped my brother's betrothed." He raked his fingers through his hair. "Elam is evil."

"He is your family."

"Yes, that he is. However, as much as I dislike it, his lack of repentance will force me to ashes and sackcloth." Even in the pale moonlight she could see sorrow in his eyes at the prospect of mourning a loved one. His brow furrowed and she imagined his nostrils flared much like they had when she and Dara had treated his wounds. "You of all people should know, Abigail, family can turn against each other."

~

Her jaw dropped and she looked toward her cousin. He didn't wait for her response. It was obvious Abigail had led a sheltered life. Sheltered enough to be ignorant of the atrocities her parents had committed against their own flesh and blood, no different from his own, but he wasn't in the mood to smooth her ruffled feathers. He wouldn't take back his words even if they did unlock mysteries better left alone. However, with the questions flitting through her eyes, he wasn't about to hang around and wait for them. He wasn't in the mood to tell her the truth. Besides, it wasn't his responsibility.

He tapped a heel to the horse's flank and rode toward the high trees. The jarring movement rewarded him with a slice to his innards. He bit down on his cheek to keep from crying out. He would not give anyone the satisfaction of knowing how difficult it was for him to remain seated on Papyrus.

Jesse tilted his head toward the sky. The bright star in the handle remained high and to his right. By his calculations they'd reach the grove before too long.

The heavy clopping of hooves closed in upon him. He looked over his shoulder. Dara's arms clung to her son's waist, as did Bilhah's to Abigail. Nathan moved beside him. "I fear we've been discovered."

Jesse twisted around. The movement stressed the stitches of his cuts. He squinted into the dark. Although difficult to discern from the distance and the dark, Jesse knew several horses rode toward them. Given they were horsed men could only mean one thing. Suph had woken sooner than expected and had discovered their absence.

"Come." He pulled the reins to the right and rode hard toward the hills for several long minutes before halting. "Head straight. Hide in the shadows of the cliffs. There is a path on the far east, just wide enough for the horses. Go slow as it is narrow. Follow it up thirty paces. Look for a cave. It is large enough for the horses. There are caverns to hide in, as well. I'll fall back. Micah," he said, twisting around. "You must go with them and help protect the women."

"You cannot think to fight Suph and his men alone. Not in your condition."

Nathan looked hesitant at Abigail's words even as he lifted Micah up in front of Dara.

"Go. Protect them well."

Nathan nodded and handed Jesse a dagger. Abigail's chin took on a stubborn tilt. This was no time to argue. He glanced at Nathan who acknowledged the silent command. Nathan kicked his heels into the horse's sides as Jesse smacked the rear of Abigail's horse.

It was not where he wanted to take them, but he had no choice. Not with Suph closing in.

Jesse rode hard toward the trees. At the quick pace it didn't take long for them to shelter him. He dismounted, his legs wobbling beneath him. Sweat beaded on his forehead and he leaned against Papyrus until he gathered his strength. He tugged the horse deeper into the grove and, unclipping the hooks from one side of the bit, tossed the reins over a low-hanging branch before making his way back to the outer edge. He crouched behind a bush and peered into the dark as he watched for the riders. He prayed the men had followed him and not seen Abigail escape.

A dark shadow bobbed up and down, then another, followed by several others. He exhaled a shaky breath. His pulse pounded in his ears. He lost sight of the riders, blinked his eyes and found them again.

He leaned left, then right. Nausea smacked him in the gut. He choked back the bile and tried breathing through his nose. This was not the time for his body to succumb to his injuries, not when Abigail needed him and Ianatos had no idea where to find her now.

The roaring in his head took on a thundering sound. The muscles in his legs began to shake. He blinked his eyes against the sting of perspiration. "Lord, I need strength for a few moments more."

The riders halted just outside the tree line and Jesse released a slow breath of air. One rider dismounted, crouching to the ground. His fingers danced over the desert as if to search for tracks.

A horse snorted. Jesse prayed Papyrus to silence, but an answering snort echoed through the pounding in his head.

The man glanced toward the shrubs. He tilted his head as if to affirm what it was he heard. He rose and draped the reins over the horse's neck and then walked toward Jesse's hiding place. Jesse prayed he'd turn right or left—anywhere but straight—but the man's feet never wavered.

Jesse swallowed. He wanted to shrink into the bushes, but if he dared move his muscles would give out and he'd be good as dead. At least Abigail was safe.

Lord, what am I to do? He squeezed his eyes shut for a moment. *If anything happens to me, please see to Abigail's safety. Help her find the truth she is looking for. And protect Joash from Suph's evil intentions.*

A sense of peace settled over Jesse's shoulders and he hoped the man would turn around and leave, but as he approached, his steps held their course, never veering. Jesse slipped the dagger from his belt, never taking his eyes from the man, not even when he stood with hands on his hips staring down at Jesse.

Jesse sucked in a breath and released it out slowly. The thundering in his temple worsened. He clenched his fingers around the hilt and prepared to strike out. The man leaned over the bush. Jesse tilted his head back. His vision grew dark. His muscles gave into their exhaustion and Jesse fell over onto the ground.

Chapter Nine

With her arms crossed over her stomach, Abigail paced the small cavern while Bilhah and Dara huddled against a wall, flax blankets wrapped around their shoulders. A lone firebrand flickered in the small cave. The incident when the horse's hooves had stumbled still left her shaken. When Nathan had realized how narrow the path was he'd helped them to dismount, commanding them to stay close to the face of the mountain. Reluctant to relinquish her perch on the back of the horse Abigail had chosen to remain seated.

What if Jesse had fallen and was in need of their help? What if Suph had captured him? "I do not like this."

Nathan's broad shoulders tensed at her words. He stood at the mouth of the cave, watching. "The blankets are the best I could do."

"I do not speak of our comforts, Nathan. Jesse is out there alone, defenseless." She would not mention her fears about Jesse falling from the ledge. It'd only cause her friend's anger to resurface.

"He has a dagger," Nathan growled.

"Ach, he can barely hold his head straight and you think he can hold your knife."

Surprised at Dara's defense of Jesse, Abigail glanced at her. The old woman smiled a toothless grin. "I did not waste my time tending his wounds to see him dead, child."

"He will not die, Mother."

"How do you know this?" Bilhah asked.

Micah tucked his knees into his chest, Abigail was certain, to ward off the chill. "Jesse is a warrior."

"I do not see how that makes a difference in this case. He's wounded, helpless as a wingless bird."

"And you chatter as such." Nathan turned around and crossed his arms over his chest. "If you will all be quiet I can stay attuned to what is going on out there. We would not want anyone to catch us unaware." He swiveled back around, his back stiff as one of the marble and bronze pillars at the palace.

"If you would only leave us and find him. I'd rest easier."

Nathan tossed a dark glance over his shoulder. "Would you rest easy without my protection here? In a dark cave where creature and man could happen about?"

Abigail bit down on her lip to keep from arguing. As much as she disliked it Nathan was right. She couldn't send him out to help Jesse. She couldn't risk Dara, Micah and Bilhah's lives any more than she already had.

She dropped her hands to her sides and paced.

"Child, you are making me nervous," Dara whispered. "Come." She stretched out her arm, holding the edge of her blanket. "Sit and rest. We'll need our strength."

Abigail glanced toward Nathan, who had yet to move, and then toward his mother and Bilhah. Releasing a resigned sigh, she took four steps and dropped beside Dara. The old woman wrapped her arm over Abigail's shoulder and tucked her head onto her shoulder.

"I do not like this waiting."

"I know, child. We have no choice."

"What if something has happened to him? What if Suph…what if he's dead?"

"We will know soon enough," Bilhah said.

"Your cousin is right. We will know soon enough if anything has happened to your Jesse."

Her Jesse? Jesse did not belong to her. He did not like her, nor she him. Did she? He was a Levite. A man who could tell her the truth about those things everyone else hid from her. He also knew this God Shema had spoken of and she wanted to hear more about, but Jesse did not belong to her. Even if she were to become queen she could not force his loyalty or his friendship, no matter how much she wished it.

"Close your eyes and rest, Abigail. Nathan will stand guard and wake us when Jesse arrives."

Abigail raised her head from Dara's bony shoulder. "What—"

"Shh, child." Dara patted Abigail's head and then stroked her hair. It was something Shema had done often, whenever Abigail was agitated.

Abigail blew out a frustrated breath. Dim light flickered off the walls from the firebrand. The light seemed to dance with the shadows. At times one would overtake the other causing the weaker to disappear, only for it to reappear once again.

Was that how good and evil worked? Had Jesse's uncle always been evil or had it been like the dark shadows overtaking the light? She could not imagine him always being evil or else Jesse's family would have known much sooner. So what happened to cause the man to change?

An image of her mother pressed into her thoughts. She'd always glided from place to place. Her beauty seemed good, but Abigail knew the viperous tongue that lashed out. She had witnessed her mother's cruelty. Her mother had been like the firebrand, beautiful, illuminating and dangerous.

Abigail drew in a shaky breath. If she were to believe all she'd heard, both her parents had been evil. Her father for having Shema killed, her mother…Abigail didn't need rumors to tell her of her mother's deeds. She'd seen them for herself—did that make her evil, too?

She shuddered.

"Are you cold, child?"

No, she wasn't, but how could she explain to Dara her fears? She snuggled closer to the warmth and comfort offered by this grandmotherly figure. The thought of causing pain to anyone left her with great sadness, but what if she were to change like Jesse's uncle? What if she became obsessed with an idea or a goal and allowed it to take over her actions? Obviously, evil ran thick in her veins.

A tear perched on the edge of her lashes and she closed her eyes against the wayward emotion. She would not allow her parents' lives to dictate her future. And if aught happened to Jesse and she somehow ended up in Suph's grasp, she'd make sure he did not dictate her future, either.

Dara's hand, stroking through her hair, lulled her into relaxation. Her breathing grew heavy and she knew sleep would soon follow if she did not get up and resume her pacing, but she could not force her aching body to move. She had never traveled before. The past few days were making her muscles ache and her body exhausted. And although she didn't fear the horse, she'd never ridden one outside her dreams. If she was aching, how was Jesse holding up? He was still out there.

Whoever You are, Jesse's God, I do not know if You hear me, or care to, but if so, if You are the Creator of heaven and earth, if You care for Jesse as he believes, please protect him from our enemies. And Jesse's God, if You are real, will You reveal Yourself to me? I do not want to live as my mother did, bowing to man-made idols.

Dara's soft snores, along with Bilhah's louder ones, intruded into Abigail's prayers, but she nevertheless felt that lightness enter her heart. It was as if it was easier to breathe, as if she knew without a doubt all would be well.

~

Jesse swatted at the annoying hand shaking his shoulder. It'd been ages since his brothers had bothered him. Why did they choose now to interrupt his dreams? He wanted to stay right where he was, reclining on furs and purple pillows, basking in Abigail's smile and her jasmine-scented domain, although he could do without that rock poking him in the back and the knife piercing his side. Why was Abigail holding a blade to his ribs? Had he said something to irritate her?

He peeled a lid back. The stony-faced jaw of a man stared back at him. He was not Abigail. Jesse covered his eyes with the crook of his elbow. His skin tugged and burned. "Would you mind removing your knife from my ribs?"

"You think I've come to kill you?" The shocked disbelief in the man's tone filled Jesse with guilt.

"Why else are you poking me with your blade?"

"There is no blade against your ribs, Jesse."

Jesse lifted his arm away from his eyes. Ianatos set his jaw, and not a wrinkle furrowed his stony brow. Jesse tried to ease up onto his elbows. The sharp pain sucked the breath from his lungs. He collapsed back to the ground. It was then he recalled his encounter with Suph.

"Where is Abigail?"

"Your woman?" Ianatos rocked back on his heels, revealing a watchful, scowling Jonathan, whose fists were jammed on his hips. His fingers twitched near the hilt of his sword.

"She is not my woman, Ianatos."

Jonathan dropped his hands to his sides, his shoulders relaxed. Jesse inhaled relief.

"Jonathan, have you seen your brother?"

"I would ask you the same?" Tension rolled back into his shoulders as he puffed out his chest.

"We saw riders fast approaching. I did not wish to take a chance with Abigail's life. I sent Nathan and Micah with the women to safety."

"Aye, there were signs of patrols as we trailed you. We could not tell if they are ahead of you or behind you, but it seems as if Suph is in the area. Can you ride?" Ianatos asked.

Jesse laughed. "I do not even know if I can sit. Suph thought to use me as practice for tossing his dagger. Fortunately for me, he missed more times than he hit his mark. Unfortunately, his poor aim angered him even more."

Ianatos pulled back the edge of Jesse's sleeve. "It seeps blood, but looks clean. How many more?"

Jesse twisted his lips. "I did not take count."

"He's at least one broken rib. Mother bound them, but he still moves like a snail." Jonathan stepped from Jesse's sight but then quickly reappeared with an earthenware flask the size of a goblet. He crouched beside Jesse and lifted his shoulders off the ground. "Here, drink this. It is water from the spring."

Jesse sipped from the opening. "My thanks. How did you find Ianatos so quickly?"

Jonathan grinned. "As I said, my brother and I know many things. I signaled to a friend and they signaled to Jerusalem using a firebrand. Ianatos met me halfway."

"My men and I were with Jonathan's friend and not in the city, so we weren't far," Ianatos explained.

"Come." A warrior almost as large as Ianatos stood behind Jonathan's shoulder. Jesse did not recognize him. "The sun is nearing the horizon. We must be going."

"You brought company?"

Ianatos nodded. "Friends. They will not harm you or your woman." He glanced over his shoulder at Jonathan. "As long as she is not a threat to King Joash."

"She is no threat." Even as Jesse said the words, he could not be sure. After all, she was the daughter of Athaliah. However, he did not think Abigail had cruelty running through her blood. She was too innocent, too pure. For some reason, Athaliah had shielded her child from her evil.

"Come, let us get you on your horse." Ianatos grabbed hold of Jesse's arms and lifted him to his feet.

Jesse could not help the groan escaping his throat. The men around him spun. Black spots danced before his eyes. He squeezed them closed. For a moment he felt as if he was tumbling, but a firm hand steadied him.

"We must get him to Mother. She'll treat his wounds."

Jesse opened his eyes. "She's done well, my friend. It's the ache in my ribs and the pounding in my head."

Jonathan stepped closer. His fingers probed through Jesse's hair.

"Ow!"

Ianatos scowled but moved closer to inspect the area in question. His fingers skimmed over the bump. Jesse winced.

"Did Mother see this?"

Jesse thought back to the wounds she and Abigail tended. "Not that I recall."

Ianatos pulled back, his scowl deeper. "You have a nasty bump on your head. Suph must have clouted you good."

"Aye, with the hilt of his sword." He recalled that moment with clarity. Suph's men had held his arms behind his back. He'd already been stabbed with the dagger multiple times, already had his face beaten. He could barely stand when Suph wrapped his hands around the blade of his sword, arced it upward and brought it down on Jesse's skull. He didn't recall anything afterward. Everything had gone dark. Next thing he knew he was standing before Abigail.

He hadn't known what Suph's plans were for him until that moment. It was obvious the captain intended to marry her and rule through her. Not if Jesse had anything to do with it. She was too good for the likes of Suph. He'd use her and then destroy her, locking her away in a cold chamber in the palace. If he didn't kill her. Some of the questions she'd asked led him to believe she'd never before left the palace until a few days ago. He wondered, by the way she asked about the night sky, if she'd ever seen stars before.

He looked at the horizon, streaking gray, pink and purple. The brilliant hues created by God each morning had always left him in awe of God's greatness. Had Abigail ever seen the sun rise? Had she seen it set? He prayed today would not be her first for he wanted nothing more than to share that experience with her. He had the sudden urge to be on his way, if only to discover other aspects of God's creation through Abigail's eyes.

"Are you two going to stand there poking at my scalp all morning?"

The two looked at each other and then at Jesse.

"No."

"No."

"Then what are we waiting for? The sun to set?"

Ianatos grumbled something unintelligible. Jonathan glared, but they both helped him mount Papyrus. He glanced at the men who rode with Ianatos. Ten. How were they going to get all of them and their horses on the path and into the cavern? He'd have to discuss it with Ianatos.

"Are you sure you can ride?"

The thought of jasmine and seeing Abigail smile fueled his strength. "Yes. However, there may be a problem." He told Ianatos and Jonathan of the pass along the rugged hills and the danger it possessed. He had been thankful for the cover of darkness when Nathan led the women, else they would have been frightened. "We cannot take all of your men."

"Where does it lead?" Ianatos asked. Jesse knew he spoke of hidden tunnels within some of the caves.

Jonathan cocked his head. "Where does what lead?"

Jesse rolled his shoulders to ease the ache from sitting on the horse. "Nowhere, my friend."

Ianatos gave him a look as if to say he did not believe him but did not press further, for which Jesse was thankful. Although Ianatos had helped them dispatch a few of the captain's men when they'd followed his brother and King Joash into the caves, Jesse was still unsure how much he could trust Nathan and Jonathan, and although he'd told

Nathan of the alcoves for hiding he doubted the man would search further, especially given his reaction when Jesse mentioned the cave.

"Have your men camp where we camped by the creek. If all goes well we will be there soon. With our numbers we should be safe enough and if we're fortunate my family will be there. If they are, tell your men to keep their distance as to not alarm them." Jesse eyed the large Philistines. "A battle between your men and my father's would not be good if there was a misunderstanding."

"Your people would be slaughtered," Jonathan said.

Ianatos burst into laughter. "Never underestimate your opponent, especially if he is a man of the one true God."

Pride at Ianatos's compliment welled within Jesse's chest, until he remembered he was responsible for their current plight. He'd let his guard down thinking all was well within Judah. Aye, his brother Ari had cautioned him against those faithful to Athaliah, but he didn't think they'd rally so soon after her death. He should have been more watchful; if he had he wouldn't now be in his current condition. If Suph messaged his father and brothers, Jesse knew they'd never give up Joash, but they'd do all in their power to rescue him, which would place them in danger.

He had no doubt his family could handle Suph's mere army but why cause them needless trouble? If he'd been more careful…if he'd been more careful, then he'd never have laid eyes on Abigail. And to what end? She was of the royal house. He was a warrior. She was obviously sheltered and knew little of the horrors he'd seen. They could overcome all those obstacles if he thought to court her. She was easy on the eyes and he admired her compassionate nature. Not just when she insisted on his wounds being treated, but her insistence on protecting an old woman and a prostitute. However, he could not overlook one thing. She did not believe in God.

"Are you well?"

Jesse blinked, bringing his vision into focus. Jonathan sat his horse beside him.

"Your cheeks have lost some of their color. I do not wish you to fall from your horse."

Jesse smiled. "I am well enough, although I will be glad when these wounds heal." Ianatos's men left. Jesse and Jonathan walked their horses toward the Philistine. "Shall we go?"

Ianatos nodded. "I sent two of my men to scout the area. They are to signal if trouble arises."

"And what of Joash?" Jesse guided his horse toward the rugged hills.

"After Jonathan informed me of Suph's plans, I sent messengers to alert Jehoiada and the others. The king is well guarded."

A little relief replaced the guilt of being caught unaware. He had no idea what plans God had in store for him, or why God had allowed Jesse to be captured by the captain. Perhaps it was to alert others of the imminent danger.

Abigail's green eyes and brilliant smile pressed into his thoughts. Perhaps God had another reason altogether. Dare he hope? If only she would call on the name of the Lord with sincerity then he would be free to explore his growing feelings where she was concerned. But then her ancestry was tainted with evil. Aye, that did not matter, as he could testify. Although a man's lineage often influenced, it did not dictate his future. The same could be said for Abigail. He'd seen the compassion in her eyes. Compassion her mother had lacked.

It would be good to know if the fluttering in his chest whenever he thought of her or spied her smile was something more than owing her a debt for saving his life.

"Jesse!"

He shook his head and glared at Ianatos, who had halted his horse. Jesse pulled on the reins. "Can a man ride in peace without your chattering?"

"If we knew where we were going." He waved his hand out in front of him. "You are about to run us into the face of the mountain."

Jesse swiveled back around. The cliff stood tall, leaving them in the cool shadows. An ibex stared down upon them, his curled horns looking deadly. An eagle, looking for the morning meal, soared above.

"We are close." He guided his horse to the east and around the rocky edge until the morning sun bathed them in its warmth.

He spied the path and began the slow, tedious climb.

"You cannot think to take us on this ledge." Jonathan's voice quivered.

"Are you frightened, Hebrew?" Ianatos's tone meant to dispel Jonathan's fear.

Jesse was tempted to turn around. He wanted to see the Philistine's face to see if he was as indifferent as he pretended to be. Jesse doubted, since he heard the hesitation in Ianatos's voice.

"Of course not."

"Do not look down, Jonathan, and you will be fine. Trust your horse's footing."

Small rocks tumbled over the side and Ianatos growled.

"I told you not to look down, Philistine. Why must you test my caution?"

"You are a Hebrew, that is why."

They climbed upward in silence for near an hour. The ledge curved one way and then the other. The salty tang of the sea clung to the air. Soon the Sea of Salt came into view. Jesse inhaled the scent of home even though it was still hours away. "We are close."

"That is what you said before we left the trees," Ianatos grumbled.

"Are you weary of the scenery, my friend?"

"It is breathtaking, although I could do without the rocks tumbling beneath my horse's hooves." Jonathan's voice no longer held a hint of fear.

"I agree," Ianatos added.

Jesse agreed too, especially since he didn't know how much longer he could keep his eyes open.

Chapter Ten

Abigail didn't think Nathan's posture could become any more stiff. He tilted his head, listened for a moment and then pierced her with a hard stare.

Her heart hammered against her chest. Nathan did not need to say another word. She shook Bilhah's shoulder and her eyelids snapped open. Abigail pressed a finger to her lips and then motioned toward the alcove they had decided to hide in should danger arise. Bilhah's gaze flicked toward Nathan and then back to Abigail. She nodded her understanding, and together they gently shook Dara's shoulder. The old woman mumbled, smacked her lips and resumed snoring. Abigail tried again. "Dara," she whispered. "Come, Dara, we must hide."

The old woman squinted. Bilhah placed her hand over Dara's mouth to keep her quiet.

"We need to hide." Abigail stood and held out her hand to Dara. Bilhah did likewise. The old woman grunted but placed her hands in theirs. Abigail snatched up Dara's bag as well as her own. Bilhah reached for hers, and then they moved as one toward the dark corridor. Abigail released Dara's hand and doused one of the firebrands illuminating the cave while Micah doused the other. With the morning light beginning to filter in, soon they would not be needed anyway. She glanced toward the opening once more. Nathan had taken a few steps back from the mouth of the cavern. Cloaked in the shadows, he drew his sword from its sheath.

A shiver of fear raced down Abigail's spine. Of all the possible dangers she could imagine, Suph was the greatest threat. *God of Jesse, if You hear me, please protect us from our enemies, and please keep the horses quiet.*

Micah tugged on Abigail's hand and she slipped into the darkness. A distinct chill crept over her limbs as complete darkness engulfed her. The air from her lungs ceased to move. It was as if her face was buried into a pillow. She'd experienced this sort of darkness before, the sort that claimed all of her senses and made her feel ill to her stomach. Even the sound of the rushing wind echoing in her ears was the same. Was the deafening noise in her head? Surely, the cave could not live and breathe the way it seemed the box her mother had locked her in had.

She forced her breaths to steady. As if sensing her fear, a small hand clutched hers, entwining their fingers. "My thanks, Micah," Abigail whispered, her words bouncing off the damp stone. She tucked the child against her side

Bilhah squeezed her other hand and Abigail was thankful for the dual reassurance. She was also thankful Bilhah did not mention the experience. No one needed to know her greatest fear, or how she was punished when she dared step from her room without permission.

The more she tried to breathe, the more difficult it became to draw in air. Abigail released Micah and tore her hand from Bilhah's before sliding to the floor. She wrapped her arms around her knees and buried her face into the crease of her arms. Abigail rocked back, then forward. She kept the motion. As long as she concentrated on the movement she did not think about the dark and how it threatened to swallow her.

"Halt!" Nathan's commanding voice carried into the depths of the cave.

"It is I—Jonathan."

Abigail stopped rocking and tilted her head, waiting to hear Jesse's voice. She climbed to her feet, swiped her hair from her face and stepped into the cave. She remained standing in the shadows.

"Brother!" A few slaps on the back and a tight squeeze between the two. A pang of jealousy pricked her nape. She'd seen the genuine affection the brothers had shared. They had once included her, but then Shema had died and they'd left her too and she had no idea why.

Jonathan led his horse into the large cavern. The horse blew out air. Its body quivered. The other horses tossed their heads as if to greet each other.

"What of Jesse?"

Nathan and Jonathan turned toward her. There was enough light for her to see the questioning glance Nathan gave his brother. Before Jonathan could say a word, Jesse ducked into the cave.

"How does Abigail fare?"

Heat rose into her cheeks at his concern. Her pulse picked up a beat. Her eyes watered at the sight of him. He was safe. He had kept his promise and returned. He had not left her.

Her relief was short-lived when Nathan pulled back his fist and punched Jesse in the face. She squeaked as her hand flew to her mouth. Jesse's head snapped back. He stumbled toward the ledge outside the cave. She screamed and raced forward. Jonathan snagged his arm around her waist, yanking her back. Nathan snatched the front of Jesse's tunic as another large man caught hold of a limp Jesse.

"What was that for?" The stranger's voice boomed off the cave walls.

"He near sent us to our death." Nathan spit.

The large man laughed. "He most likely saved your lives."

"Pfft." Nathan crossed his arms over his chest.

"Ianatos does not lie, brother. There are signs Suph's men have been scouring the area. It is fortunate they did not find the path."

"Bah! It is fortunate we did not tumble to our deaths." Nathan eyed a limp Jesse. "Perhaps, that was his will."

"Nonsense." Abigail moved closer. Her gaze shifted from Jesse to Ianatos. The man's size alone settled fear into her toes. "Jesse would not bring us harm."

"I wouldn't be too certain about that." Nathan's jaw set to stone. She thought to ask him what he meant, but Jesse groaned.

"Bring him in and lay him on the mat." She pointed to the flax blankets spread on the floor. "Dara, we need your help."

The old woman peered around the edge of the alcove. She lumbered forward. "I will be needing that light again, Micah."

Abigail blinked. She'd never seen anyone light a firebrand. A fire had always been present. How were they to light the firebrand when there was no fire? "I am sorry. I only thought to hide us. I did not realize we'd need the light." She folded her hands together and hung her head. "I did not consider how we would relight it."

Dara glanced at her, the papery skin around her eyes wrinkling. Abigail looked around the room; they all looked at her as if she were a two-legged, mangy dog.

"Child, Jonathan will see it is lit. You need not worry yourself." Dara dug in her bag and handed Abigail a small earthen jar. "Here, come see to your Jesse's wounds. Dip those strips of cloth from my bag into the honey and replace the soiled bandages. The honey will keep them sealed and prevent them from festering."

Abigail knelt on the blankets beside Jesse. Red splotches seeped through his tunic. Dara draped a blanket over Jesse's thighs. "Nathan, come help remove his tunic."

Nathan grumbled something about leaving Jesse alone, but he obeyed his mother's wishes. They tugged on the corners of his tunic until it was gathered around his hips. Nathan lifted Jesse's shoulders from the ground as Dara untied the belt and then lifted the tunic away from Jesse's scarred chest.

"It is good the sutures have held." Dara clucked. "Micah, fetch that cruse of water."

Abigail's cheeks warmed and she dropped her gaze. Even with all the slices crisscrossing Jesse's upper body, he was still well formed. Of course she'd not seen many men outside of those who paid court to her mother and those she'd seen from a distance. However, Jesse was much more handsome than Suph. Strange how the features of Jesse's face weren't discernible yet she thought him more handsome. Perhaps it was because she suspected a kind heart beneath all of his brawn.

"Abigail." His cracked whisper drew her attention. She looked into his eyes. He rewarded her with a smile followed by a grimace. "You are well?"

"Yes, of course, Jesse. I am well." Her cats would purr whenever they were content and Abigail felt the need to purr. All because of Jesse's smile. No, his smile had nothing to do with the lightheartedness she felt and everything to do with the fact he cared enough to ask her if she fared well when he lay wounded and bleeding.

She didn't care what Nathan and Jonathan said. Jesse was a good man. Much better than the likes of Suph.

"What happened?" he croaked.

Dara pressed a cup of water to his lips. Abigail glanced to Nathan.

"I lost my temper and clouted you," Nathan responded.

Jesse flicked his gaze toward Nathan. "For what purpose?"

"Abigail near fell to her death on that path you sent us on."

Jess sat up, wincing as he did. He grabbed hold of her hand, his thumb gentle against her skin. She sucked in a sharp breath at the contact as locusts seemed to buzz in her ears. "But you are well?"

She pulled her hand from his. If she'd left it there, she would have begun to purr and that wouldn't do. "I am. It was nothing. My horse remained sturdy on the ledge at all times."

"Bah, rocks tumbled and his hooves slipped. If it weren't for Micah's quick thinking, you would have slid over the edge." Nathan scowled.

"I was not that close." She sent Jesse an apologetic smile. "Nathan's back was to us and it was dark—he could not have seen what happened."

"It is as she says," Bilhah added, surprising Abigail, given her cousin did not seem to like Jesse much.

Jesse lay back down, his breaths ragged from the exertion of holding himself up. He placed his palm on his jaw and moved it around. "Then I deserved what you doled out, even if it does hurt."

"Ach, enough chattering like old women. We must see to the boy's wounds so we can be out of this damp hole."

"Dara's right." Jesse scrubbed his palm over his jaw once more. "We need to be quick. Ianatos's men are waiting for us."

Abigail dipped a strip of linen into the honey and smoothed it over the smallest cut first. Dara applied a balm to Jesse's swollen and cut lip.

Jonathan crouched near Dara's side. "He has a bump on his head. It would be no cause to worry except…" He looked from Ianatos to Jesse.

"'Cept what?"

Jesse squeezed his eyes shut for a moment. "My eyes do not see like they should."

"What else?" Dara prodded.

"My muscles feel weak." Jesse grimaced, but Abigail did not think from pain. She had a feeling it was difficult for this brawny man to admit weakness.

"Is that all?"

There was silence for long moments. Only the shifting of the horses could be heard.

"He fell asleep." Ianatos's voice rumbled through the cave.

Abigail glanced over her shoulder. The man stood with his feet hip-width apart, his arms crossed over his chest. "What do you mean he fell asleep?"

"One moment he was looking at me, the next he was laying on the ground. He slept."

She turned her gaze to Nathan. "And you hit him!" She shoved him, knocking him a step back. Honey stuck to the front of his tunic. Good, let the flies congregate around him. "You could have injured him more. You could have killed him!" She shook with anger. "What were you thinking?"

Nathan gaped. His mouth opened and closed. "You were almost killed."

"No. I. Was. Not! Even if I was, my life is not worth that of a man of his standing." Abigail wrapped her arms around her midsection.

"What do you mean, a man of my standing?" Jesse's tone was hard; it raked down her nerves.

"You are a Levite." How could she tell him what was truly in her heart? That she thought him good, kind and noble. If she uttered those words, everyone here, including Jesse, would think she liked him more than she should, and she couldn't allow that. If she did, then he'd abandon her.

"Just because I was born into that tribe does not mean anything. It does not give me any more standing with anyone than if I were a Philistine."

Ianatos grumbled. His fists clenched at his sides.

"My apologies, my friend. I meant no offense. I am only trying to make a point. My ancestry does not make me any more special than if I were born of the tribe of Dan." At her confused look he explained. "Dan, the son of the great patriarch Jacob, sold his brother into slavery out of jealousies. I am not but a man, Abigail, a man born into the tribe of Levi."

"But you know God."

"And you can too, Abigail. Just like Nathan and Jonathan. Just like Ianatos. All who call on the name of the Lord can."

"How is that even possible?"

~

Seven pairs of eyes stared at him and Jesse froze. What was he to say to them? Not one of them believed, for certain, in the Creator of heaven and earth. His brother would have known what to say. And he would not have hesitated.

Jesse sniffed, his breathing no longer an even cadence of a man comfortable in his surroundings. Their waiting faces closed in on him and began to swim before his eyes. He did not lie when he said his eyes didn't see properly. At times, he'd seen two Nathans and two Jonathans. He had to get away. He needed to gather his wits. Odd, given how he'd never been one to run, but rather face adversity head-on. Now all it seemed he was doing was running.

Jesse sat up. He snatched his tunic and draped it over his shoulders. Drawing the blanket around his hips, he grabbed his belt, stood and pushed past Ianatos.

"Jesse, where are you going?"

He ignored the concerned plea in Abigail's cry and stepped out into the daylight. He draoed the blanket over his shoulders, donned his tunic and then tied the belt around his waist. He leaned back against the stony rock face, closed his eyes and drew the salty air into his lungs.

Her sharp inhale alerted him to her presence. He snapped his eyes open and glared at her.

"It is lovely. The most beautiful thing I have ever seen."

Pushing away from the rock, Jesse tore his eyes from the Sea of Salt surrounded by the rugged cliffs and looked at her. "I guess that depends on whom you are asking."

She turned her head. Her gaze settled on his. Her lips parted as if she understood what it was he was saying. Her cheeks flushed and she dropped her gaze. "Oh, my. It is narrow."

"You understand why Nathan was so angry with me?"

She shook her head and then nodded. "I suppose, but he still had no right—"

"Abigail." He moved closer, drawing his hand along the side of her face. He cupped her chin and forced her to look at him. "Nathan is your protector. Your life has meaning to him."

"Only because he believes I am the rightful queen of Judah." She pulled her chin from his hand and looked out across the sea. "The longer I am away from the palace, the more I do not want to return. The more I want to believe Joash is the rightful heir."

Jesse would not force the truth upon her. She would have to come to that realization on her own. "I understand. Obligations often feel like a prison."

One corner of her mouth slid upward, and even though he could not see her eyes he knew great sadness clung to them. "What is it, Abigail?"

She hugged her arms around her waist. "I do not know what it is like to be a prisoner, not like you. I've not been tortured or wounded."

"A man can be a prisoner and never have had manacles on his wrists, Abigail."

"This I know." She raised her head and looked him in the eye. "I have seen very little outside the palace walls. Very little outside of my chambers."

"It is often such with princesses. They are meant to be protected, guarded against their kingdom's enemies, and groomed for marriage to kings."

A tear slid from the corner of her eye. He wiped it from her cheek. The smoothness of her skin warmed the top of his finger, daring him to linger. Her lashes fell against her cheeks as more tears streamed. "My mother kept me hidden, not because she sought to protect me, but to protect herself."

Jesse was not surprised by Athaliah's jealousy, even of her own daughter. Athaliah no doubt feared her daughter's beauty would take attention away from her. "Your mother was jealous."

"No." She shook her head. "I shamed her."

He stroked his hand through her hair. "I do not know what you could have done—"

Abigail jerked away. "All I have seen of Judah is beautiful. Even this place with its dangers and rugged terrain." She darted a glance his way. "My mother was beautiful. She surrounded herself with beautiful things. Exotic. There were tigers in the palace. Monkeys even. She invited people from all over just to dine with her, but never me."

Jesse's heart lurched at the sadness and longing. He wished he knew how to ease her sorrow.

"I never dined with my mother, Jesse."

He jerked as if he'd been slapped. Her words formed a pit in his stomach, but it was the words she did not say that left him reeling. "Abigail, you must know…" The wind blew over his heated skin and he shivered. "Exquisite…"

"Jesse?"

His knees began to buckle. He reached out and grasped hold of a rock. It loosened. Jesse rocked from one side to the other. He pitched forward. She screamed and he waited for the jarring pain of his body as he fell to his death. All he could think of was that he should have told her how she could know God. And tell her once again that she was beautiful.

Chapter Eleven

Her heart stopped when Jesse began to fall. She had feared what he had been about to say and had failed to see the beads of perspiration on his brow until he shivered. It was by providence that Ianatos had grabbed hold of Jesse when he did. Or was it?

She tipped her head back and looked up at the blue sky. She had no idea where the heavens were but that seemed the obvious place. "Jesse's God," she said, dropping her hands to her side. She shrugged her shoulders and gazed out at the sea nestled below. "Wherever You are, thank You for Ianatos's presence and rescuing Jesse."

"Who is it you are speaking to?"

She glanced over her shoulder to see for certain who spoke, since Nathan and Jonathan's voices were so similar. "Jesse's God."

Nathan glanced around.

"You have to wonder, Nathan, if there is something out there greater to worship than wood and bronze. Wood rots and burns, and bronze, well, it can be reshaped and loses its shine after a time. Its beauty disappears."

"You are right, Abigail. I remember the stories my mother used to tell about the great God."

"Dara?"

He snapped his gaze to her. Shock, and then sorrow flitted through his eyes. He shook his head. "We should not speak of such things. Come, let us check on the prisoner."

She took a step toward the entrance, and Nathan halted her with a hand to her arm. "I am sorry that I hit him. Not because I could have harmed him further." He dropped his gaze to his feet. "I do not wish to distress you, Abigail."

She smiled. "You are forgiven, Nathan. As long as Jesse is with us we are to treat him with kindness. Just like when we found that wounded bird when we were children. Remember?"

A twinkle danced in his eye. "Of course. How could I forget how you and Bilhah cried when he recovered and flew away?"

Abigail laughed.

"Your tears left us bewildered. Jonathan and I had no idea what to think. You cried when he was broken and cried when he was well."

"Bilhah stared out the window for days waiting for the bird's return."

"Aye, it broke my heart to see her as such."

Abigail laid her hand on his forearm. "You were a good friend to us, Nathan. As was your brother. We have never forgotten your kindnesses. Why did you and Jonathan leave?"

He stiffened and his eyes bored into hers. "We were not allowed to return." He disappeared into the cave.

Abigail stepped into the cavern. "How is he?"

"Ach, the bump on his head is not too good. I have done all I know how to do." Dara wiped her brow then looked at each of them. "Do not move him until he wakes on his own else you risk killing him."

"We cannot—"

"Jonathan, we will stay." Abigail glanced at his brother. "Nathan, will you keep watch with Ianatos? Bilhah and I will prepare some food while Dara tends Jesse's wounds."

"There is not much else I can do. I will help Bilhah while you sit beside him and keep watch."

"She is right, Abigail. You should not be preparing meals." Bilhah smiled. "I would wish for edible food. I do not think you have made anything before."

Heat rose into Abigail's cheeks. Her cousin was correct. She would not know where to begin, but was it not something she should learn? Especially if Joash remained King of Judah.

As if reading her mind, Bilhah laid her hand on Abigail's shoulder. "Do not trouble yourself, cousin. Tomorrow has enough worries of its own. Even if you are never to be queen, you are royal and will never have to do such things."

"But I want to. I want to learn. What if..." Her gaze landed on Jesse and then back to her cousin. "What if I chose to marry and not live in the palace? What if I have no choice but to live outside the palace? What then?"

Bilhah laughed. "Then we will teach you how to cook."

It was obvious they were not going to allow her to help. She sat in the place Dara had occupied.

"Watch his chest. Make sure he breathes."

Abigail felt her eyes go wide.

"Fear not. He did not escape Suph to die." Dara began to move away and then stopped. "Dip the sponge into that cup and moisten his lips. He needs water and rest to renew his strength. I have already applied honey to reseal the wounds that split. It will take some time for his ribs to heal."

Time was something they did not have. Suph would search until he found them.

"Abigail?"

Jesse's eyes slit open. Lines of pain etched his brow. "I am glad you are well."

"My thanks. You must rest, now."

He shook his head. "No. You must listen. If I cannot—"

"You will be—"

"Please." He reached for her hand and squeezed. "I do not understand the wounds plaguing my body. I do not like this weakness." He closed his eyes and swallowed. "You must do all in your power to stay away from Suph. He is not a kind man. He will treat you poorly."

"What choice will I have if you do not take me to Jerusalem?"

"Abigail." He opened his eyes and tried to sit up. She placed her hand on his shoulder, pressing him back down.

"We need not worry, Jesse. You will be fine."

"If I am not, have Jonathan and Nathan take you to Hebron. Ianatos knows the way. The journey will not be easy. Ask for..." His lids slid shut and the hold on her hand relaxed.

"Jesse?" The beat of her heart caught as she thought he had perished. She glanced at his chest. It rose and fell, but he did not reopen his eyes. She leaned her head against the cave wall and sighed, thankful he had not passed from earth.

There were too many questions he had the answers to, and she trusted him enough to give them to her. She held onto his hand, the little pulse at the base of his thumb beating against hers. The contact brought her peace and comfort, something she had not truly felt since Shema had been taken from her life.

Why had her father killed Shema? Had he discovered the stories she'd told? What had he to fear of such stories to kill her? She thought back to the last time she'd seen Shema and then the look on her father's face when he'd come to check on her. Shema had been there. Her father had snapped his fingers and she'd immediately left the room, but there hadn't been fear in her nurse's eyes. But then Shema had never shown anything but joy. Was it because she had loved Jesse's God?

What was it about this God that caused such passions? Some would die to worship this God, yet others, like her father, killed those who would worship Him. It was another question she would ask Jesse when he was well enough.

"Abigail." Bilhah's voice broke through her musings, causing her to jump. She jerked her hand from Jesse's and was rewarded with a slight groan of protest. Did she bring him as much comfort as he did her?

"What is it, Bilhah?"

"Your food is ready." Bilhah walked toward her and handed her a wooden bowl filled with various fruits . She glanced to Abigail's hands folded in her lap. "You should be careful, Abigail. Your life has not been such as his. You do not have the experience to know who to trust and who not to trust."

"This I know, cousin. However, I believe there is only good in him."

"You may be right, Abigail, but even good people cannot be trusted when they lack good judgment. What will you do if you discover he is not all you think he is?"

Abigail shook her head. "Do you think I am so trusting?"

Bilhah crouched beside her and pressed the flat of her palm against Abigail's cheek. "Abigail, how many people have you spoken with in your life?"

The skin between her eyebrows scrunched together. "I do not understand."

"Dear one, I have encountered all sorts of people. Some good. Many bad, most evil. I can see it in their eyes. Jesse is a good man, but there is something in his eyes that keeps him guarded."

Abigail laughed. "Would you not be guarded if you were surrounded by those who were once your enemies? Besides, what if all you see is the agony of his wounds?"

Bilhah looked down at Jesse. "Be careful, Abigail. It is obvious you are taken with the man. A man's affections are not as easily given as a woman's."

Bilhah rose and walked away. Nathan's eyes followed her cousin and she wondered if her cousin knew of Nathan's affections for her. Abigail might have been sheltered, secluded from much, but she could tell Nathan loved Bilhah. Even when they were children he had claimed an undying love for her, but then according to servant gossip most of the men in Jerusalem did. Perhaps that was why he had the look of sadness.

Jesse mumbled something in his sleep, drawing her attention. Did she feel something for this man? Something beyond caring for a weak and wounded vessel? She drew her finger over the warmth of his brow, skirting along the edges of the purple swelling and the cuts. She outlined his beard, now cleansed from dirt and blood. She could not discern the natural shape of his lips or his cheeks. Did this man have a stony jaw, or were his cheeks rounded? Had his nose been straight, or was the bump on the ridge natural?

"Why is it you wished to rescue me from Suph, Abigail?"

She startled, jerking her fingers from his skin. Heat filled her cheeks. "I told you, I want the truth."

"And what truth is that?"

"My brothers and cousins, my father. My mother. The whole of it." *Your God.*

"What if you do not like what you hear, Abigail?"

She breathed in the dank, salty air. Moisture caught in her throat, causing her eyes to water. She already knew what her father was capable of, but why? And was she capable of the same sort of evil? "Then I will deal with it."

"I will not tell you rumors, Abigail. I will only tell you what it is I know. Jehoiada must tell you the rest." He turned his head toward the others and then back to her. "But not now. I must see you safe from Suph's grasping hand before I tell you the truth."

~

Jesse did not think himself a coward. Abigail deserved to know the truth, but if she discovered it and Suph got his hands on her, forcing her into a marriage, her hatred toward him would make married life difficult for her. Besides, he cherished his time with Abigail. The more time he spent in her presence, the more he thought of holding green-eyed sons and daughters. He had no doubt once she discovered what he'd done she wouldn't want anything to do with him.

"I have thought myself a patient person. However, I find I am anxious to know the full truth."

"I understand, Abigail. Waiting has never been one of my strengths. I have always rushed headlong into situations, but trust me when I say this is for the best, even if you never discover what it is you wish to know."

"I do not understand." She curled her legs beneath her. Her green eyes pleaded with him, tugging on his heartstrings.

"Abigail, there are those who were faithful, not to your parents, but rather to their ideas. They would see those ideas protected, even kill for them, sometimes even do worse things."

"What could be worse than death?"

He ignored her question. If she did not know, he wouldn't tell her and he prayed God would protect her from such evils. "Tell me, Abigail, have you ever seen the sun rise or even set?"

She glanced toward the opening of the cave and blinked. Her lips twisted. "I do not know."

He smiled at her. "Once you do, you'll never want to miss another one as long as you draw breath."

He had the sudden urge to watch her as she witnessed her first sunset, more now than he had earlier. Her eyebrows furrowed. Perhaps she did not understand what it was he was trying to say. "Right now we have the freedom to choose to stay here, travel to Jerusalem or return to Suph's camp. We are not forced to one or the other. No matter the course, it is ours to decide."

"I have not had the liberty to choose. Leaving camp was the first decision I've truly made on my own since I was a child, and even then I paid a price."

"I wish to know more, but I fear we must be leaving soon."

She smiled. "First you eat, Jesse."

Jesse rose up on his elbows while she folded a blanket behind his back. She pressed her bowl into his hands. "You cannot regain your strength without sustenance. Besides, I am learning that what will happen, will happen."

"I guess you are correct." However he knew the longer he tarried, the more likely they risked being found. He had not thought of it at first when he sent Nathan here, but Elam might guess he'd hide here and inform Suph. "I will eat, then we must go."

"I will get you some water." She rose from her seat and Jesse immediately missed her presence. There was something about her that drew him. She was kind and tender, yet wounded deep in her heart. He did not know if he could offer her words of healing, but somehow he knew he must try. Perhaps that is why God allowed him to be captured, to help her not be so sad.

"Here," she said as she handed him a cup. "Ianatos has gone to check the pass. I will help gather our belongings. When you are ready we will leave."

He nodded. "I would like some time to pray. Then I will be ready." It seemed ages since he had given thanks to God and it was time to do so, before he took another step. Too often he made decisions without seeking God's direction.

She stood there, looking down upon him, wariness in her eyes. "How is it you speak to your God? He is not here. There is nothing to pray to."

He laughed. "In that you are wrong, Abigail. He is everywhere. Do you think so little of the God Almighty, the one who created the heavens, the one who created the very mountain you seek refuge in, that He could not be here with us now?"

She shook her head. Strands of hair fell loose from her veil. "I do not know this God enough to know what He has done or what He is capable of doing."

"Then come, sit beside me and we will pray together."

Tears welled in her eyes. Her lips parted as if to say something, but she drew in a shaky breath and walked away.

An ache, not caused by any of the wounds Suph had inflicted, tore at his heart. What would it take for her to acknowledge God as the one true God? Jesse closed his eye and bowed his head. "Father God, thank You for guiding my paths. Thank You for Abigail and Dara's healing hands. Forgive my stubbornness and having not called on You sooner. Father, I weep for these people. My wish is that they would know You. Moreover, I weep for the whole of Judah. I thought once the rightful king was restored to the crown all would be well, but it is not, is it, God? It will not be well until Your people call on Your name and acknowledge You as their God. Father, may it be so. May Your people call upon Your name and may my actions, whether word or deed, glorify You."

He felt her eyes on him. He raised his head and glanced at Abigail. With jerky, angry movements she stuffed goods into a bag. His offer of praying together had angered her, but why? Perhaps, she was not yet ready to seek God.

"Do not forget this." Bilhah handed Abigail a small earthen jar, but Abigail did not take her eyes from his. It was if she was searching for something, but it felt as if she was distancing herself from him and she did not even know it.

God, soften her heart and show me how to reach her.

Jesse waited for the peace Ari had spoken of to settle in his being, but nothing came. He felt weak and not from his wounds, but from sorrow. He wanted her to want to know God. It was that choice he told her about. It seemed, however, the false gods were too rooted in her past to be removed.

A shadow passed before the entrance of the cave. Ianatos stood, hands on hips, his muscles tense. "Is Jesse awake?"

"Aye, that I am. What troubles you, my friend?" Jesse climbed to his feet.

"Travelers are ascending the pass."

Chapter Twelve

Abigail's heart hit the rock floor along with the linen bag she'd been holding. She'd feared the moment when Suph caught up to them. Not for herself, though; she'd be willing to do as Suph asked as long as Jesse was not harmed any further.

"Jesse," she said as she neared him and laid her palm on his arm. "You must hide in the alcove."

One of his eyebrows rose and his muscles tensed. A tinge of color, the first bit she'd seen since she'd met him, painted his cheeks. "I am no coward."

Her jaw dropped, and then she snapped it closed. Abigail had not fought back nausea as she diligently stitched each of his wounds just so his pride would see him killed. She jammed her fists onto her hips. "I never implied as such. You are wounded and weak. You can barely hold your head up let alone stand on your own two feet." She glanced over her shoulder to insure it was still only them. "Now hide."

"I will not." He slid the dagger Nathan had given him earlier from his belt. The stubborn man wavered on his feet. She braced herself to steady him as he leaned forward, the glint of the blade between them.

"You will." Abigail smacked the flat of her palm against Jesse's wrist. The blade clattered to the cave floor. The color of his eyes took on the fire of the torch. His nostrils flared. She stepped back, eyed the dagger and then him. His chest rose and fell in smooth, controlled movements. He pressed his palm against the cave wall, she was certain, to steady himself.

"I will not cower in the dark like a babe, Abigail. I have made a vow to protect you."

"Ha!" She threw her hands in the air before fisting them on her hips once again. Her pulse thumped, whether from anger at him or from the danger bearing down upon them, she did not know. Perhaps it was both. "You are not invincible, and you have made no such vow to me, Jesse the Levite, as if you could keep it in your condition."

In one swift movement he grabbed hold of her arm and pulled her to him. Singing metal echoed off the stone walls, but she paid them no heed for his warm breath scented with honey and cinnamon caressed her lips, making her knees weak and her toes curl. She swallowed past the knot in her throat.

His gaze shifted beyond her shoulder. "Tell your dogs to put their swords down."

She shivered, not because of the command in his tone. Nay, he loosened his hold on her arm and replaced it with a gentle swirl of his fingers, soothing the bite of his earlier grip. Abigail couldn't form a coherent thought, let alone speak. She heard the swords being sheathed and closed her eyes in thankfulness.

"Abigail." His soft whisper jerked on her heart. She opened her eyes. An emotion unknown to her swirled in the depths of his gaze, an emotion somehow connected to her knees, for they seemed to melt like warmed honey. "Do you doubt my prowess, lovely Abigail?" He removed his hand from the stone wall and drew it down the length of her hair; his eyes left hers, following the trail of his hand.

Jesse held on to the ends, twisting them in his fingers. "So soft and beautiful." His gaze bored into hers once more. "I, Jesse the Levite, vow to protect you, Abigail, Princess of Judah, daughter of Athaliah. I will protect you from your enemies even at the cost of my life."

She swallowed and blinked.

"Do you understand what it is I am saying, Abigail?"

No one had ever made a vow to her. Aye, she knew Nathan and Jonathan would give their lives for her, but never had they vowed it. Not in the way Jesse had.

"Jesse, if you are done playing court you have company." Ianatos's hard tone had Jesse releasing his gentle hold on her. He bent at the waist with a barely perceptible moan, picked up the discarded dagger and stepped past her. She did not move. She stared at the spot he had vacated, bemused by the instant change in strength. However, she did not miss the lines of distress that proved his wounds continued to bother him. Jesse was a mystery, one she intended to unravel before they parted ways.

"Nathan, you are the fighter, yes?" Jesse took command.

"Yes."

"Jonathan, take the women and their belongings to the alcove."

Ianatos cleared his throat. "That will not be necessary, Jesse. I believe it is your brothers."

Abigail spun around on her heels. "Your—brothers?"

Jesse's spine stiffened at her raised tone but he did not turn and acknowledge her question. Anger warred with relief. Her worry that Suph had found them had been for naught, but how had his brothers found him? Now that they had, surely Jesse would no longer need her. Surely his promise to protect her from her enemies, men like his brothers, would be forgotten. She pressed her palm to her chest. How would his brothers feel about her? Would Jesse hand her over to them? Would they seek to kill her as they had her mother?

She stepped forward and was halted by Bilhah. "Now is not the time, Abigail," Bilhah pleaded.

"But—"

"No." Bilhah grabbed hold of her arm and took her to the edge of the alcove. "I know of Jesse's family. Do not argue with him. Do not cause him shame."

Abigail glanced at her cousin and then to Jesse, who spoke with Ianatos and Nathan. "How?"

"I cannot answer that question for you, Abigail. What I do know is you should not question him as you have already done. You crossed bounds no woman would dare, not even with her husband."

"He is not my husband."

"This I know, dear one. However, you have wounded his pride by calling him weak."

"I did not…"

"I know this." Bilhah glanced toward Jesse and then back to her. "I believe your Jesse knows this, as well.

Unfortunately, when a man's pride is wounded sometimes it is worse than the physical wounds we can see with our eyes."

Heat rose into Abigail's cheeks.

"If you wish to redeem yourself in his eyes, do not question him further. Allow him to take the lead. He will answer your questions in due time. However, if he tells you to hide, hide. If he tells you to run, run. And if he vows to protect you with his life against your enemies, he will do so even against his family."

Bilhah moved away from her and began helping Dara finish gathering their supplies. Abigail stood there watching the activity move around her in slow motion. Too many things of this world she did not understand. Bilhah knew more than Abigail could ever imagine, and like the rest of the people in her life she tried to shield Abigail from the horrors. Well, no more. Jesse had said she had a choice, which meant she could choose the truth if she wanted or she could chose to remain ignorant.

However, she would listen to Bilhah's wisdom and would bide her time. She would obey Jesse's lead for now and hope she didn't lose her life doing so.

~

Jesse knew family could mean Elam. However, if Ianatos had seen his uncle, would he have not said?

"How many?" Jesse asked.

"Three come up the pass. Many more are down below." Ianatos responded.

"My traitorous uncle Elam?"

"This I cannot be sure of, Jesse. I only recognized the man in front as he looks like you only…smaller." Ianatos glanced at his feet as if embarrassed at his observation.

Jesse smiled, knowing Isa would greet him. However, if his brother had not heard of Elam's wickedness he would not know to distrust him. Precautions must be made. He turned to Jonathan. "Take the women to the alcove and remain hidden. There is a chance Elam is with them. If he is, that means Suph is not far behind. Nathan, stay in the shadows. Do not let them see you. If Elam is with them and he sees you, he'll know Abigail is with us."

Nathan started to move away, but Jesse halted him with his hand. "I know you will guard her well."

Nathan nodded and then slipped into the shadows. After they were gone Jesse faced Ianatos. "My friend, if anything should happen to me, take them deep into the mountain. These passes lead to many places. Follow the signs. The ibex drawings will take you to the spring. Take her to my brother Ari. He must get her to Jehoiada. I do not have to tell you how important it is that she not be captured by Suph."

"No, that you do not, my friend."

"Good, shall we greet our visitors?" Jesse stepped out onto the ledge with a quick prayer on his lips that Elam and Suph were far from here. Warm air encompassed him. The salty sea filled his senses. He glanced toward Manna, the city hidden within the mountains that his family called home. A place he hadn't called home in years, even though a part of him longed for its seclusion. It would be easy enough to go there and take refuge from the chaos ruling Judah. However, his heart beckoned him to stay with Abigail and help her in her quest for truth.

He exited the cave and began descending the pass. It was not easy to keep his feet firm, not with his head spinning with each movement. But he'd made a vow to Abigail and he'd see it through, if only to prove to her he was not a coward, nor a weakling. He shook his head. If he had not been beaten to a bloody pulp, she'd not have asked him to hide. He stretched his chest and arms, testing his muscles.

"Will you get over her insults?" Ianatos asked from behind him

"I was not offended."

"So you say. If you ask me, her words struck you where it would hurt you the most."

"And where is that, my friend?"

"Your pride."

"Aye, she did sting my pride a little."

Ianatos laughed. "You near crossed boundaries. I thought I was going to have to kill her friends in order to save you. Not that I would have had a problem, mind you."

Jesse thought back to his anger and regretted the emotion. He did not, however, regret touching her arm. Her tresses. Her eyes with his. He did not regret making his vow to protect her. In fact, his vow, albeit hastily spoken, soothed his wounded pride a great deal and humbled him even more.

She was a treasure to behold, one he had no right thinking of possessing. Unfortunately, his heart seemed taken with her.

He blew out an exaggerated sigh.

"What is it that bothers you, Jesse?"

"Nothing." Everything. Abigail. Somehow he had had the fortitude to hold back. The jasmine cloaking her had drawn him in until his eyes focused only on her lips. He had grasped her tresses in an effort to distract himself. He had wanted to kiss her, had thought to kiss her. However, once he crossed that line he would give her his troth, and that he could not, would not do. Not as long as she denied God. Then why had he angered so easily? Not because she had wounded his pride, but because as long as she denied God, Jesse couldn't allow a simple kiss between them. He could not be yoked to a helpmate who did not love God the way he did.

"You grumble much for a man who has nothing bothering him. If I were to guess, it would have to do with a stubborn princess."

Before he could respond, rocks tumbled from the side of the mountain. Jesse and Ianatos halted their steps and listened. Muffled voices reached Jesse's ears. His muscles tensed and he fortified his nerves for the encounter. He held his breath as he followed the pass around the curve. At two boulders' distance, three men sat in the middle of the pass, their feet dangling over the edge. The older of the three drank deep from an earthenware flask. Jesse smiled, thankful Elam was not among the threesome.

"Come, Ianatos. I would have you meet my brothers Isa and Melchiah, and my uncle Seth." Jesse rushed forward. His head began to spin. He reached out to steady himself against the rock wall and met air. Fortunately for him, Ianatos grabbed hold of his tunic and settled him.

"You are weak, my friend."

Jesse started to grumble.

"No. I do not insult. It is the truth. If you wish to see your woman safe you must slow down until your strength renews itself."

"You are right. I am excited to see my brothers and Uncle Seth." He smiled. "It is a great joy to see them after the ordeal I have been through. And of course," Jesse sobered. "I must inform them of Elam's betrayal."

"Do not allow your excitement to dictate your steps, or you will meet your death before you greet them."

"You are correct," Jesse laughed. "You do have a way with words, my friend. Brothers! It is I," Jesse called out.

Isa and Melchiah rose to their feet, shielding their eyes with their hands. Seth, his blind uncle, continued to sit, grinning up at the sky.

"Jesse?" Melchiah approached him. "What has happened to you?" His brother gave Ianatos an accusing glare.

"I found a bit of trouble. Tell me Mother is not with you. I would not have her see me this way."

"It is not as if she hasn't seen you with purple eyes before." Isa shook his head. "No, she is not with us. She is with Abba and our other brothers celebrating Ari and Mira's marriage."

Isa reached out and hugged Jesse. "When Ari discovered you had not returned to Jerusalem he became worried Elam had somehow brought you harm. Where were you? It is not like you to shirk your duty. Even we became worried."

Jesse looked at his brothers, relieved he didn't need to tell them of Elam's betrayal. "Athaliah's former captain has gathered forces. He came upon me and Elam. The captain promised Elam he could be the high priest if he allowed me to be used in exchange for our new king."

"What did he intend to do with King Joash? Rule through him?"

Ianatos cleared his throat. "Turns out Queen Athaliah had a daughter."

Jesse told them of all that had happened and how Abigail had rescued him from further torture.

"And now you feel indebted to her," Melchiah said, more of a statement than a question.

Jesse furrowed his brow. Was that what drew him to her—he felt indebted to her? "Perhaps. It does not matter. She is not like her mother, nor her father. Somehow she has been shielded from their evil ways. I would hate to see her innocence destroyed by Suph. I do not need to tell you what will happen to her if she chooses to defy him after he forces a marriage upon her. He needs her to rule, at least until she bears his children."

"What will you have us do, Jesse?"

"Abigail needs sanctuary until Suph and his men can be dealt with."

"We will take her to Manna then. He will never find her there and she will be well guarded."

"No." Jesse could not take her from one prison fortress to another. Besides, those who lived at Manna had pledged their lives to God, something Abigail had not done and seemed set on not doing. "She has people who are loyal to her with her. A healer, the healer's two sons, who seem capable enough at guarding their mistress, a small boy of ten or eleven and her cousin."

"Her cousin? Was not all the royal family killed?"

"It seems Bilhah was given a fate much worse than death." His brothers furrowed their brows.

"You have the shrine priestess with you, Jesse?" Seth asked.

Jesse firmed his lips together and nodded. "Aye," he added, knowing his uncle was blind.

His brothers gasped. "We cannot—"

"No, we cannot," Isa added. "Our wives would not understand."

Jesse stared at his brothers, dumbfounded. "Forgive me if I am wrong, as I did not pay as close attention to our studies as you two did, is it not written in the scriptures that to any who call upon the Lord that he draws nigh?"

"And these people, they have called upon the Lord in truth?"

Heat flamed Jesse's cheeks and he bowed his head. "No. Although I have hope. They willingly left behind their idols without hesitation to save me from further torture and my eventual death."

"Until they place their lives in the hands of our God, we cannot entrust them with the secret of Manna," Seth said as he continued to bask in the sun.

"I know, Uncle." Jesse did not like it, for he wanted nothing more than to share the home he loved with Abigail, to see it through her eyes.

"Then what is your plan?"

"Jerusalem," Ianatos said from behind him.

"It is the obvious choice," Melchiah agreed.

"Abigail wishes to speak with Jehoiada. She is under the belief that he killed her brothers and cousins."

Isa's brow rose to his hairline. "Why would she believe such a thing of her sister's husband?"

"Seems that is what her mother told her." Jesse swiped the beads of perspiration from his brow. "And I am not certain she knows Jehosheba is her sister."

"Are you certain she does not wish the king harm?"

"No. However, I do believe that she will listen to what he has to say. She already has doubts about her family."

"So Jerusalem it is, then. Do you not think Suph will have the gates watched?" Isa asked.

"Yes, of course," Ianatos answered. "But as you can see, Jesse can hardly stand. He will not be able to battle Suph's men, even with Nathan and Jonathan's help."

"Nathan and Jonathan?"

"They are twins."

"Well, then, brother," Melchiah said, gripping Jesse's shoulder. "Why don't you sit and rest beside our uncle? I will go down to the camp and explain to them why there are Philistines crawling all over and Ianatos will return and fetch Abigail. We will help you get to Jerusalem."

The spinning in Jesse's head worsened and he swayed on his feet.

"On second thought, why don't I take you to camp where you can be taken care of."

"He can hardly walk," Isa said.

"That is fine. I will carry him if need be." Melchiah turned to their uncle. "Seth, are you staying here or coming with?"

"I believe I will stay right here. I want to meet this daughter of the queen and the shrine priestess."

"And I will wait with you, Uncle." Isa sat beside Seth. "I do not care what Jesse says. I want to see these people with my own eyes, too."

"Aye, and you can tell me if they have horns growing out the side of their heads." Seth chuckled.

"That I will do, Uncle, that I will do."

"Uncle Seth?"

"Yes, Jesse?"

"Try not to frighten her. Up until a few days ago she'd never been outside the palace and then rarely out of her chambers."

"Would you have me cover my eyes?"

"No, Uncle." Jesse laughed. "Never. Perhaps Ianatos would prepare her beforehand." Jesse glanced at the Philistine.

Ianatos grinned. "And why would I do that?"

"I believe I like you. Philistine." Melchiah laughed.

Melchiah grabbed hold of Jesse's tunic and guided him forward. Jesse did not dare glance over his shoulder to see if Ianatos went after Abigail. He would have to trust the Philistine. Of course, he knew the risks as much as Jesse did and if it had not been for his diligence in protecting Joash and helping save Ari's betrothed, Mira, Jesse would not trust him, but the man had proven himself.

"I cannot believe you allowed yourself to get caught."

"Do not think I have not beaten myself over the head, Melchiah." He paused. "I have. However, I'm coming to see God's plan is much greater than my own, even if I did let my guard down."

"Do not be so hard on yourself, Jesse." Melchiah kept a firm palm on Jesse's shoulder. "We all did, even with Ari's warnings. What of Elam?"

Jesse twisted his lips. "Unfortunately, as I mentioned he has become friends with Suph."

"Why did you come this way?"

"There was a risk, I know. However, I prayed our people would soon return home. There is safety in numbers, is there not?"

Melchiah grumbled.

"You do not have to worry over Bilhah much. She has kept her head covered since we left, and Melchiah, she helped rescue me. Of course it was at her cousin's insistence, but even so, I owe her my gratitude."

"Then for that I will give her my thanks, as well. Mother would not be too happy if her youngest son had not been found."

"By the way, why was it just you, Isa and Seth coming up the pass? Why not the entire camp?"

"Some of our people went with Ari. Abba did not want to risk losing him when we could not find you. As for the others, well, Seth could smell the Philistines at a good distance." Melchiah laughed.

Jesse joined him. "The truth?"

"Seth and Isa went out to the Philistine camp. They explained to us why they were there and that they were waiting for Ianatos to return. After a few questions we discerned the numbers in your party. We did not know if they were friend or foe. So we pretended to be travelers."

"So you knew where I was?"

"Aye, of course, we just did not expect your pretty face to be so ugly."

Jesse winced. "Is it that bad?"

"It is not pretty, Jesse, although, your cuts seem to be healing without infection. You must have a capable healer."

Jesse laughed. "Capable, aye. I'm quite certain she was around when Noah built the ark. She is a grumpy crone, but there is a big heart behind all of her crassness."

A slight breeze blew across his skin, causing him to shiver.

"Brother, are you well?"

Jesse fell to his knees. Small rocks pricked his skin.

"Jesse?"

Jesse touched his fingers to the pounding in his head. A burst of light flashed into his eyes.

Melchiah hefted him to his feet. "Come, little brother. Let's get you home."

Home. Jesse couldn't go home. He needed to see to Abigail.

"Aye, Abigail will follow shortly." Melchiah bent down and pressed his shoulder into Jesse's stomach. Jesse howled in pain as his ribs sliced his innards.

Chapter Thirteen

Abigail steadied her hand against the face of the rock, her feet rooted. Jesse's pain reverberated through her heart and straight to her toes. She held her breath, waiting for another sound. Another cry of pain, his laughter, Jesse's body hitting the rocks below. Anything.

"Ach, child, what are you waiting for? Me to perish in this hot sun?"

Abigail looked over her shoulder at Dara. Had the cry of pain only been her imagination? She glanced to Ianatos, who continued in his trek down the pass. He showed no signs of distress.

She inhaled a ragged breath, thankful she was not riding a horse on this narrow slope. "It is sorry I am, Dara. I fear the treacherous travel is wearing on my nerves."

"As is it on mine. If you do not mind me reminding you, the sooner we get back down there—" she pointed toward the valley rising before them—"the sooner we can rest."

Dara was right. More importantly, the sooner they made camp, the sooner she could see for herself that Jesse was fine. Ianatos had tried to reassure her that Jesse was well enough now that he was with his family. Abigail had her doubts. She did not know this Philistine whose fealty belonged to the child believed to be her brother's son. However, Jesse seemed to trust him. But what did Abigail know about trust? Had not Bilhah suggested she was too naive to know who to place her faith in and who not to?

All the sudden Ianatos stopped, then Micah, and then Bilhah. Abigail craned her neck to see around them, but detected nothing other than sky, rock and the sea.

"What is happening?" Abigail climbed on her tiptoes.

"I do not know." Bilhah craned her neck.

Oh, God, please let Jesse be well.

She clapped her hand over her mouth. Had she just prayed to God? Really prayed to Jesse's God as if He were her own god too? It seemed strange that it came naturally, as if God had been there all the time. A sense of inner joy filled her heart at this revelation. She dropped her hand to her sides and smiled to herself.

Somehow she knew Jesse was fine. Whatever halted their travels had nothing to do with his well-being. Micah mumbled to Bilhah, and then her cousin turned to Abigail. "It is Jesse's brother and an uncle."

Abigail stiffened, thinking Elam had found them, but then Bilhah said something she never expected. "A blind uncle, one who wants to meet the shrine priestess?"

Abigail thought her cousin might be hurt by the name, but laughter danced in her eyes as she said, "I shall not disappoint him."

Bilhah scooted between Micah and the rock wall, until she stood beside Ianatos. She bowed her head as she dropped to her knees. What kind of man was Jesse's uncle to command such respect from her cousin?

Bilhah waved Abigail forward. "Come."

She ignored Jonathan and Nathan's protests and patted Micah's head as she passed him, then she glanced at Ianatos, still unsure if she could trust the Philistine. She relaxed a little when the corner of his mouth curved upward, not in the same sinister way that Suph usually did, but in a reassuring manner.

She lifted her eyes. Two men stood before her. Both tall, one with a graying beard, his eyelids scarred and sealed shut. The other was not as tall as Jesse, but his eyes had the same look. She wondered how much Jesse looked like this man when he was not so badly bruised.

"Abigail, this is Isa, Jesse's brother." Bilhah pointed toward the younger man, and then smiled as she gazed upon the older one. "And this is Seth, Jesse's uncle."

Seth reached out his hands, indicating Abigail should place hers in his. He wrapped his warm fingers around hers. "It is my gratitude I give you for helping my Jesse."

"As is mine." Isa bowed his head. "My mother would be none too happy if we did not have good news of her youngest son." He lifted his head and winked, easing some of the tension building in her chest.

"Then it is glad I am to have helped." She looked around, hoping to catch sight of him.

"Our brother Melchiah has carried him to camp."

Her lips parted. Fear thumped in her heart. "Is he well?"

"Aye, Jesse's received much worse training for battle. He will be back to his duties in no time."

"Duties?"

Isa glanced at Ianatos, who shrugged his shoulders. "Jesse is a temple guard. Once Jehoiada begins rebuilding, Jesse will need to see that all goes well."

Abigail knew Isa spoke of the temple to God, not the ones her mother had erected to her false gods. She just never imagined Jesse a warrior, even though Suph had said as much. He was big enough and fit enough, but his character was honorable and kind. She swallowed past the knot in her throat; it twisted in her stomach. No wonder she had angered him when she tried to force him to hide. It was not in his nature.

"I see. I am certain your temple will be set to rights in no time, then."

Seth, Isa and Ianatos laughed. Abigail's cheeks burned.

"Why do you laugh?"

"Have you not seen the temple?"

Bilhah wrapped her arm around Abigail's shoulders. "Forgive my cousin. She has been sheltered from much of what Jerusalem has endured."

Abigail shrugged her away. "I am not a child. It is true I have not seen God's temple, but I have heard stories from the servants. I just could not imagine…"

"Neither could we, child." Seth reached out his hand and drew her alongside him before turning his feet down the path. "Even now I cannot fathom the damage that was done, but Isa told me." He lowered his voice. "I made him tell me every detail. However, I think he exaggerates. I would discover for myself, but alas, the boys will not allow me near the temple for fear I'll injure myself. "

Abigail's jaw dropped, but she had the feeling Jesse's uncle was testing her mettle. "You navigate this pass better than those of us with sight."

He burst out into laughter and patted her hand. If he had eyes Abigail was certain they'd be filled with merriment.

"Jesse will have his hands full with you." Seth released her arm, stepped around a rock and then helped her to maneuver it. "Tell me, Abigail, how bad are Jesse's wounds?"

"No—"

"The truth, if you will. My brothers and nephews seem to think it best to shield me. Why, I ask? It is not as if I will become further distressed. I have learned to listen to what it is they do not say."

Abigail drew breath in and then out. How many times had she felt the same? How many times had she only wanted the truth? Did those around her not realize that being kept in the dark only caused her more anxiety? *God, forgive me. Here I am complaining of the dark when this gentle, courageous man beside me is truly in the dark.*

"Jesse has many cuts. Some deep, some not so much. My healer bound his ribs for fear they were broken."

"Aye, broken ribs can make a man wish for death, but they heal easily enough. What else?"

"His face has been beaten. It is almost hard to discern he is a man and not a leper."

"Ha, there have been times when Jesse has wished for such a curse."

"Why would anyone wish a thing? From what I have heard, it is horrible. Those who suffer do so alone for no one will go near them."

"You are correct, Abigail. And such was Jesse's wish. Mothers and their daughters often plagued Jesse's footsteps. No matter. What else is wrong with my nephew?"

"He's a bump on his head. It seems to cause him to grow faint."

"Hmm, now that is bothersome. No matter, you and your healer will see to him shortly while I'll pray."

Abigail nodded.

"I'm glad you agree."

She glanced at the man, intrigued by his wisdom. "How…how did you know?"

The corners of his mouth curved upward. "As I said, I hear what is not spoken. The brush of your hair against my shoulder told me you bobbed your head. You did not shake." He firmed his lips together much as she'd seen Jesse do. "The way Isa paced waiting for you to arrive, I could tell Jesse was not good. Isa was anxious to see to his brother."

"I will not lie. His wounds worry me. They are not pretty. If they fester…"

"Let us pray they will not."

They walked in silence for a while before Seth halted. He raised his face to the sun and then dropped it as if he could see the valley below. "We are almost there, Abigail. Whatever happens, stay close to Jesse. He will gain his strength from the need to protect you. I fear he will need it for the battle to come."

"Battle? What battle?"

Seth did not say another word as he led her into the valley.

~

A breezed brushed over him. The sound of linen buckling beneath the desert wind met his ears. The distinct scent of jasmine teased his senses. He groaned as he sought to open his swollen lids. Discomfort kept them closed. He turned his head and tried to make note of his surroundings. The last he recalled, Melchiah had hoisted him onto his shoulder. Familiar sounds from many years of traveling to and from Manna with his people kindled a fire within his chest. The pestle grinding into the mortar. The sharpening of swords. The deep rumble of chatter.

They were a part of him. They were home.

Even the hand cradled in his palm gave him a sense of home. It reminded him of the nights when his mother sat beside his bed reciting stories from their ancestors. But the palm resting in his did not have the same callused feel from days running a household. This hand was smooth, soft. The fingers twined with his were long and graceful.

"Abigail?" He opened his lids with a groan as the bright daylight greeted him. A white canopy fluttered in the breeze. He lay on a soft mat of wool. He turned his head. Abigail reclined against pillows, her eyes closed. Besides the tiny mark next to her right eye, her olive complexion was without flaw. It was much lighter than his. Most likely from her lack of days spent in the sun. It suited her, however, suited the color of her exotic green eyes.

She did not have the freckles his sister, Lydia, sported, nor did fine lines crease at the corner of her eyes. Her linen veil, dusty from their travels, hung lopsided, revealing a wealth of her cedar-colored tresses. His fingers itched to touch the fine silkiness once again.

He pressed up on his elbows, the pads of his fingers remaining in hers. He reached up with his free hand and smoothed her hair from her shoulders. Her eyes snapped open.

"Jesse?"

He smiled.

"You are awake?"

"Aye."

She pulled her hand from his and he immediately regretted the loss of her touch. She poured water into a goblet. "You must be thirsty."

"That I am." However, it was not water he thirsted for, but the simplicity of holding her hand. All these years he'd been looking for his sense of purpose. Melchiah taught the law, Isa was content living at Manna with his wife and children. Ari had been a guardian to Joash, and Jesse…well, he wandered. Did as he was bade and wandered. Never before had he felt a sense of rightness that all was as it should be. Until now. However, he had not a clue what that rightness was. All he knew was it was tied to her.

She pressed a cool cloth to the wound on his head, and then drew the damp linen along his brow. "Dara says the coldness should lessen the swelling. She left to retrieve more honey. Once she cleans your wounds she'll slather them again. I'm surprised your people allowed Dara to touch you when they have their own healer."

"Abigail, do I make you nervous?"

Her lashes brushed against her cheeks. "Why…why would you make me nervous?"

"You are chattering like my younger sister does when she is overly nervous. Do I make you nervous?"

"No…yes. A little."

"What has changed?"

"Noth…your family. They watch me closely. They watch you closely. I feel like a meaty bone being eyed by a pack of wild dogs."

Jesse laughed. "They have that affect, don't they?" He sat up. His ribs ached but did not hurt as much as they had. He rubbed his hand over the bandages.

"Your brother wrapped them tighter. Dara did what she could, but I fear her strength was not enough."

"She did well, as did you."

She dipped her chin and stared at her folded hands resting in her lap. "My thanks."

"Abigail, you have no reason to fear my people. They are my family and fiercely protective, but they will cause you no harm. Not as long as I am around."

She lifted her gaze to his. "I did not mean to imply they would, Jesse. You must understand, outside the servants, Bilhah, Dara, Micah and the twins, I have had very little dealings with people. I am learning to discern their actions. I do not think your people wish me here."

"Do you blame them, Abigail?"

Wrinkles formed between her eyebrows. "I do not know, Jesse."

"You seek the truth. These people have been scarred by your mother and your father. Some have lost loved ones, others have wept because their altars to God have been demolished. They have not been free to worship God as they choose, but have been told they must bow to wood, clay and bronze. Things made and destroyed by man's hand."

He swiped the tear from her cheek. "As much as you do not trust them, they do not trust you, but they are willing to try, and they will respect my vow to protect you."

Her eyes grew wide. She seemed to shrink in on herself. "Yes, Abigail, I have told Melchiah of my vow, and I'm certain he told them. They will honor my vow as long as you do nothing to cause them to do otherwise."

"What," she gulped. "What could I possibly do to make them turn on me?"

"Slit my throat." He winked. "Even though I have vowed to protect you, they will do all to protect me. As long as you do not hold a threat to me or to Judah, you have nothing to worry."

Shadows flickered in her eyes and he wondered if she could be a threat. He doubted it, else she would not have wasted her energy tending his wounds. What was it that bothered her?

"Where are Ianatos and the twins?" He glanced around the mulling people and then back to her. She toyed with her hands in her lap, her lips twisted together.

"Abigail, what has become of them?"

"I am afraid Nathan would not leave my side and I would not leave yours. Your brothers and Jonathan returned for the horses. Some of the men demanded Nathan lay down his weapon. When he would not, Ianatos joined him." Her gaze skittered to his. "I am surprised the commotion did not wake you. Ianatos was escorted outside of the camp to his people. Nathan is bound to a tree. Jonathan and your brothers have yet to return."

Anger burned in his gut. After he had just told her they would protect her, they took her only anchor away from her. At least Dara, Bilhah and Micah... "Where is Bilhah? Micah?"

"After much coaxing, Micah left with Ianatos. I did not wish the boy to do something rash and—" she paused, her cheeks turning red "—I do not know your people, Jesse. I do not know what they are capable of, so I sent him with Ianatos.'

Her trust in the Philistine surprised him.

"He went to great lengths to protect Joash. I cannot see him harming a child."

She was right. "And Bilhah?"

"A woman sent her away. She followed Ianatos, but I do not know if she was allowed in their camp either."

The anger in his gut turned into a raging inferno. He rose to his feet and stepped from beneath the canopy. Abigail placed her hand on his forearm to stay him. No wonder she was frightened of his people.

"Is this the payment you give for kindness?" he bellowed. "If her family is not welcomed here then neither am I." He grabbed hold of her hand. "Dara! Dara!" He hollered for the old woman until she stood before him. "Gather your things. We are not welcome."

He stalked away from the canopy, weaving through gaping and stuttering people. His head pounded but not as fiercely as it had before. He halted at the edge of the camp. "The horses?"

"Did you not hear me? Your brothers returned for them."

"Aye. Which way did Ianatos go?"

She tilted her head as she twisted her lips. "I do not know."

Jesse blew air from his nostrils, scrubbed his hand over his face and then looked up to the heavens. He released her hand and glared at Dara to silence the outspoken sarcasm he knew was on the tip of her tongue before he began to pace. "What now, Lord?"

"We wait," Abigail said.

He halted his feet, snapped his head toward her and near fell to his face. "What is it you said?"

"We wait. That is what I was doing while you were sleeping. We wait for your brothers to return."

Abigail's calmness sank into his bones. "Fine. We wait then." He turned on his heel and headed back to the canopied area. "Where is my uncle?"

"Ach, the old man is taking a nap," Dara grumbled.

Jesse swiped his hand over his face. Beads of perspiration were back and this time nausea roiled in his gut. He rocked back on his heels. Abigail caught his arm and steadied him.

"Jesse, you need to lie down. Dara will tend you and I'll find something for you to eat."

He glared down at her, unwilling to send her into a den of wild dogs ready to chomp at the first chance. "You will stay here."

"Jesse—"

He moved close and stared down into her wide green eyes. Something flickered in them, drawing him closer. She drew in a breath. Like a droplet of water being pulled to another, he dipped his head closer. His lips hovered above hers. He wanted to kiss her, to know what it was like to share such an intimate touch with a woman. To share this, her first kiss with her. His first kiss.

But he could not. She did not know God. Did not love Him the way Jesse did. He closed his eyes and leaned his forehead against hers. "Abigail, I know it is difficult for you to understand, but if you ask for food among my people—"

The tips of her fingers hovered so near his bottom lip he could feel the warmth of them. The temptation warring within his chest won out. He cradled her hand and brought her fingers to his lips. What was it about this woman that drew him like no other? His father had not held to the ways of arranged marriages and always encouraged his children to seek love. He could not feel such an emotion with her, could he?

No, it was only because he was beholden to her for all that she'd done for him. She had not needed to risk her life to save him, but she had. Only because she wanted the truth. What happened when she discovered the full of it? What happened when she discovered he was the one who had killed her mother? Not just by command, but by deed.

Her fingers trembled within his hand and she pulled them away, dropping them to her side as she took two steps back. "I have suffered much worse at the hands of my mother." She tried to smile but her efforts were in vain. He knew the little bit she revealed about her childhood had cost her a great deal. It was evident in the pain reflected in her eyes. Whatever her mother had done to her did not change the fact that he was the one responsible for her parent's death. "If you insist on seeing your vow through, you can only do so if you are alive. If you do not rest, the wound on your head may not heal. Then where would I be? At the mercy of Suph."

The blood in his veins grew cold. He knew she only teased him to prod him into rest. However, her words were like dousing a fire with frigid water. He narrowed his eyes. Duty called. He would not, could not think about her as anything more than a vow he must honor. Once he saw her to Jehoiada's protection, he would be free to wander once again.

Chapter Fourteen

He wobbled farther away from her and winced as he raked his hand through his hair. His shadow no longer loomed over her. No longer granted her security. Abigail bit her tongue. She should not have mentioned Suph or Jesse's current physical condition. For that was the exact moment he pulled away, shielded himself from her and turned to stone like the very rugged mountains on the horizon. The way he closed himself off from her, like those cedar doors gracing her bedchambers, caused an ache to form in her chest. The kind of ache that occurred whenever she craved her mother's presence. The same kind of ache that closed in on her when she'd been locked in a box to teach her not to sneak out of her room.

That kind of ache brought tears. Tears brought ridicule and more pain. Holding her head high like the queen she was never meant to be, she stepped around Jesse and went in search of sustenance. Once she insured he was on the mend, she would have Nathan and Jonathan take her to Jerusalem. Or maybe she would leave as soon as Jonathan returned, and maybe she would have them take her elsewhere. Someplace where Suph would never find her. Nor would Jesse, if he so chose to look for her. After all, Jesse said she could choose her destination. Her own future.

She skirted around a pen filled with sheep and swiped the tears trailing down her cheeks. She sat on a small log and stared off into the horizon. She did not need Jesse. Did not need his protection. Did not need him to discover the truth; nor did she need him to seek out his God.

"Abigail?"

She crossed her arms around her legs and rested her chin on top of her knees. "Leave me be, Jesse."

"I did not mean to upset you." He ignored her plea and sat beside her.

They remained in silence for long moments. His gaze warmed her. She wanted to look at him, to see the emotions swirling in his eyes. However, if she did, she knew she'd lose more of herself. To what, she did not know, for she did not understand the joy encompassing her whenever he was around. The joy of holding his hand. The *need* to be near him. Bilhah had said a man's affections were not as easily given as a woman's, but it seemed Jesse was more than willing to touch her hand, to soothe *her* wounds.

His fingers tangled in her hair and her stomach tumbled. How was it that a simple touch caused her such turmoil? She swiped at a wayward tear.

"Do not cry, Abigail. I beg of you, do not cry." He curled his fingers around hers and pressed his mouth to the back of her hand. Shivers shook her at the intensity of the unknown emotion shining in Jesse's eyes. Pulling her hand from his, she crossed her arms over her middle.

Another tear escaped, then another. She waited for him to laugh at her. Instead, he grasped her chin with gentle fingers and forced her to look at him. "Abigail, your tears tug at my heart. Your beautiful green eyes were meant for joy, not sadness."

She winced as she tried to blink back the welling tears, but they slid past her lashes and down her cheeks. The color of her eyes had been a curse. She would not mention that lest it bring more pain. "All of this!" She waved her hand at the desert before them. "It is new and I do not understand the emotions building inside me. One moment I want to dance, another I want to curl in a ball and cry. At times I believe I can conquer Suph's evil on my own, others I want to hide and never be found." She tucked her chin back onto her knees. "I just want to breathe, Jesse. I do not want to consider what is real and what is not. I want to breathe."

"Then breathe, Abigail." His words were a bare whisper, but they struck her heart like a hammer to a rock, shattering into many pieces. He rose from the log and crossed his arms over his chest. He was giving her what she wanted, and yet it hurt more than if he remained beside her.

He drew in a ragged breath. "Have you ever seen the sunset, Abigail?"

Jesse had asked her that very question earlier in the day. She glanced up at him, but he stared off into the horizon. She followed his line of sight and sucked in a breath.

"Breathe, Abigail." He turned and stepped over the log.

Brilliant hues of colors she could only imagine stretched across the sky. Blues splashed with royal purple, reds and oranges, mingled with pinks and grays. It was as if the heavens burned, yet the soft glow did not consume—it caressed. She watched as the colors faded, watched as the blue melded into the black as the sun dropped beyond the horizon. Was it as such each night? Was this the doing of the one true God?

If so, thank You, God.

How had she lived her days without ever knowing such beauty? She breathed deeply and closed her eyes. She tried to brand the image into her mind lest she never see it again. What else had she missed locked away like a prisoner?

A small cry called to her. She lifted her head and searched through the waning dark. The screech of a great bird drew her attention skyward. Within its clutches a small animal struggled. The bird dropped the animal, and Abigail rushed forward. The bird rose high and then dove back toward the tiny creature. Abigail ran, yelling while waving her arms in the air trying to scare off the predator.

It screeched and cawed. Abigail covered her head with her hands and ducked. The bird missed its target and came back for another round. Abigail stumbled, falling to her knees. She hunched over the tiny animal, protecting it from the bird.

"Abigail!"

Her heart thundered against her chest. She could imagine Jesse's anger, but she did not care. She could not allow this tiny creature to perish at the hands of the giant bird. Wings batted against the air, swooping over Abigail's head. Her veil ripped from her hair. A whack and a screech.

Jesse lifted her from the ground and cradled her against his chest. "Are you all right?"

She pulled back and glanced at the ball of fur tucked in her hands and then at him. "Yes, I think so, but it's injured."

"What is injured, Abigail?"

She lifted the tiny creature for him to see. "Abigail," he growled. "You risked your life to save a rodent?"

"I did not know what it was, Jesse. I could not let that beast have it. Not after it dropped it."

"You could have been severely injured." He tightened his arms around her. "Have you ever seen what one of those birds can do to a man? No, of course you haven't. It is only by the grace of God you were not maimed or worse killed."

"I know." Her voice sounded shaky even to her own ears. "But I had to rescue it."

He set her down on her feet and held out his hand, but she refused to hand the animal over to him. "What are you going to do with it?"

"Let it go."

"Jesse, he is hurt."

He scrubbed his palm over his beard, something she realized he did whenever he was irritated. "All right, then. Let us see if Dara can mend it."

Abigail squealed, wrapped an arm around his neck, rose up on her toes and kissed Jesse on the cheek.

~

Jesse froze. The touch of her lips against his cheek sent a wave of shock clear to his toes. He'd forgotten all about the fear of seeing her run, then daring to combat a griffon of all things. He forgot the anger surging through his blood when he realized she was trying to rescue a wild animal from the deadly talons. Forgot his disbelief when he discovered it was a mere rodent. Weren't women afraid of such creatures?

Obviously not his Abigail. His Abigail?

He set his hands on her waist, his fingers clenched, daring him to pull her closer. He took a deep breath and…cleared his throat, untwined her arm from his nape and took a step back. The merriment dancing in her eyes had him wanting to pull her back into his arms. Instead he crossed his them over his chest. "You better get that thing to Dara. Although I do not think she will like it one bit."

Abigail giggled. "Dara? Oh, she is used to it."

Jesse scratched his beard. "What do you mean?" Did this woman take on wild beasts often? Most likely not. What kind of wild beasts could be found in the palace? An image of a spotted cat forced its way into his thoughts. Athaliah had collected whatever her heart desired.

"Only that she has treated my pets whenever the occasion arose." Abigail skipped away like a child with a joyous secret. Something he'd seen his sister do a time or two.

He caught up with her in two long strides. It was amazing how he forgot about his own aches when he thought her in danger. He knew, even though she'd asked him to leave her alone, he could not. He had to make sure she was safe, and when he heard her screaming…

She glanced at him. "Thank you."

A genuine smile lit up her face, making her beauty radiant. The blood in his veins halted. He hoped he had made her happy and not the creature cradled in her arms. The fist-sized knot forming in his chest had him wanting to keep making her happy. He glanced at the furry creature once more. The ball of fur wasn't what he thought it was. With the waning light it had been hard to discern its features, but it definitely did not have the pointed pink nose of a rodent and its ears were too big.

"The setting sun was…I do not even know how to describe it. All I know is that I don't want to miss another. Are they like that always?"

"Huh?"

"The sunsets, are they always so breathtaking?"

"Yes. Each evening is something different. Never are they the same. I try to never miss one, even on a cloudy day."

"It was a gift. Thank you, again."

He tugged on her arm, halting their steps. He stared down into her eyes. "Abigail, the gift was not from me, but from the Creator of the heavens and the earth. It is the one true God you should thank."

Her eyes crinkled in mirth. "That I already did, Jesse."

"What are you saying?" Had he heard her correctly?

"What I witnessed could not have come from anything other than an almighty Creator, so, I thanked your God."

He released her arm and shoved his fingers through his hair. He winced when he touched the knot on his head. "He can be your God, too, if only you call upon Him."

"I know." She winked at him, then turned and skipped into the camp.

She knew? Was there hope between them? Only if she chose to allow Joash to remain king. If she contested his kingship, Jesse could not court her, not even if she was the only woman his heart seemed drawn toward. But he would not try to convince her, no matter how much he wanted to. She must make her own choice without his influence, for only then could he be sure of her integrity.

He scrubbed his palm over his chin. How could he doubt the integrity of a woman who took on a griffon to save a...

"Abigail, wait a moment."

She stopped and faced him. "Yes, Jesse?"

"Do you realize that is not a rodent?"

She laughed. "Of course it's not."

"Then why did you not tell me?"

"If I told you it was a baby lion, would you allow me to bring it into camp?"

"Abigail," he growled. What was he going to do with her?

"It needs mending, Jesse, or it will die."

"And what of its mother?"

Abigail cast a glance toward the desert, then back to him. "I do not know, Jesse. All I know is that I can not bear it to suffer an excruciating death. No more than I could bear the thought of you being tormented by Suph."

He stared at her as she walked away, the sting of her words penetrating his pride. The woman saw him as nothing but a wounded animal in need of rescue. He released a sigh and hardened his jaw. He hated being perceived a weakling. All through his childhood he had striven to prove himself to his brothers. He'd been the runt. His mother often coddled him, but then one day he outgrew Melchiah and Isa and even Ari, who had been near a head taller than their older brothers. He trained longer, harder, until he beat them at their games. If he hadn't been outnumbered ten to one, he would have beaten Suph as well and then Abigail would not have seen him as incapable of protecting her. But then he would never have known she existed. That such a humble, beautiful and caring being existed outside of his closet kin amazed him.

Even if he could not court her, if she would not accept his attentions… He pulled his eyebrows together. How long had he hoped that there were women like his mother and sisters by marriage. Women like Abigail. Women who cared enough to risk their lives for a wounded animal. Women who walked away from everything to save an enemy. Would she have done the same if she knew the truth of what he'd done?

Chapter Fifteen

"What has you anxious, Jesse?" Isa sat beside him in front of the fire.

"Besides the fact that we sit in the open waiting for our enemy to find us?"

"Melchiah and I have scouted the area. There are no signs of Suph's men."

"My thanks for retrieving Ianatos and Bilhah. I know it was not easy."

Isa dropped his hand onto Jesse's shoulder. "Listen, little brother, these people have done nothing to be treated as such. It is our father's will and that of the elders that we treat strangers with kindness." He dropped his chin. "It is shame I feel that their kindness has been rewarded with prejudice. But all is well, now, yes?"

Jesse gave his brother a tentative smile.

"What is it, Jesse?"

Jesse rested his head against his folded hands and stared at his sandals. "When Melchiah was young he was sent to the temple to learn. You were the greatest of all warriors trained by the Philistines."

Isa laughed. "Yes, until Ari came along."

Jesse turned his head. "Until Ari came along, and he even excelled over Melchiah in his studies. It is why he was chosen to guard King Joash all this time."

"And you cared for Ma-maw."

"Yes." He had cared for his father's mother in Jerusalem.

Abigail strolled past them and waved, the cub cradled in her arms.

"Jesse, you must know you surpassed Ari's greatness in battle. You are not only quicker and, do not tell Ari this, but stronger."

Jesse rolled his eyes.

"Maybe not at this moment, maybe not tomorrow, but when you are in good health, it is you I want protecting my back. Aye, Ari would do, but I know you'll not allow an enemy to sneak up on me. Besides, Jesse, our lives are not about our great deeds we've accomplished. It's about how we honor God and love those whom he has placed in our lives. It does not matter if that person is a leper or a lost princess."

Jesse snapped his head up. "The only feelings I have toward Abigail are ones of gratitude. If not for her I would be carrion for the vultures."

Isa wrapped his arm around Jesse's shoulders once again and hugged him. "That may be what you think, little brother, but I see the way your eyes light up when they rest upon her."

"Even if I did like her, Isa, she does not worship God."

"Perhaps that is because she does not know how. It is a husband's duty to lead his family by example. No!" He held up his hand. "You may deny she is part of your family, but she is your friend and as you watch her, she watches you."

Jesse glanced over his shoulder and caught her looking at him. She quickly dropped her gaze to the cat lying in her lap and then said something to Bilhah.

"Our father's children love him greatly because he loves us. He is a paragon, an example for his children. He treats our mother as if she were a queen. He loves her above all else, excepting God. Those who meet Father are charmed by him, because he treats them with respect, whether they believe in God Almighty or not, Jesse. His faith and the way he honors God has drawn men to believe in our Father in heaven, even some of the Philistines we've trained with."

Isa rose from his seat. "I must find my wife and children. Seek your rest this night as we do not know what tomorrow holds."

The words Isa left unsaid hung in the air above the crackling of the fire. They were not that far from the city gates, but Jesse knew as well as Isa, that Suph could be anywhere. Jesse scrubbed his hand over his face.

"Are you tired?"

Abigail sat beside him in the spot Isa had vacated.

"Truth be told, I am more anxious than tired. I wish to be at peace with my enemies."

"Of course. I have only known about such enemies for a few days and I am weary. I cannot comprehend years of turmoil."

Jesse nodded toward the cat in her lap, not much bigger than his foot. The cub couldn't be that old. "How is he?"

"Fat." Abigail giggled.

"Fortunate for him, else the griffon would have carried him away."

"Yes. Dara lathered honey where the talons had broken the skin. Now he sports bandages around his waist much like you." She held the cub in the air and smiled.

"Odd the griffon took a live cub. They tend to hunt for dead things."

"Why is that?"

"I do not know, but I imagine it is God's way of ridding the world of death and decay so disease does not spread."

"Interesting. I never thought about that, but then I never knew such animals preyed on the dead. Bilhah brought me a bird once. Dara helped mend its wing. Bilhah and I thought it would be a good idea to play with it and the palace cats."

Jesse shivered at the thought of what could have happened to the young girls if they'd tried to save the bird. "I have seen those cats. They would have devoured two little girls."

Rocking back, Abigail laughed. "Not the large spotted cats my mother kept. They frightened me."

Jesse glanced at the cub in her lap. "But you are not scared of that one's mother? She cannot be far." He did not tell her the mother was most likely dead or had abandoned the cub, else she would not have allowed the cub to be taken. If she'd only been out hunting they would have heard her cries of distress by now, for he was certain the griffon had not carried the cub far from where he found it.

"I am surrounded by capable warriors. Besides," she said, looking into his eyes. "You will not allow anything to harm me, even a lioness."

He narrowed his eyes. "You believe me capable?"

Her gaze roamed from his feet, rested on his arms for a moment and then moved to his head. "Are you not?"

His chest expanded. The muscles in his arms twitched. "Of course, I just thought you believed me…weak."

"Jesse, I've seen my mother's soldiers parading through the palace. I've seen Suph exert his cruelty on the servants. When the temple guards stormed the palace I watched out my window. I was frightened, but the temple guards did not kill those who surrendered. The palace guards would not have done such a thing. I've heard of them killing servants simply because they did not bring them sustenance in a timely manner."

"I am sorry you had to witness...you must have been frightened."

"Yes and no. I wanted freedom. I was not allowed out of my room without consequences. That is how much my mother despised me."

"I do not understand."

"Neither do I—it is why I must discover the truth. It is why it is important to me, so I can understand."

"And what if the truth only brings you more sorrow?"

"Then I will be sorrowed for a time, but at least I will not fear being locked in a box if I leave my chambers."

Anger surged through his veins. He clenched his fists, rose from his seat and stormed to the edge of the camp.

"Jesse, what is it I said? I did not wish to anger you."

He spun on her, the cub cradled in her arms. Abigail's eyes creased with worry. He drew his hand along the side of her jaw, swiping away the lone tear. How could a mother lock her child in the dark? How could she not have loved Abigail, treasured her for the gift she was?

"You do not anger me, Abigail. The treatment your mother bestowed upon you, that is what has angered me. If she were not dead..."

"Do not." The palm of her hand pressed against his chest, the tunic and bandages a poor barrier for the warmth searing him. His head spun, and not from his wound. It was as if he did not draw enough air into his lungs. And his knees grew weak, not the sort that came right before he passed out. No, this was exhilarating. It was as if he stood on top of a mountain, reaching toward the sky with his hands. As if she felt it, too, she leaned closer, her lashes fluttering closed.

Drawn by the scent of jasmine wafting from her, he dipped his head closer. His heart pounded against his rib cage as he sensed her pulse increase. Air caught between them, daring not to move as their breath mingled. Like an ibex drawn to a cool creek in the heat of the day, Jesse pressed his mouth against hers.

He had wished for this touch between them, this intimacy, but he had not been prepared for the intensity pooling in his gut, curling his toes. It threatened to consume him.

Jesse jerked back and raked shaking fingers through his hair.

"Abigail, I..." He needed to tell her the truth but he could not, and until he did so, he should not, could not touch his lips to hers again, not until he knew she would forgive him for his sins against her and her mother. He was quite certain that sort of forgiveness would never come. Some things were beyond grace. Such as killing another's mother, even if she had been beastly. "I am sorry, Abigail. We must return to camp. If all goes well, tomorrow you will have your truth and then you can live in freedom."

Jesse knew, however, that freedom for her would not come until after Suph was captured. And peace would not come for him until he knew without a doubt Suph would no longer threaten Abigail's well-being.

~

Abigail had never known the touch of a man's lips to hers. She'd never known a kiss other than the few Jesse had pressed to her hand, not even one to her brow by Shema as she'd done to the twins. Abigail blinked. Why was that? Shema had been like a mother to her, but the boys... "You are right, Jesse. You need your rest if you are to help me get into the city. I will see you on the morrow."

Jesse raised his hand as if to stop her, but he quickly dropped it back to his side. She wished for him to ask her to stay. Disappointment curled in the pit of her stomach when the words did not come. Sadness settled on her shoulders. However, she would not allow the emotions to rule her. She eyed him. Once again he was a fortress of stone. Unmoving. Impenetrable.

Stiffening her backbone, she walked to the tent she shared with Dara, Bilhah and Micah. She slipped between the folds and handed Micah the purring cub. "See to it he does not tear his bandages."

"Yes, Abigail." A grin split across the child's face and Abigail knew the boy would see to his duty.

She ducked through the opening and looked for Nathan and Jonathan. They sat eating roasted meat, laughing with several of the men. She stood, watching, hesitant to break up the revelry. She twisted her lips, ducked her chin and turned back toward her tent.

"Is all well, Abigail?"

She startled. Looking up, she stared into Jesse's eyes.

"I can see you are troubled. Perhaps if you shared it with me."

She looked back at the twins and then to Jesse. "Yes, of course."

He led her to the place they'd sat before he'd become angry about her mother, which even now perplexed her, knowing her mother was dead.

"What is it, Abigail?"

She tucked her hands into her lap, twisting her fingers. "I had a nurse when I was younger."

She glanced at him but he did not say a word, only waited for her to continue.

"I loved her and I know she loved me. She is the only person I knew who did love me, besides Bilhah. One day she disappeared. My father said she left. My mother said it was because—" she hesitated, ducking her head as heat filled her cheeks "—I was not beautiful. I was too ugly to care for and I was cursed."

Jesse grasped hold of her hand and tucked it between his. "That cannot be true, Abigail. Why, your beauty surpasses even that of your mother."

She sucked in a breath. "I do not know if I can trust you, Jesse, when you tell such lies."

His gaze bored into hers. "It is no lie, Abigail. I have seen your mother and, yes, she was beautiful, but you, especially when you smile, are unlike anything I've ever seen."

"My thanks, but that does not change the fact that I believed my mother. I believed Shema left because I was too ugly. The twins left, too. I never saw them again, but I knew they were around. Little things they left here and there that they knew I liked. It wasn't until yesterday that I discovered my father had Shema killed and I believe it was my doing."

"You could not have been very old, Abigail."

"I was seven, old enough to know certain things were not allowed to be spoken of. I just...if I would not have asked for another story, Shema would not have told one and my father would not have caught her."

"Abigail, you are not responsible for Shema's death. That was your father's doing and his alone."

"Yes, but if I had not spoken about God, then my father never would have known, and then—" she glanced toward the spot where Nathan and Jonathan sat "—the twins would not have lost their mother."

"What is this you speak, Abigail? Dara is here with us, she has not left her sons."

"Shema used to hug and kiss them on the cheeks. Whenever they did something that made her happy, she would press her lips to their heads. She never did that with me, and I loved her. I know she loved me."

He squeezed her fingers. "I am sure she did love you, but that does not mean she was their mother, Abigail."

"You have a mother, Jesse. Did she pick you up when you scraped your knees? Did she kiss you and wish you well before bedtime?"

He nodded.

"Shema did those things with the twins. She did not do so for me and she was like a mother to me. I remember her saying that if she ever had a daughter then she'd want her to be just like me, Jesse. Like me." Tears welled up in her eyes. "I know she was their mother, I know it here." She thumped the tip of her finger against her chest. "And I took that from them. Oh, how they must hate me." She buried her face in her hands and sobbed.

The warmth of Jesse's hand seeped through her tunic as he rubbed comforting circles on her back, for the night air had begun to chill with the lack of sun.

"Abigail, you must know they would not be here fighting to protect you if they hated you. They are loyal to you. I have seen it in their eyes."

Abigail lifted her head and searched his eyes for the truth. She swiped the sleeve of her tunic across her eyes and sat up straight. "You mean it?"

"Yes, Abigail. I have not excelled at the ways of battle without discerning a man's loyalty."

"Why would they?" She hiccuped. "Why would they do that after what I have taken from them? Shema was the kindest of people, gentle and full of joy."

"Then you do her proud, Abigail."

"What do you mean?"

He tucked a finger beneath her chin and raised her eyes to meet his. "You are the kindest of people, gentle and full of joy."

She shook her head. "It is not—"

"It is, Abigail. How many people do you know who would steal a meal from a griffon?"

She gave a little laugh. "Shema would have, the twins. And as grumpy as Dara is, she would have, too."

"They leave a legacy that will carry on through you. As for the twins, they do not blame you, Abigail."

"Unless they do not realize my part in her death."

"Abigail, my beautiful, beautiful Abigail." Jesse cupped her cheek in his palm. "Do not allow the sins of your father to steal your joy. Shema would not wish it, and I am certain the twins would not, either."

"It remains, I must beg their forgiveness and then seek this God who makes beautiful sunsets."

The corner of his mouth slid upwards. "Abigail, the God who makes beautiful sunsets is the only living, breathing God. The only one worthy of your prayers and worship. Hear the song?"

She nodded.

"It is a song of praise unto our Lord, Creator of the heavens. *'Oh Lord, our Lord, How excellent is Your name in all the earth, who have set Your glory above the heavens.'* It was written by your ancestor King David. He loved the Lord, even in his sin, and trust me when I say he had many, yet he always sought reconciliation with God."

"How can I do this, Jesse? How can I make amends with God?"

"David wrote, 'Lean your ear to me, O Lord, hear my cry.' All you must do is call out to the Lord and have faith he will hear you."

She glanced to the wide expanse of the heavens. A multitude of lights winked down at her.

"Those who seek refuge in the Lord will find rest."

She dropped her gaze to his. "Even the daughter of Athaliah?"

"Even the daughter of Athaliah."

Chapter Sixteen

Jesse stretched his arms. The sting from the cuts had lessened as had the pain in his ribs. The soft sounds of the camp slowly coming awake brought him comfort. Soon they would be on their way to Jerusalem. And he was quite thankful there had been little grumbling since his people had just left the city. For the most part, they were willing to help, especially since it furthered the cause of Judah, secured Joash as king.

Some, however, were leery of returning Abigail to Jerusalem for fear she'd try to seize the crown. Of course, they did not know her motives for wanting to return. They did not know she wanted truths. If they did, they might not have agreed, especially if they knew what the truth entailed.

He scrubbed his hand through his beard, sat up and rested his elbows on his knees. It did not matter how he felt—she deserved the truth, even the part he played in her current situation. He was glad of Athaliah's death. He only regretted having been the hand who had shed her blood.

He speared his fingers through his hair. The bump had grown smaller overnight. He had not noticed the lack of thundering in his head until this moment. He was thankful for the attention and care Dara had taken. If not for her and Abigail, he would have perished and missed this morning's sunrise.

He slipped from his tent and stood. He arched his back and stretched again.

"Did you sleep well?"

Something kicked against his chest and he smiled. "Good morning, Abigail. What is it you are doing awake?"

"I did not wish to miss my first sunrise."

He held out his hand. "Come, shall we?"

She entrusted her hand to his. He navigated his way through the sleeping bodies and tents until they reached the east side of camp. He did not want any man-made objects obscuring their vision as they watched God wish them a good morning.

"I should have grabbed one of the blankets for you to sit on."

"I am well, Jesse. I think I would prefer to stand. That way I am closer."

They stood there for long moments, watching in silence as the darkness gave way to tender shades of dark blue. Purple streaked to the south. Pink to the north. A bright orange oval pressed into the horizon, bringing with it colors indescribable.

"Do not stare at the sun, Abigail. Its brilliance will momentarily blind you."

He felt her eyes upon him. He turned and looked at her. "'Twould not be such a bad thing, would it, Jesse? Your uncle seems to find his way around better than those of us with eyes to see. He is wise, that man."

His breath caught in his throat as something burst in his chest and shot to his knees. He drew his fingers down the side of her jaw, tucking her hair behind her ear. Somehow she understood his uncle when many would only see a blind man. She saw beyond the ugliness of his scarred eyes.

He glanced back toward the horizon. "It is why I try to never miss a sunrise or sunset." He gulped. "It is the one thing my uncle claims to miss the most."

The shuffling of feet reached his ears. Jesse turned to see Seth walking toward them. Jesse let go of Abigail's hand and made toward his uncle. "Good morning, Uncle."

"Good morning it is, Jesse. How is it this morning?"

"Beautiful as ever," Jesse said as his eyes sought out Abigail, her eyes closed, face tilted upward.

"I meant the sunrise, nephew."

"Of course. It is breathtaking as usual. The blues are more tender this morning."

"Tender? Is that what it was?"

Jesse smiled. "They were deep, near the color of blackness. However, they have smoothed together as if there is no barrier between them."

"Magnificent. Good morning, Abigail," he said as Jesse brought him to a halt.

Abigail placed her hand on Seth's shoulder. "Good morning, Seth."

"Come now, I have asked you to call me Uncle."

She leaned forward and pecked Seth on the cheek. "Of course, Uncle."

Seth smiled, his age seeming to dissipate as he basked in the morning sunlight and Abigail's affection.

"My thanks for pleasing an old man with your description, nephew. I never tire hearing of God's goodness."

Abigail clapped her hands together. "Oh, but it is beautiful. I cannot imagine they are different each morning."

"Have you never seen the sun rise before?"

She dipped her chin, her cheeks pink. "I have always known there was day and night. Knew the sun rose and the moon appeared in the dark along with the stars, but no, Uncle, I have never witnessed such a brilliant sight." She looked at Jesse. "I now understand why so many believe there is a supreme God. How else could such a thing occur?"

"In that you are correct, Abigail. Only a loving God, the God Almighty, would provide such a gift to his creation."

The look in Abigail's eyes as she spoke with Seth captivated Jesse. She spoke to him as she spoke to anyone. Her eyes did not shift away, only when she felt shame, such as her having never seen a sunrise before this very morning.

Jesse's heart smiled. There was no other way to describe it. He was glad he was able to share this first sunrise with her. He hoped it would be only one of many, but first they had to get to Jerusalem.

The sun was near halfway above the horizon, and as much as he regretted it, it was time for them to begin packing up camp. "I hate to bring an end to this moment, but it is time. We must gather our belongings and make our way to Jerusalem."

They turned toward the camp. Jesse acknowledged many as they wove through the throng of people. He guided Seth to his tent. "I will see you soon, Uncle."

Abigail gave Seth a parting kiss on the cheek.

"May God grant thee safe travels."

"To you as well, Uncle."

It had been decided the night before that two of the younger boys would lead Seth and Suph's horses back to the cavern to wait for their people to return home. Jesse had been reluctant to give up Papyrus, but, as Isa had pointed out, it would not do for Suph to recognize his own horse. Of course, Nathan and Jonathan grumbled as well, but they eventually saw the wisdom in leaving them behind. It helped that Jesse vowed to return them once Abigail was safe. Now he had to speak with Ianatos and explain the plan for the Philistines. Ianatos would not like it, but what choice did they have?

He stopped outside Abigail's tent, reluctant to leave her presence for even a moment. "Until I see you again."

He turned to leave. "Jesse," she said, halting his retreat.

"What if I do not wish to return to Jerusalem?"

He grabbed hold of her shoulders. Had she decided to return to Suph? "What is it you are saying?"

"What if I do not wish to know the truth, Jesse? I fear it will destroy the peace I am finding here among your people."

His people had not been so kind to her cousin, but he understood. He did not wish to take her to Jerusalem, either, but in this they had no choice. He could not tell her what it was he had done until she heard what it was Jehoiada had to say. It was his only hope of receiving her forgiveness.

"Abigail, if you do not return, you will always wonder about your cousins and your father's sons. You will always wonder if Joash is the rightful King of Judah. You will always wonder if you were responsible for Shema's death."

Shadows of pain flickered in her eyes.

"It is sorry I am, Abigail, but I do not believe you will live in peace, not with yourself, if you do not find the answers you seek."

She stepped back and crossed her arms over her chest. "I am scared."

He tipped her chin up until she met his eyes. "Abigail, you were brave enough to stand in the face of a griffon's deadly talons in order to save a cub."

"I did not know what it was I was facing."

"As so in this, Abigail. You do not know what the truth holds, neither do I. What I do know is you are brave enough to face the truths before you, no matter what they may bring."

She drew in a ragged breath. Tears welled on the edge of her lashes. He watched her fight for strength and courage. She straightened her shoulders and nodded. "Jesse, will you pray?"

He smiled and grabbed hold of her hands. Here she was prodding him to be an example. "Of course."

He knelt on the ground outside her tent, drawing her down beside him. He closed his eyes and bowed his head.

"Heavenly Father, God of all creation, we praise You above all, for You are the only God who breathes and gifts His creation with sunrises. Lord, You alone know our days. You alone know what our purpose is here on the earth. Lord, Abigail and I beseech You to go before us, to hide us from Thine enemies and grant us understanding in the face of our own fears. Seal our future in the palm of Your hands, God. Amen."

Jesse opened his eyes. Abigail's hair draped around her shoulders, shielding her. Peace surrounded her. Peace encompassed him and he knew no matter what happened in the next hours, the next days, all would be well. He did not know if he loved her as Isa had suggested, but he knew in this one small moment he wanted to try.

And, Lord, I pray Thee, grant Abigail the ability to forgive me for my sins against her.

~

Something—she did not know what—calmed all of her fears as Jesse prayed. He'd quit speaking, but she did not want to move from the comfort surrounding her. She wanted to bask in this moment and never let it go.

He squeezed her fingers and guided her to stand. She opened her eyes and looked into his. They were filled with an emotion she did not understand but had seen when Nathan looked at Bilhah. Perhaps it was that affection Bilhah suggested a man did not give easily. If that was true then why had Jesse kissed her?

Did Jesse feel something for her?

Would he kiss her again?

He winked. Her heart dropped to her stomach and rolled around. She felt…happy, joy. Laughter bubbled up into her throat, but she tamped it down. Jesse would only ask her the cause of such joy and she had no answer for him, not yet.

"It is time." He gave another reassuring squeeze and then dropped her hands. "Help Bilhah and Dara gather your belongings, and do not forget the cub."

She gave in to the laughter. "I do not think Micah would allow me to do such a thing. He is quite taken with the beast."

Jesse pressed his lips together. He looked as if he wanted to say something.

"It is all right, Jesse. I know the cub cannot stay. It is too dangerous. Surely someone at the palace will know what to do with it."

It would not be the first time a big cat prowled the courts of Judah.

He nodded. "I will see you once the camp is broken down. Do not leave or wander. Wait here and I will come for you, Bilhah and Dara. I will not send a messenger. I will come myself. Understood?"

She twisted her lips.

"Abigail, if the twins arrive before I do, make them wait here with you."

"I will not leave."

"For nothing, Abigail. It is important. You do not know everyone here. If a stranger were to come into camp and ask you to go with them, you would not know them from any other here."

"I understand, Jesse."

He grabbed her hand. "If you have need of me, send Micah."

Stepping closer, he leaned forward. She thought he was going to kiss her, the glint in his eyes like that of a polished stone telling her so, but the shine dulled and became guarded. He released her hand and walked away. His rejection reminded her of all the times her mother had paid her little heed.

She watched him skirt around one tent then another. She caught glimpses of him as he moved toward the tent he'd spent the night in. He moved like the big cats she'd seen at the palace, lithe, graceful. Yet strength and power laid at rest in his shoulders and upper arms. She'd felt his strength when he'd cradled her after her encounter with the bird. She'd seen the strength vibrate through him as he fought to control his anger.

"Princess, will you care for the cub while I fetch some things for Dara?" Micah looked reluctant to give up the animal. She would have offered to do Micah's chores for him, but she'd told Jesse she would stay.

"Of course." She held out her hands from the cub. "How is he doing today?"

"He keeps his eyes open longer and has had some goat's milk. He still does not move much."

Abigail laughed. "Soon you will be wishing he did not move at all. Go do what Dara has asked. Do not be long, we must be ready soon."

"Yes, Princess." He scratched the top of the cub's head, bobbed his chin and then ran off.

Abigail took a deep breath before ducking into the tent. "Are we almost ready?"

Dara rolled a wool blanket and tied a cord around it. "I sent Bilhah for Nathan and Jonathan, and then sent Micah after Bilhah. I need my boys to take our things and load them on the donkeys."

"Yes, Micah just left a moment ago, but I did not see Bilhah anywhere." She snuggled her face into the cub's fur. His purring tickled her cheek.

Dara's wrinkled brow wrinkled further. "She left shortly after you did, Abigail."

Abigail peered out the tent flap and then back to Dara, Jesse's warning firm in her thoughts. Was it possible Suph or one of his men had snuck into camp? "You do not think anything has happened to her, do you?"

"I would not panic, yet, although she has been gone longer than necessary. Unless she still searches for Nathan and Jonathan."

Abigail closed her eyes and prayed for Bilhah's safety. *Lord, please send Jesse to me. Something does not feel right.*

"Dara, I do not like this."

"Do not fret, child. She is most likely giving some of these women a difficult time for sending her away as they had."

Abigail's cheeks burned. She recalled Jesse's anger over Bilhah's treatment, but she knew Bilhah would do no such thing. Not now.

Abigail ducked through the tent flaps. Standing on her toes, she scanned the area for Bilhah or Micah.

Micah ran toward her, and she breathed a sigh of relief. "Abigail?"

She looked down upon him with great affection. "What is it, Micah?"

"I cannot find Bilhah, nor Jonathan and Nathan."

Abigail hugged her middle as fear replaced her early relief.

"Go find Jesse, and ask him to come quickly, please."

The child took off running in the direction Jesse had gone earlier. Abigail ducked inside the tent. Urgency vibrated through her muscles. "Dara, Micah can't find Bilhah." She laid the cub down next to the old woman and began grabbing a few items. She tucked her cloak over her shoulder and then snatched up a small dagger one of the twins had left on her window ledge several years earlier. She dug for the cedar box, opened the lid and pulled out the gem that belonged to Jesse. She slipped the repaired cord over her neck, tucking the stone beneath her tunic.

Abigail bent and kissed the old woman on the cheek. "I will return."

"Abigail, you cannot think to go on your own."

"What is it, Abigail?" Jesse ducked his head in between the flaps. Ragged breaths puffed out his cheeks.

Although her heart weighed like a stone in her chest, the sight of Jesse eased the tension. "No, Dara. I do not intend on going alone."

"I will be right out, Jesse."

He slipped from the tent, his shadow large and imposing. She rose from beside Dara. "Stay with the camp and Micah. Where they go, you go, Dara. Do you hear? Jesse and I will find Bilhah and your boys."

Even though Abigail was certain the boys were not hers, but rather Shema's, the old woman cared deeply for them. It was evident whenever she spoke of them. "Micah will care for the cub."

She slipped between the flaps and saw Jesse pacing, wearing a path through the valley dirt beneath him. "Micah, help Dara."

Jesse grabbed hold of her shoulders and stared into her eyes.

"Abigail, what is it? The child would tell me naught, only saying it was urgent."

"It's Bilhah—" Before she could say another word, Jesse began to storm away.

"Wait!"

He spun around.

"Dara sent Bilhah for the twins just after we left to watch the sunrise. She has yet to return. Something tells me Suph has her."

"Lord Almighty, what are we to do?"

"Jesse, we have prayed, do we not need to trust God will see things to the way they should be?"

He stared at her as if she'd grown a tail and sharp talons.

"You are right, Abigail." He speared his fingers through his hair. "It does not mean I like the possibility that Suph has infiltrated our camp. It is one thing to use me to gain what he wants, another thing altogether to use a woman."

She laid her hand on his arm. "Jesse, all will be well. Perhaps Bilhah only searches for the twins."

"I am not so certain, Abigail."

The hints of anger twitching at the corner of his eye worried her a little. She'd only known him for a few days, had come to care for him during that time. Still, she did not know what he was capable of, especially when his body was on the mend.

"The swelling around your eyes has disappeared."

He shoved his fingers through his hair. "Stay with Dara while I search the camp.

She shook her head. "No. I am coming with you."

"It will take less time if I go alone."

"Two sets of eyes are better than one, Jesse."

"If there is—"

"No! Everyone I've cared for has disappeared, except for Dara and Micah and I refuse to believe they will be the only ones left."

Light danced in his dark eyes. He took a step closer to her and she thought for a moment he might embrace her, but he clenched his jaw and crossed his arms over his chest. "Very well, Abigail. You will go with me. You will obey every word I say, do you understand?"

"I will obey as long as your orders are within reason."

"Abigail." His growl sent shivers racing down her spine but she pretended not to hear.

"If you ask me to be quiet, I will. But if you ask me to do something that goes against my newfound faith, I will disobey."

He gave in and took that step forward. Tucking a strand of hair behind her ear, he leaned toward her. His mouth hovered above hers. Something palpable snapped between them. His chest expanded as if he held his breath as she did her own.

Waiting, hoping, needing to know he cared for her, she dared not move lest the moment slip from them. Her lashes fluttered shut, waiting for the touch of his lips against hers.

"I do not expect anything less of you, Abigail."

She pushed aside her disappointment when he pulled away. "Come, let us find my brothers and Ianatos." Jesse took hold of her hand, the strength and warmth against her palm gave her confidence that he would find Bilhah and the twins.

They rounded one tent, turned left and rounded another. She'd been surprised when he hadn't slept outside her tent the night before and a little disappointed, although she knew he needed his rest in order to heal. If his stride was any indication, he had gotten his rest and then some.

"Jesse, what if we do not find them?"

"We will, Abigail. Isa is one of the best trackers in all of Judea. And I am the second best." He glanced down at her and gave her a teasing grin. "Besides, we have God on our side. We will pray for guidance and as you said, trust He will help us."

"My thanks, Jesse."

He stopped, his hands gripped her arms. "For what, Abigail?"

"For not making me stay with Dara. For not teasing me about my fears. Not laughing when I have cried."

"Why would I laugh at your tears?"

She dropped her gaze to her feet. "Is that not what people do? Laugh when others cry?"

"Abigail, tears should not be laughed at. Not unless they are tears of joy and laughter bubbles forth, but your tears, the kind that comes with sadness, are not meant for laughter." His thumb drew lines along her cheekbone as if to wipe away her tears. "I will never laugh at your tears of sorrow."

"I am trying to believe all will be well, Jesse. This is all new to me. Truth be told, I am frightened that something horrible has happened to Bilhah."

He leaned his brow against hers. "I, as well, Abigail. However, the longer we tarry, the longer it will be before we discover her whereabouts."

She had difficulty imagining this man being scared of anything, but the empty look in his eyes proved his words.

He resumed walking, holding her hand between them. "Isa," he hollered as he came near a large tent. "Isa! Melchiah!"

His brothers released the cords from the stakes. Their wives released the poles they'd been holding and the side of the tent collapsed to the ground. "What is it, Jesse?" Isa stepped forward, Melchiah followed.

"Bilhah, Nathan and Jonathan are not to be found."

The brothers straightened their shoulders, crossed their arms and looked at each other. The resemblance between the older two was like that of the twins. She glanced at Jesse and wondered if he looked just like them beneath the bruises and swelling.

"Are you certain they are not with the Philistines?"

Jesse looked down at her, and then back to his brothers. "No, but my instincts tell me they are not. Bilhah was sent just before sunrise to look for the twins."

Isa shoved his fingers through his hair. Melchiah worried his beard. Abigail couldn't help but think how similar all three of the brothers' mannerisms were.

"You are wise to come to us, Abigail." Melchiah tugged on his beard. "It is possible someone knows you are here and is seeking to draw you out of camp."

Isa quirked an eyebrow. "Jesse, I am surprised you did not run off on your own to look for them."

Jesse looked to his brother, at Abigail and back to Isa. "There is more than just me to consider. If what I fear has happened, then it would not do to leave Abigail alone without protection. Besides, I do not think I could have stopped her from following me if I chose to go alone. And then we'd both be at the mercy of Suph."

Abigail's hand involuntarily squeezed his. He smiled down at her.

"In this I believe you are correct, Jesse. Let us formulate a plan." Isa faced Melchiah. "Would you keep Abigail with you while Jesse and I search the Philistine camp?"

"Of course."

"How do you do their bidding so easily?" Abigail asked. "Are you not the eldest?"

Isa laughed as he nudged Melchiah with his elbow. "That he is, Abigail. However, he trusts mine and Jesse's abilities when it comes to warfare."

Chapter Seventeen

"I do not like this." Jesse jumped down from his horse and knelt. It was obvious the Philistines had been camped here, but now there was no sign of them. Even the charred wood, which should have remained warm, had been long ago cooled.

"What do you think has happened to them?" Isa asked.

Jesse shook his head, thankful Abigail had agreed to stay with Melchiah and his family while he and Isa scouted the Philistine camp. "There were ten Philistine warriors with Ianatos. As far as I could tell, even if Suph had thirty men, he did not have a large enough following to take down the Philistines."

"You know as well as I do that we cannot underestimate our enemies."

Jesse dropped the reins and walked around the camp. Slight indentations where the bedding had been left him scratching his head. Ianatos was supposed to have met them shortly after they broke camp. From the looks of it the Philistine camp had been broken long before sunrise.

He released air from his lungs. "There is no sign of a struggle, Isa."

"The Philistines would not go without a fight."

"Unless…" Jesse tugged on his beard and thought hard about all of the possibilities.

"Unless what, Jesse?" Isa prodded.

"Unless they were told to leave by their commander."

"Jesse, I thought Ianatos was trustworthy."

"He is. Which means something…why did he not come and tell us?"

Isa dismounted and stood beside Jesse. They stared at the white ash in the fire ring. "Are you suggesting Ianatos knew of a threat, and instead of alerting us he skipped out?"

"No." Jesse scanned the horizon toward Jerusalem. His eyes searched for anything that should not be there. "I am saying he is watching from a distance. He did not warn us because he could not without alerting those who watched him or us."

"How do you know this, Jesse?"

He looked at his brother. "Did you spend time with the Philistines during your training?"

"Of course, we all did."

"Do you see the indentations the bedroll left on the north side of the fire? It lies differently than the rest. Then there is another." Jesse walked around the fire and toward the second marked indentation. "Here and a third, there." He pointed.

"What does it mean?"

"It tells us that is the direction Ianatos went."

Isa gazed toward that direction, then turned on his feet looking in all directions. "Where are our enemies?"

"They are near, watching us." Jesse walked back to the fire and kicked at the ashes. "We travel on toward Jerusalem and keep our eyes open."

He would not tell Isa he was anxious to get back to Abigail. He had full confidence in Melchiah to keep her safe. However, some of his confidence in their plans had waned with the disappearance of the Philistines and he still had no idea where Nathan, Jonathan and Bilhah had gone. What few tracks they were able to detect had gone farther than Jesse was comfortable leaving camp to follow.

They mounted their horses. "I guess there is no sense in sending Seth to the hills with the horses," Jesse said.

"It is just as well. He longs for the city. He does not say as much, but I hear it in his voice when he asks how it has fared over the last seven years."

"He would have made a great priest," Jesse mused.

"I agree, but he has served us well. Perhaps his tragic accident was not part of God's will, but it has all turned out well enough."

"I dislike he will never see another sunrise or sunset."

Isa laughed. "Yes, but Seth has seen greater things without his eyes then we have with our own."

Jesse pulled up on the reins. Isa did likewise. "Abigail said much the same earlier this morn."

"Is that so?" Isa smiled. "She is a wise woman."

Jesse burst out laughing. "Excepting she is willing to fight a griffon in order to save a lion cub."

"You jest?"

"No," Jesse said as he pressed his heel into Papyrus's flanks. "I do not think I have ever been so scar—"

Fire shot across the sky in front of them. The line arced from their camp. Jesse looked toward the direction the firebrand had flown. Had their camp been attacked in their absence?

They urged their horses into a gallop and raced back to their family. Jesse's mind whirled as another firebrand flew across the sky. "I pray all is well."

"I pray you are right." Isa urged his horse to run faster.

Jesse chased after him. It did not take them but a few moments to reach camp. Much to Jesse's confusion and relief, their warriors had not sent the firebrands. Who had sent them? He would have time enough to discover that mystery, but first Jesse longed to lay his eyes on Abigail, to insure she was well.

He was surprised to find no signs of his nieces and nephews running around or of sister-in-law, Isabel, chasing after them. He dropped to his feet. Thorns pricked his nape as he reached for Melchiah's tent. Afraid of what he'd find, he pulled back the flap. What he saw left his heart hollow, his veins cold.

Falling to his knees, he rent his tunic in two.

~

An ache settled deep in Abigail's heart. She longed to return to Jesse, longed to sit and watch the sunset when nightfall came, but worst of all she longed to turn back the days before she had met him.

If she would have chosen to seek refuge with the temple guards instead of allowing Suph to sweep her from the palace then perhaps Jesse never would have been captured. And if he had, she never would have known him, never would have placed his family in peril.

"You did not have to hurt Bilhah."

The arm around her waist banded like steel. "You gave me no choice, Abigail."

"There is always a choice, Suph."

He jerked his arm around her waist, cutting off her air. She was certain if his other hand did not guide a horse he would have done much worse. However, at this moment she welcomed the pain he doled out. "If I did not need you, Abigail, you would have met a fate worse than your cousin."

What could be worse than death? Suph had left her cousin gasping for breath, lying in a pool of blood. The thought of her possibly dying because Abigail had chosen to leave Suph sickened her. "What of Nathan and Jonathan?"

"They are well. For now, Abigail." He pulled the reins, leading the horse away from where they had been camped. Fear clawed at her throat. "If you do not do as I say, they will meet the same fate as Bilhah."

Abigail wasn't certain what plans he had, but she knew they would not see fruition. "I have no power in Judah, Suph. You must know this."

"That is where you are wrong, Abigail."

"The people of Judah do not even know of my existence—and if they did, I am nothing but a woman. As a son, Joash is the rightful heir."

"That may be true, Abigail. However, the prisoner will come for you and when he does he will do whatever it is I wish to see you unharmed. Even hand me the king, and then the child will be of no consequence."

A bitter laugh rose up in her throat and passed her lips. "Jesse would never betray his king, Suph."

"You underestimate your allure, Abigail." He shifted his hold on her. "Do you think I did not see you and he? I watched him take hold of your hand." He laid his hand atop hers and squeezed, causing fear to creep into Abigail's gut. "A hand he has no right to touch, for you belong to me."

"We are not betrothed, Suph."

He laughed. Pricks like a kitten's claws climbed up her spine. "Of course we are, Abigail. All of my men bear witness to our contract. Being that you have no male relatives, I had to call on Elam to agree to give you to me. Nevertheless, Abigail, you have no choice in the matter."

She bit down on her lip to keep from spewing venom and making matters worse. There was always a choice and she'd stick a blade in his poisonous heart before he took her as his wife, of that she was certain.

Suph moved toward the base of the mountains and then rode between two rugged hills. Encompassed in their shadows, Abigail felt as if she were being locked in a box. She shivered and squeezed her eyes closed against the tears threatening to spill over her lashes as she recalled the words Shema had taught her to speak whenever she felt scared when she was but a child. "You are my rock and my fortress and my deliverer. My God, my strength—"

"What nonsense do you spew, Abigail?"

"—in whom I will trust, my buckler, the horn of my salvation and my high tower."

"Blasphemy, Abigail! Has that rebel turned you from your mother's ways?"

"I will call upon the Lord." Her voice became louder, echoing off the mountainous walls as she remembered the love pouring from Shema's heart when she spoke the words to God. "He is worthy to be praised, and I shall be saved from my enemies."

Suph's arm trembled. "You are mad, Abigail. No wonder your mother kept you locked away."

Awareness dawned on her like the rising of the sun. Is that why her mother had kept her locked away? Because she believed the stories Shema had told her? She searched her memories, for she had not always been isolated. Memories of running through the palace halls flashed into her mind. They were quickly followed by the cramped darkness of the locked box.

Perhaps it did not matter why her mother had treated her so. All that mattered now was that she continued to call on the name of the Lord and worship him. Even though Suph had left the last of her family for dead, even if he killed the twins, she would worship God because He loved her, loved her enough to give her a sunrise each day. Even if Suph brought harm to Jesse, she would choose to worship God. That was one choice Suph could not take from her.

She giggled. Her giggle bubbled into laughter. Joy overflowed her heart and into her eyes. She wiped the tears of joy from her cheeks and glanced over her shoulder at her captor. His eyes darted to and fro as if seeking a threat, or mayhap he was scared of her. "Perhaps you are right, Suph. I am mad. Mad with love for the one true God. God Almighty, Creator of heaven and earth, and that is one thing you can never take away from me, Suph. As long as I breathe life into my body, I will worship Him."

He released his arm from around her waist and clouted her on the back of the head. The impact propelled her over the side of the horse. She would have fallen if Suph hadn't grabbed hold of her tunic and jerked her upright. "We will see about that."

Chapter Eighteen

"Jesse, would you slow down?"

He pulled up on the reins and glared at Isa. "We have wasted enough time retrieving the Philistines."

"We will not get there at all if you ruin our horses."

Jesse raked his fingers through his hair. "It is sorry I am, Isa. After what Suph did to Bilhah, I fear for Abigail's life."

"It is fortunate Bilhah is alive."

"For now." The bitterness of revenge clung to his tongue.

"Dara is a capable healer, as is our own healer. They will work together." He blew an exaggerated breath. "It is fortunate Melchiah and his family were left unharmed."

"Aye, I do not think I could have swallowed that sour grape. I should have been there. I should not have left her. I should have taken her with us."

"Jesse, if you would have, it is certain Melchiah, his wife, and the children would have been taken or murdered. It is by the grace of God, Abigail pleaded for their lives."

Jesse swallowed the bile in his throat. Melchiah had told him that she held a knife to her own throat and threatened to slit it if Suph harmed a hair on their heads. His brave, courageous Abigail, the woman he had vowed to protect and failed. How could he?

"I should not have left. Not when I had known Suph had more than likely stolen Bilhah from camp. I should have been more vigilant. I should not have rested."

"Enough! You can think of all the things you should have or should not have done, but that does not help us now. It does not change our circumstances at this moment." Isa moved closer to him, his gaze roaming over the Philistines. "If you do not get your emotions under control, I will have them tie you up and leave you for the birds while we rescue Abigail."

Ianatos rode up beside them. "It does have merit. You cannot go into a battle led by your emotions, Jesse. You know this. Besides, Suph will be expecting you. He believes you are the key to removing Joash from the throne."

"What is it you suggest, Ianatos?" Jesse growled.

"I like your brother's suggestion. I weary of listening to you whine."

Jesse narrowed his eyes.

"You cannot ride into the pass, Jesse."

"You will not go without me."

"We will lie in wait. Suph will grow impatient and he will come down. When he does, we will be ready."

Jesse scanned the cliffs. "How do we know he does not have men watching for us?"

"I have already sent men to scout the area earlier this morn. My men will signal soon. If I am correct, Suph believes he's outsmarted us. You forget your reputation, Jesse. You are known for your rashness. You often rush headlong into battle." Ianatos shifted his weight on the back of his horse. "It is what makes your prowess renowned. It's what makes you dangerous. It also makes you predictable."

"Patience is not a virtue I possess."

"Then we will tie you up."

"I do not like this. The more time he has Abigail, the more time he has to harm her." Jesse did not think she could survive what Suph put Bilhah through. "I cannot bear the thought—"

Isa reached out and dropped his hand on Jesse's shoulder. "Jesse, where is your faith? Have you prayed for Abigail? Have you sought God's guidance in this?"

Jesse closed his eyes and lifted his face heavenward. "We prayed together this morn."

"Then trust God to carry us through. No matter the outcome."

"And if Suph harms her," Ianatos said, "I will personally take care of him so you do not have his blood on your hands."

Jesse dropped his head to his chest. "Forgive me, Father God." He drew in a long breath and glanced at his brother, then to Ianatos. He nodded. "So be it. I will trust your lead in this."

It was difficult for him to hand over leadership to these two men, not because he did not believe they were capable, but because his emotions demanded he rush in and take Abigail back. However, he knew they were right. He knew he would do Abigail no good if he were captured. He wished this heaviness weighing on his chest would disappear, but understood that would only occur if he fully placed his trust in the Lord. God was more capable of protecting Abigail than Jesse was, that was for sure.

"You can inform me of your plans when I return." Jesse dismounted and tossed his reins to Ianatos. He removed a flask of water from a leather bag and drank from it. He walked toward a grove of trees and knelt beneath what little shade was available. He leaned his forehead against the trunk. "God, forgive me. Please forgive me for my lack of faith. I do not know what has overcome me. Is it because I care for Abigail, because I have broken my vow to her?

"I pray she will forgive me for my lack. God, I ask You to help me to redeem my vow. Enfold her in your wings, Father. I beseech You, keep her from Suph's cruelty. May he not be able to lay a hand on her. Guide my footsteps, I ask You grant Ianatos and Isa wisdom in their plans.

"Father of Abraham, Isaac and Jacob, praise You for Your greatness, Your goodness and Your faithfulness to a faithless people. Anoint my steps and my words, keep my actions pure. May they reflect what is in my heart. Help me to forgive Suph for the evils he has committed against your people."

A screech cried out overhead. Jesse leaned back from the shadows and looked to the evening sky. Several griffons circled above, looking for their evening meal before they sought their perch in the mountains. An image of Abigail flinging her arms in the air trying to frighten such a great bird in order to save the life of a cub forced its way into his thoughts. He smiled when he recalled thinking it had been a mere rodent she had risked her life for. Most likely it would not have mattered if it had been a rodent. His Abigail had a big heart, full of courage and compassion. She would have done the same for such a miserable creature, had done so for him. He prayed her heart had not been shattered by what Suph had done to those she loved.

The cold seeped into her bones. Suph's hiding place in the mountains left little room for a large fire and she refused to move any closer, lest she smell the stench of blood on his hands. Even now his tunic was stained. He wore it like a badge of honor, which made her nauseous every time she laid her eyes upon him.

Nathan and Jonathan were nowhere to be seen. She had no idea if Suph told the truth about their captivity, or whether they were even alive. Given his actions so far, she had little hope.

However, she refused to allow her circumstances to rob her of the joy she had gained from speaking with God. Three nights now, she had spent cuddled in fleece praying to the God of the Heavens. There was little to be seen entrapped as she was between the tall craggy mountains, but she could see the stars twinkle down upon her. And although the sunrises and sunsets had been obscured, she did her best to recreate them in her mind's eye when the time arrived.

Suph seemed to know whenever it was she began to pray in earnest. Once he tossed water in her face, another time he yanked her to her feet and made her stand for what seemed like hours. His eyes had grown wide with fear when she began praying louder until he pushed her back to the hard ground. She sported a few scrapes and bruises, but she welcomed them, knowing this man had delivered much worse to others. To Jesse. To Bilhah.

The more she prayed the more agitated Suph became. He paced often, even gashed his own arm with his blade. His faithful soldiers began to eye him with distrust. Many kept their distance and made as little noise as possible. Abigail could only hope they would tire of this barren place with no springs and leave him. Could only hope they had the courage to leave Suph to his madness. She giggled to herself.

"You are mad, woman. Why is it you laugh?"

"I am filled with joy, Suph. Why is it you scowl and pace like a wild animal?" She lifted an eyebrow, daring him to answer.

He stalked toward her like the very beast she accused him of being. Crouching low in front of her, he grabbed her by her nape and pressed his nose against hers. "The longer it takes for your Levite to arrive, the longer it is before I can make you my bride, Abigail. I am anxious to see the deed done." He curled his lip and looked her up and down, before rising and walking away. "Why, I have no idea. You haven't the beauty of your mother, but one must sacrifice for the good of his kingdom, I suppose."

"The only kingdom you possess is those few souls who have followed you into this barren land. If you look closely, Suph, you will see even they wish to abandon your side. No, you will never rule over Judah, for you will never rule over me."

Anger filled his eyes and he came at her with a roar. He was mad, crazed. His eyes were wide and darting as he grabbed hold of her and jerked her against him. Afraid, she slipped the dagger he had failed to remove from her tunic after she'd threatened to slit her own throat and pierced it into his flesh. Suph rocked back on his heels with a howl of pain. He jerked the dagger from his upper arm. Fire burned in his eyes and she feared what it was he might do to her. He arced the dagger upward. A hand caught his before he thrust it down.

"You forget you need her alive." One of Suph's men stood over his shoulder.

The hardness of Suph's jaw relaxed. "Bring me one of our prisoners."

Frantic, Abigail searched the area. What prisoner? Did he have one of the twins here? Worse, had he captured Jesse?

The soldier climbed higher into the mountain and disappeared around a bend in the pass. Her pulse beat hard against her chest.

"Scared, my beloved?"

Bile rose into her throat at the endearment. She flicked her gaze toward him and glared. "I will fear no evil for Thou art with me, Thy rod and Thy staff, they comfort me."

Suph swung his hand back and smacked her across the cheek. Abigail reeled backward. The palm of her hand landed on a sharp rock. She sucked in a breath against the pain, gripped the rock and clouted Suph's jaw with it.

Grabbing a fistful of her tunic, he jerked her forward, pressing his face into hers. "You do something like that again, and I will kill you, Abigail. I will find another way to secure Judah as my kingdom."

She spit in his face. He tossed her from him and then wiped his tunic over his bearded jaw. "Ah, here we are."

Suph's soldier led a small boy by his neck. The child's hands were tied in front of him. Abigail squinted, unable to tell in the waning light if she knew who this child was. He was much smaller than Micah was, younger. She shook her head, glanced at Suph, to the boy and back to Suph again. "I do not understand."

"Do you not, Abigail?"

Did Suph know her well enough to know she would do anything to protect a child? The soldier brought the child closer and released him. Suph wrapped his arm around the boy's shoulder and then mussed his hair. The smile Suph rained down upon the child left Abigail feeling sick. There was no possible way Suph had kidnapped Judah's rightful king. Was there?

~

After three nights of trying his patience and praying, Jesse finally convinced Isa and Ianatos that Suph might not come down. Ianatos's men had kept watch over Suph's little hideaway and reported that the man had not moved but seemed to grow more agitated by the hour.

Isa believed Suph would come down soon, but Jesse was not too sure. When a man was led by his emotions, even he did not know what his next actions would be. Jesse could testify to that.

Now he crouched behind a rock, above Suph's position. Isa and Ianatos were positioned close by as were Ianatos's men. The plan had been for two of the Philistines to make as if they were passing by. However, when Suph began to torment Abigail, Jesse near gave up their positions. It was only the staying hand of Ianatos and the grace of God that had kept him rooted and his jaw clamped shut.

He could not believe his little Abigail had the tenacity to fight her attacker. Although he hated that she had drawn blood, for it was not an easy task to handle, he applauded her courage and strength. His heart roared to life when she spoke God's word aloud. He knew her heart belonged to God, and if she could forgive him for killing her mother he would court her; if not she would be beyond his reach.

"Who is this?" Isa pointed toward a small child tied at the hands.

Jesse squinted. It was not easy to tell in the dusk, especially since the child was hidden within the shadows of the mountain.

"It cannot be King Joash." Ianatos leaned forward for a better view.

Every fiber in Jesse's being froze. Anger, fear, dread... "Are you certain? I cannot tell from here."

"This child's hair does not curl like our king's does."

"It does not matter. It is obvious Abigail has angered Suph. He will use the child against her, to make her suffer and assure her cooperation." He looked from Isa to Ianatos. "We cannot allow him to harm the child."

Crouching low, Ianatos scrambled away from them toward the opening of the pass and then came back. "My men are close. They are making merry."

"Not merry enough if they have not drawn Suph's attention."

"What do you suggest, Jesse?" Isa asked. "It is not likely we can do anything from here."

Jesse glanced at Ianatos. The Philistine nodded, then lifted his hand high, signaling to his men across the way. Suph's soldier drew close; the boy trembled. Jesse was certain tears streamed down the child's cheeks. Ianatos stood and drew his bow, arrow poised. Suph wrapped his arm around the child and then teased the boy's hair. Jesse held his breath.

Suph released the boy, turned and said something to his soldier. Abigail screamed and clambered toward the boy on her hands and knees. Suph grabbed hold of her. She pounded him with her fists, kicked him in the shins. "No, no, no!" she cried.

The soldier drew his sword. Abigail gripped the edge of Suph's tunic, pleading with him for the boy's life. Jesse's heart ripped from his chest. The soldier flipped his sword around. The moment before he would have thrust it into the child, an arrow sped from Ianatos's bow and pierced the man's heart. A second later, the soldier released the child and fell to the ground as Ianatos bellowed out. Suph looked up. He grabbed hold of Abigail, using her as a shield. His knife was at her neck.

Jesse stood, arms crossed over his chest.

"It is about time you arrived."

"You are surrounded, Suph. I suggest you release the woman."

Suph spun one way then the other, spying each of the men standing above his camp.

"You cannot think to leave here alive," Jesse bellowed.

"No. What say you, Abigail?" Suph's words were said against Abigail's ears but Jesse heard them as Suph meant him to. "Do you think we can make it? If they shoot an arrow, they will not miss you, will they?"

Jesse blew air out through his nose. He narrowed his eyes. He was too far up to do anything. He hated feeling defenseless. Even though Suph was surrounded, he still had the upper hand because he had Abigail. "Release her and we will let you leave alive."

Jesse felt Isa's gaze on him. He heard Ianatos grumble. Jesse widened his stance.

"You will let me go with her, not without. She is my betrothed."

Abigail frantically shook her head.

"She may deny it all she likes but I have the contracts to prove it. Since she has no male relatives alive I appointed your uncle Elam as her guardian. Of course, he was only too happy to accommodate my wishes." He breathed against Abigail's ear. "After all, I am the only one suitable who is willing to marry her."

That was not true. Any man would be honored to have Abigail as his wife. "As King Joash's guardian, Jehoiada is the only one who can draw up the marriage contracts."

"That imposter?" Suph laughed. "What do you have to say, Jesse the Levite? If you care for her, you will let her go. You will allow her to reign as Queen of Judah with me by her side, not that imposter you support."

"King Joash is not an imposter, Suph. If you opened your eyes you would see he looks like his father. His grandfather."

Jesse prayed Suph's words had not seeped doubt into Abigail's thoughts.

Suph pressed the blade tighter against Abigail's throat. "If you wish to see Abigail live, you will come down. I believe there are things we need to discuss." He turned his mouth toward Abigail's ear. "Is that not right?"

Jesse glared.

"You cannot think to do as he requests, Jesse," Isa pleaded with him.

Without taking his eyes from Abigail, Jesse responded, "She deserves the truth. The entire truth. Besides, if I am down there I can better rescue her."

"You risk your life, Jesse. Mother would not be happy with me if I did not bring you home."

Jesse wrinkled his nose to fight the tears pricking the back of his eyes. He never once took his eyes from Abigail. "Mother would understand and would expect nothing less from me."

"You love her?"

Jesse snapped his gaze to his brother. Did he love her? It was not a question he could fully answer, for he did not know. "All I know is I vowed to protect her and I would not see her harmed by Suph. Life with him will not be easy for her and she deserves happiness. Judah deserves to know her kindness."

"I do not like it. Judah deserves your service as well."

Jesse glanced back toward Abigail. So beautiful and full of life. "Judah has known me, Isa. I have done what God has willed me to do. If He chooses to continue my life, He will do so. Right now I must appease Suph."

Abigail cried out in pain. Jesse did not need to see the trail of blood sliding down her neck to know Suph had nicked her.

"What will it be?" Suph hollered.

"I will come."

"Alone."

"Of course."

Jesse turned to scale down the rocky cliff. Ianatos halted him. "Jesse, Suph has not seen my men in the pass. By my count he only has ten or so. There may be another where the boy was kept."

Jesse shook his head. "Do what you can to save Abigail and get her to Jehoiada. He will take care of her as the princess she is. She is a descendant of King David."

Ianatos stared at him, pressed his lips together and then dropped his hand. "As you wish, my friend."

Jesse climbed down the mountain. Rocks slid beneath his feet and tumbled below but he paid them no heed. He wanted only to be near Abigail. To stand near her and smell the hint of jasmine wafting from the warmth of her skin. To look into her green eyes and know she was truly well. To experience the sense of home she created in him.

Even if they were to leave the pass alive, they could never marry. Wandering in the desert, he could believe they could marry, but the truth was even if she forgave him for killing her mother he was a warrior. She was a royal princess, worthy of a king's hand. Worthy of love. If he were more than a simple temple guard, if he were a king, like Solomon, he'd move these mountains to court her, to love her.

The beat of his heart pounded against his chest. Did he love her? If he did, it did not matter. He could not love her. Would not love her because it would only cause them both unneeded pain.

He jumped down the last bit and stood tall. He spied the area where he had spent the past few days in prayer. Odd how he did not feel a comforting peace that all would be well. He dropped to his knees and bowed his head. "Yahweh, lend Your ear to me. I do not know what it is I ask or even how to ask it. All I know is my heart is filled with sorrow. If I see Abigail lives, then surely I will die at the hands of our enemy. If I live, she dies and that is a burden I cannot fathom to bear." A tear slid from his eye and into his beard. "If I were to choose, God Almighty, I choose her life over mine. May her heart rise like that of the sun and spread her joyous warmth over Your people."

Chapter Nineteen

Her heart filled with that growing familiar emotion as Jesse appeared around the pass, and then it hit the ground. He came to save her. Surely he had to know there was little hope of meeting a good end. Jesse was immediately surrounded by several of Suph's men. His arms were jerked behind his back and then he was dragged forward.

Abigail could not take her eyes from him. She loved this man she had come to know during their journey. His gentle caring of her even when she did not believe in the one true God, even when he did not know if she would cause his family harm—he had taken her in and treated her as he had anyway. And how did she repay him, by bringing harm to him and his people?

"You should not have come, Jesse." She tried to convey her apologies for all the trouble she had caused his people.

Suph sneered.

"I could not stay away, Abigail."

"He will kill you." Tears coursed down her cheeks.

"With great pleasure." Suph kept her shielded in front of him. His gaze searched the crags above. "Where are your Philistines?"

Jesse glanced upward, scanning the same high places. He shrugged. "How should I know?"

"You command them, do you not?"

Jesse furrowed his brow. "No. They are Carite men bound by a vow to preserve King David's ancestry. You should know more than most that they will do what they must to meet that end, Suph." Jesse narrowed his eyes. "Even if you were to ransom me for the king, it would make no difference. If you threaten Abigail's life, it would make no difference. The Carites' ultimate goal is to see Joash remain where he is, on the throne, King of Judah."

"And what is your goal, Levite?"

Jesse's eyes flickered to hers. She sucked in a breath at the emotion swirling in his dark eyes. Her knees wobbled. The sorrow in his gaze sliced through her.

"To see Abigail is returned to her home in Jerusalem where she belongs."

"If she were to marry me, I would see she returns to her home."

Suph made a gesture that Abigail could not see. One of his men pulled his sword from his sheath, and just like the other soldier had done before he had died from an arrow, this one prepared to slice Jesse's neck. "What will it be, Abigail? Will you marry me or trust the man who killed your mother?"

The words that spewed from Suph's mouth were of no consequence, not until she witnessed the truth in Jesse's downcast gaze and slumped shoulders. Facing the man who had murdered her mother should have left her cold and angry. However, she had no emotion. No sorrow. No hatred. Not like she had experienced when Suph dropped Bilhah's limp body at her feet. There was nothing toward Jesse other than hurt that he had not confided in her. Could she blame him, though, for not telling her? It could not be an easy burden for him to bear, even for a man as brawny as he. He promised the truth and yet he had withheld so much from her. Now, she understood why.

"Abigail…" The pleading in his voice cut deep, but if she showed any concern toward him, Suph would use it against her. Against Jesse. And he'd already suffered much at the captain's hands.

Tears pricked the back of her eyes and bubbled to the surface. She shook her head against Suph's shoulder, disbelieving the impossible choice thrust upon her. Suph relaxed his hold and turned her to face him. "You cannot think to trust him, Abigail. Not after he took your mother from you."

Closing her eyes, she drew in a breath of air as the tears gave way and trailed down her cheeks. Her mother had never belonged to her to be taken. She hardly knew her beyond the brief visits where she made clear her dislike of her only daughter. Abigail blinked her eyes open, and if she did not know Suph better she would say he actually looked pained at her sorrow. If only he truly understood her loss.

"I need time to consider your offer."

Reaching out, he gripped her upper arms. The hilt of his dagger dug into her flesh. She bit down on the inside of her cheek to keep from crying out. "We do not have time, Abigail."

She glanced over her shoulder at Jesse, and then back to Suph. "As long as you hold him, there is no danger to us. Give me this night. That is all I ask. Come the morrow I will have an answer for you."

"You have no choice in the matter, Abigail. The contracts are in order." He brushed his finger down the side of her jaw, eliciting a wave of sickness, and she knew at that moment she could never willingly become the captain's bride. Not when Jesse's touch made her feel alive instead of wish for death.

She bit down on the corner of her mouth. "There is always a choice, Suph." Jesse had taught her that bit of wisdom.

His mouth curled into a sneer. He looked as if he was about to argue, or something worse if the clenching of his fists were any indication. "I prefer a willing bride and will give you this night."

"My thanks, Suph." She buried her hands into the folds of her borrowed tunic. The one that still smelled of sandalwood. Still smelled of Jesse.

"Do not thank me, Abigail." His tone brought her eyes to his hard, cold ones. A shiver raced from her nape to her toes. "Either way, you will be mine, as will Judah."

The knot lodged in her throat thickened. With Suph's determination to rule Judah, she did not see a way out of her and Jesse's predicament. She could not see how she would make it to Jerusalem with her life's blood intact. If she did not agree to marry Suph and go along with his plan, she had no doubt he would kill her. If she did and became a threat to King Joash, then she had no doubt Jesse or his family would end her—in that he had not lied.

~

Jesse's teeth ground together as Suph ordered her hands and feet bound with heavy rope. The guard in charge of the duty was none too nice and even tied a lead from her hands around his waist. Her poor treatment caused his blood to boil. Even if she would not forgive him for her mother's death he could not stand by while a Princess of Judah was treated no better than a wild dog. However, what could he do? Somehow he needed to rescue her.

He scanned the high places. One sign from him and this little camp Suph had erected would be crawling with Philistines. However, Jesse did not know for certain how many men Suph commanded. The Philistines and his brothers would, no doubt, be victorious, but Jesse did not wish to take achance with Abigail's life. He much preferred that the battle to come was out in the open where he could better assess his opponent.

The captain slithered closer until his nose was but a few inches from Jesse's. "If you attempt anything, Levite, she will die."

Jesse kept the retort burning on his tongue to himself. It would do no good to goad the captain.

Suph rested his chin against his curled fingers. One eyebrow rose into his hairline. "Have you no words? What kind of man uses a weakling to escape his captors?"

Hands tightened around Jesse's upper arms as a low growl emitted from his chest. "What kind of man forces an innocent into marriage to gain a kingdom not rightfully his?"

The captain bellowed. "We are no different, you and I."

"We are far from the same."

"No," Suph said, shaking his head. "We both take what we want by any means possible."

"That is where you are wrong, Suph. I have not killed harmless people for ill-gotten means."

The smile disappeared from the captain's face. His eyes darkened and Jesse knew he looked into the eyes of evil. "Have you not, Levite? As I recall you confessed to killing the Queen of Judah. You ousted a harmless woman to serve your own purposes." He flung his hand into the air as if to toss Jesse away. "It is useless to argue the matter."

It was useless. Jesse would not argue Queen Athaliah's harmlessness. She was guilty for many innocent deaths, if only for the pleasure of frightening her people into submission.

"In that we agree, for I will always fight for the greater good of Judah and that means restoring God back to our land."

Grabbing the neck of Jesse's tunic, Suph pressed his face close. "Your God will see you dead."

"Then I will die a man of honor."

Suph shoved him away; only the hands holding his arms kept him from stumbling back. "If Abigail knows what is good for her, she will not choose to side with a dead man." Suph took a few more steps back and looked at Jesse's captors. "Bind him, keep him from Abigail. If he escapes, you will die."

Jesse raised his hand to scrub his jaw but found his arms jerked behind his back and bound. What had he been thinking when he decided to enter the enemy's camp? An image of Suph's blade pressed against Abigail's neck and the red rivulet running down her flesh had taken all thought from his mind. But to enter unarmed? And somehow he had convinced his brother and Ianatos his plan had been brilliant.

The guard led him away from the camp and up a path before halting outside a small cave. "Beware, the captain will kill your woman if you try to escape."

"As well as you," Jesse replied.

"As well as me." The man shifted his weight. "And my wife and child."

Jesse drew in a breath of air. Kindness often begat loyalty. "You've no need to worry, my friend. I do not wish any more blood to spill."

"My thanks." The man turned to go.

"What do they call you?"

"Reuel."

"Reuel. Friend of God." Jesse smiled. "It is fitting. Now, let me warn you, when the Philistines ambush Suph's camp, lay your weapons down. They will not harm you, and then you can return to your wife and child."

The guard did not say a word. He just turned and walked away, leaving Jesse to make his way in the small cave. The sound of heavy breathing met his ears and Jesse waited for his eyes to adjust to the darkness. He detected the outline of a bulky body slumped against the rocky wall. If it hadn't been for the jerky rise and fall of the mass, Jesse would have thought it a part of the cave.

"Shalom," Jesse called.

A shadowed head lifted and bobbed before rising again. The clank of chains echoed as the man swiped at his eyes. "Oo's thar?"

"Jesse, the Levite."

"Je—sse."

"Jonathan?"

The man coughed. It sounded as if he were drowning in a pool of water. "Aye."

Stepping farther into the cave, Jesse knelt beside him. "Where is your brother?"

Jonathan's chin dropped back to his chest; the harsh breathing resumed. Jesse sat beside him and crossed his legs. His arms, stiff from being bound behind his back, began to ache and grow numb. If he found a jagged edge in the wall he could try and cut through the ropes. But what of Reuel and the twins? What of Abigail?

He settled against the wall. If he could, he would whisk Abigail away from this place, from the choices that lay before her. Let her live in peace, away from Suph's evil. From his. If only Abigail would forgive him! But he had no right to ask it. He would bide his time, see if he could rescue Nathan. See if he could protect Abigail, to discover what her choice would be. If she chose to marry Suph, Jesse would walk away and leave her to her fate. The temple guard would catch up with the captain before he entered Jerusalem, if he remained determined to usurp Joash. However, if Abigail chose to marry Suph, she'd no doubt meet her death. If not by the temple guard, then by Suph's own hand.

He clenched his jaw. The thought of Abigail lifeless left him chilled. If she showed any hint over the next few hours that she would trust Jesse, even after all the pain he'd caused her, he'd move mountains to see her released from Suph's wickedness.

Chapter Twenty

The blanket did little to serve as a barrier between her and the hard ground. However, she could not blame her sleepless night on the lack of comfort. The air had turned colder, causing her to shiver throughout the long hours as she lay awake thinking.

Her tears had dried long before the murky darkness gave way to the soft pink hues. Eyes focused on the twinkling lights most of the night, she recalled Jesse's belief in a Creator. Even now, in her anguish and in the face of Jesse's betrayal, she could not deny that the Almighty God existed. She could not deny Jesse forgiveness, either.

In the brief moments after Suph revealed Jesse's misdeeds, she had seen the ache in his eyes. She held no misconceptions that Jesse felt remorse over killing her mother, only regret that he'd caused Abigail pain. If only she could tell him otherwise. Aye, she had mourned the loss of her mother, but Athaliah had never been a mother in truth. Not as Shema and Dara had.

She pressed the palms of her bound hands to her eyes and choked back the sob threatening to spill forth. The time for tears was over. Somehow she needed to find the fortitude to face Suph and convince him of her plan, all the while pretending her heart did not belong to Jesse. Pretending she harbored ill will toward him.

Footsteps crunched against loose rocks. Abigail dropped her hands to her stomach as Suph approached. He stared down at her, hands on hips. His lip curled and nostrils flared. How had she ever thought him handsome?

"It is time, Abigail." He reached down and gripped her arms, lifting her to her feet. "Have you made your choice?"

He cut the ropes binding her and tugged her toward the center of camp. She stumbled at the sight of Jesse's proud bearing. His muscular chest seemed broader with his arms extended behind his back. She was glad his wounds were mending. Her gaze flicked to his and she near lost her resolve. The blank, indifferent stare cut her to the core. It was as if he did not see her, as if they had never been friends. As if he had not treated her with affection. As if he had never kissed her.

Had it all been a lie? Had he only pretended affection to meet his end? Her eyes stung. Her throat burned. If only she could tell him what was in her heart, but it did not matter. If all went according to her plan, Jesse would return to his family, Joash's throne would be secure and she would most likely meet the same end as her mother. And only Almighty God would know the truth of her heart, the truth of her deception.

She choked down the knot forming in her throat and stiffened her spine. The years of parading in her room, pretending she was the daughter her mother was proud of, one who forced nations to war over her beauty, stole into her being. She pretended indifference, pretended she was a palace cat stalking its prey.

Suph halted her a few feet in front of Jesse. Her heart thumped against her chest as it welled with love for Jesse. Thorns pricked her nape as Suph drew closer. She dropped her gaze to Jesse's feet and allowed a lazy sneer to form on her lips as she followed the lines of his wrinkled tunic to his beard, and then to his dark eyes, the color of Lebanon cedar.

"Your night was restful, I hope, Abigail," Suph said.

Flicking her gaze to Suph, she smiled. "Well enough."

"What have you decided? Will you remain loyal to this Levite, or willingly become my bride?"

She glanced at Jesse and curled her lip, and then gazed into Suph's evil eyes as she fought the wave of sickness roiling in her stomach. "Neither."

Narrowing his eyes, Suph gripped the hilt of his sword.

"Patience, Suph. I have thought about this all night." Forcing a calm she did not feel, she rested her palm against the captain's bloodstained tunic. Swallowing back the bile, she lowered her voice an octave, something she'd seen

Bilhah do whenever she wanted something from the palace guards. "I have spent time with his family and the Philistines. We have no chance of entering Jerusalem alive."

His fingers tightened around her wrist, nearly crushing her bones.

"If you will but listen to me, Suph," she whispered for his ears only. "The Levite was to take me to meet Joash. It's our only way."

The corner of his right eyebrow twitched as he narrowed his eye. His fingers bruised her upper arm and he dragged her away from Jesse. "You ran from me, Abigail. You have a soft heart, even pleaded for the lives of his people."

"Yes, I did this. I was a fool." She pulled back and tossed a glance over her shoulder at Jesse. Folding her hands in front of her, she raised her chin and forced calm into her limbs. "I have had much to consider. What kind of God would send my mother's murderer to rescue me? I admit I am naive, having rarely left my chambers. The Levite preyed on my innocence and deceived me into believing you wished me only harm, which has left me angry. Vengeance boils in my blood. I now realize how much my mother's daughter I am. I want to rule Judah for her. For my mother. I will go with him. To Jerusalem. I will kill Jehoiada and then I will kill this imposter just as my mother had all of my cousins."

"And what, my dear, will you kill them with?"

"If only you return my knife…"

His eyes narrowed to mere slits, cutting off her words. She drew in a breath to fortify her nerves and waited as Suph considered her for a moment. "I do not trust you, Abigail. Even so, I see no better plan." He slipped her knife into her hands as he motioned to one of his soldiers. With his chin resting against his knuckles he began pacing. She glanced toward Jesse, his jaw as forbidding as the crags surrounding them.

Her skin crawled with shame at her deception. However, it was the only way she saw to save Jesse. The sound of chains broke the silence and Suph's arm rested over her shoulder. Out of the corner of her eye she saw Jesse's muscles expand, becoming the dangerous warrior everyone claimed him to be. A chill of dread snaked down her spine.

"You will inform Nathan of your decision. I know his loyalty lies with you. He will see you protected and your plans followed."

Abigail drew in a shaky breath, relieved that her plan might work.

"If you deceive me, Abigail, Jonathan will suffer far worse than the Levite."

A chill raced through her life's blood as Suph turned her and the surrounding soldiers parted, revealing the source of the chains. Revealing a shell of the man she had called friend. It took all her self-control to keep up her pretense. She clamped down on her lip to keep from crying out in protest at the sight of her friend.

"I know how much you care for him. I see it in your eyes, feel it in the way you shake, even now. And do not think it went beyond my notice all the times those two boys snuck into the palace to grant you treats." He drew even closer, his wine-soaked breath assaulting her senses. "When news of the child's death reaches my ear, I will release him unharmed."

Unharmed? Jonathan was near death as it was. His head hung to the side. His knees brushed the ground as he was unable to stand.

"My thanks, Suph." She blinked back a wayward tear as she acknowledged the little bit of mercy he granted her.

"You must know, Abigail, if I do not hear in seven days' time of the king's death, his torment will begin."

The knot forming in her throat grew, suffocating her. She sucked in air and forced the knot back to her stomach. "There will be no need."

She turned toward Jesse. The pain evident in the brown depths of his eyes was worse than when she'd treated his wounds. She had no way to reassure him of her motives or inform him of her plan, which was now certain to fail. Would he trust her?

A scowl stressed the corners of his eyes as she moved closer, telling her what she needed to know. If only the truth did not cause so much pain. She had hoped he'd come to know her, to know her heart.

~

Jesse did not know what sort of game she and the captain played, but he wanted no part of it, especially since Jonathan seemed to be yet another battered pawn. However, it seemed he had no choice in the matter. As long as Suph remained alive he posed a threat to King Joash and the good people of Judah.

As Abigail moved closer her eyes pleaded with him, but the thorns pricking his nape gave him caution. He wanted to trust her, but he dared not. Not after what he'd done to her mother. Not after witnessing the whispered conversation between her and the captain. A conversation that had left the captain looking as if he'd been handed the crown.

She halted mere inches from him. The scent of jasmine caused his chest to pound. Her nearness left him weak in the knees. Left him feeling as if he could move mountains to make her smile. To draw his hand through her chestnut tresses. To feel the softness of her cheek beneath his fingertips, the curve of her lips against his.

"I will go with you."

Her words were as if a boulder had slammed against his stomach. He pressed his lips together to keep his thoughts from spilling off his tongue. Did she think Suph would allow them to just walk away? The muscles in his chest expanded as he drew in air and chose his words with care. "For what purpose?"

"The captain has seen to reason. I am no good to him. Not when he's surrounded by your people and the Philistines." She worried her hands together and bit down on her lip, evidence she was not as confident as she pretended. Suph would not give up his pawn so easily, of this he was certain. What purpose was there in revealing Jonathan's condition to her? "Suph will never enter the city gates alive. He now knows this. He is freeing me of the contracts. Allowing me to do as I please."

Jesse glanced over her shoulder. The captain's eyes remained hard and unmoving. Jonathan collapsed to the ground unconscious. Anger thundered like a thousand horses racing to war in Jesse's blood.

"He is granting you your freedom, Levite."

It took all of his self-control to keep from flinching at her cutting word. The lack of his name could only mean she had not forgiven him for her mother's death. Just as well. He could never court her, not even if he was inclined to do so, especially as callous as she now seemed to be. How could she ignore Jonathan, the man she had called friend, as he fought for his life?

"You would travel with your mother's murderer?" He kept his tone hard, commanding. Accusing. He gave her credit for not flinching, but she needed to know he did not trust her. Not now. However, that did not mean the loss of color in her cheeks did not make him feel regret and a great deal of guilt. His wish was never to cause her further pain.

Composing herself like the princess she was, he watched her gather her fortitude. A bit of pride welled in his chest before he tamped it down.

She stared him straight in the eye. "You promised me the truth."

"Aye, and the truth you shall have when we reach Jerusalem. What of Jonathan? What of your captain? He will not just allow me to leave."

Abigail twisted around and glanced at Suph. "Unbind him."

The captain laughed. "I think not, Abigail. Your Levite is correct. I cannot allow you two to walk away. Not yet."

She clenched her fingers at her side. "But I thought—"

"Yes. I will release you both." His eyes scanned the high places. "But not until I am certain his men will not pounce upon me once I do." The captain crossed his arms over his chest. "For now, we will travel together. It is my understanding, Levite, that you and this traitor have become friends." He nodded toward Jonathan.

"I would not call us friends." Jesse did not wish to give this man any more power over him than he already had.

"Whatever it is you call it, I am certain you would not wish to see him harmed further. As I informed our dear Abigail, if your men descend upon us after your release, he will be the first to die."

Tears threatened to spill from Abigail's childlike green eyes and somehow he knew, no matter what she had planned with the captain, it was not meant to cause anyone harm, least of all the King of Judah, especially given her reaction to the child the night before. But he had to play along, even if it caused her more discomfort. "Why does this man's life matter to me?"

Suph yanked on Abigail's hair, eliciting a cry of distress from her. Jesse leaped forward, but was yanked back by his bound arms before he fell to the ground. "It matters to you, Levite, because it matters to her. I did not become captain without observing things. Do not think it has gone beyond my notice how you watch her. How she watches you. Perhaps the two of you have already become man and wife."

Abigail sucked in a sharp breath as Jesse growled, "As a man of honor, I would not take her to wife without the permission of her closest kin."

Suph released her and knelt down in front of Jesse. "A man of honor, you say. What sort of man kills the Queen of Judah? One of honor? I think not. Perhaps, one bent on revenge."

Jesse climbed to his feet and stared down at the captain. "I have no need for revenge. The queen was killed out of duty. If I had not done it, someone else would have. Perhaps, even you, Suph."

Abigail's gaze darted between them. Suph smiled as he rose. "You know more than any man should."

"Do I?" Jesse kept his eyes on Suph's. It would not do him or Abigail any good if he revealed all he knew about Suph. Like how Athaliah's faithful captain had grown weary of waiting for her to make good on her promise to marry him. "Then again, mayhap I know nothing and only speculate. There were many attempts on the queen's life before the temple guard stormed the palace. I just happened to be successful."

He disliked the way Abigail cringed and seemed to pull away. How she seemed to sidle closer to the captain.

"None of that matters. What is done is done." Suph flicked his hand in the air. The sound of chains being dragged along the rocks told Jesse Jonathan was being moved. "We will leave within the hour. You will signal your men to stand down. If they attack, Jonathan dies. Abigail dies, and then you die."

"You do realize, Captain, our lives are of no consequence. Not in comparison to that of King Joash."

Suph chuckled. "That is where I believe you are wrong. You see, your life means something to your brothers. Abigail's life means something to you and Jonathan's means something to her. Your men will allow us to leave this area. Once we are in the open, I will cut you free and you can take this—" Suph flung his hand toward Abigail "—this pitiful excuse for a woman with you."

The inward wince at Suph's insult caused Jesse's fingers to twitch. He might not understand what was going on, but Abigail was anything but pitiful, nothing like her mother had been. "What of Jonathan?"

"I will allow Nathan to attend you. Jonathan will stay with me until I am certain your men will not attack." Suph slid his gaze toward Abigail. She dropped her chin to her chest and worried her hands in her tunic. What were these two hiding?

"And then?"

"I guess we will see, won't we, Abigail?"

A tear slid down Abigail's dusty cheek. Jesse's heart lurched and his arms ached with the need to pull her close and comfort her. Suph had been correct about one thing. Her life did matter to him. More than it should. If it didn't, he would have no problem signaling to Ianatos and Isa to rain arrows down upon Suph and his men. But it did matter. His emotions had been taken over by the curse of love. Every fiber of his being froze. Did he love her? He tilted his head and considered the woman being led away from him. She was no doubt beautiful and compassionate and loyal to those she cared about, but was that enough for love? Even now, knowing she loved God? He just did not know. To love her would cost him a future, for he could never become her husband. Not when he was responsible for her mother's death. Not when she deserved to marry a king. And he would never marry another if his heart belonged to someone else. To her.

Chapter Twenty-One

"He is watching."

Abigail tore a piece from her cake of bread and tossed it to a hovering bird. "Of course he is." She tucked a small bite into her mouth and chewed, ignoring the stale taste. "After my defiance, do you expect Suph to trust me? He may think me a child, easily swayed, but he will not be caught unaware by me again."

Nathan scrubbed his hand over his beard. "I do not speak of the captain."

On its own accord, her chin rose. Her heart hitched as she focused on Jesse. His eyes remained blank, hard. Dropping her gaze, she toyed with the flat bread. "Should I have Suph bind his eyes?"

And hers. Everywhere she turned, Jesse was there. She had tried to avoid him ever since they'd left the pass, but with so few traveling amongst them, it had been impossible. When she walked behind him, she often found herself staring at the curls gracing his shoulders. When she walked in front of him, she'd felt the touch of his gaze. And the scent of sandalwood clinging to the tunic she wore was a constant reminder of the man who possessed her heart.

Her friend rolled his neck before crossing his arms over his chest. "What game is it you play, Abigail?"

If she was to convince Suph she was agreeable to his plan, she needed to convince Nathan, which meant she could not tell him her true intentions. "It is not a game, my friend. If you have not noticed, I am soon to be married."

Nathan took a sip from a flask and then rested his arms against his knees. "Why, Abigail? Suph has no affection for you. He only wishes to use you to gain something that is not rightfully his."

Her fingers gripped the bread tight until it crumbled. "You surprise me, Nathan. I did not think you liked the Levite."

"It is the captain I do not like. There are things—"

"And there are things about the Levite you do not know. He is no different than Suph when it comes to using me to gain his will."

"The captain is cruel."

"And the Levite murdered my mother. Whose sins are greater?" Her heart pounded at her own words. She did not harbor resentment against Jesse, but she could not let Jonathan know, lest he discern the truth of her plan to rescue Jesse and King Joash from Suph's wickedness. If Nathan discovered her ruse, Suph would sense it because her friend had never been able to tell falsehoods, and then they'd all lose their lives.

Nathan drew in a harsh breath. "Is this a lie Suph told you? He will say anything to gain your trust."

"Suph did not lie."

"Are you certain?"

"Aye, Nathan. The Levite confessed his deed." She recalled the look in Jesse's eyes, the way he had closed in on himself. She willed her tears to remain hidden. He had vowed to protect the rightful King of Judah. She knew Jesse's heart, knew his kindness. If her mother would have turned from her wicked ways, Jesse would have spared her. Abigail had no doubt.

"It is sorry I am. I know you love him."

She shook her head against the truth burning her ears, tearing at her heart. "I cared for his wounds, Nathan. I brought healing to the man who killed my mother. I helped him escape."

And she'd do it all over again, but if she was to gain Nathan's help in getting Jesse to safety, she needed him to believe in her revenge. "A marriage to Suph is a just punishment, is it not?"

"You have never been one to watch a being suffer and you should not be punished for offering help to a wounded man, Abigail. No matter what Jesse has done, I think he is a good man."

As did she. She rubbed the toe of her sandal against a pebble. "Suph holds your brother. If we do not convince Jesse to take us to Jehoiada and the king, he will torture him." She did not need to tell Nathan what that meant. He'd seen Jesse's wounds and he was much more capable of handling such torment than Jonathan.

"What is your plan, Abigail?"

"Jesse needs to believe Suph is giving us our freedom so he will take me to Jerusalem as promised." She drew in a shaky breath and prayed Nathan would believe what she had to say next. "Then we do away with the king."

She felt Nathan's gaze on her. "You think to kill the king, to have me do it? What of my brother? No matter what you do, Suph will still kill him."

This she feared, but she could do little else to save him. However, she would try. If she failed, at least she would remove herself from Suph's talons so she could no longer be used against Jesse to threaten the good of Judah and King Joash.

"You must know Jesse is not a stupid man. He will wonder why Jonathan is not with us."

Tilting her head, she looked at Nathan and laid her hand on his forearm. "Your brother was not well when I last saw him. Suph left him in the mountains. Jesse will think him dead."

"Then why carry out Suph's will? Once we are free—"

Her fingers dug into his muscles, willing him to understand. "I have to hope Suph will keep his word to me. I have to hope he will not bring further harm to Jonathan. You two are all I have left."

And Jesse, even if she was about to make him believe she was about to betray him. She was not proud of the deception but it seemed necessary if she was to save his life.

"What of Bilhah and Micah? My mother?"

She shook her head. "Shema was your mother, was she not?"

His jaw slackened. "Yes."

"My father had her killed because of my disobedience. Suph left Bilhah for dead because of my disobedience. I will not allow Jonathan to be further harmed because of the same."

"You were but a child, Abigail."

"And now?"

"You did what was right."

She wasn't too certain. If she'd done what was right, then why had God allowed those she cared for to perish? Why did Jesse, even now, seem to be at the mercy of their enemy?

"If you wish to stand by my side, I welcome you. However, if you have no stomach for what we are about to do, then I beg you to stay."

Nathan's gaze flicked toward Jesse and then to her. "I have no stomach for what you ask of me, but I will not allow you to do this alone."

"My thanks, Nathan."

"The captain will likely not allow us to go alone."

Abigail glanced across the camp at Jesse, the memory of his kiss warming a place in her heart. "He has no other option if we are to convince Jesse of our freedom." She looked at Nathan. "That is why Suph must believe you are loyal to me without any question and will do as I ask."

A wide grin split his mustache and beard. "This I can do, but I will pray to Jesse's God and all will be well. You will see."

She prayed her friend was right.

~

He had long lost the feeling in his arms, no longer felt the burn of the ropes cutting into his wrists. How much longer would they travel before Suph cut him loose? The sun, no longer above, would not light their path much longer, which meant another night camping with his enemies.

Fortunately, he'd seen signs from Ianatos and, if Jesse understood correctly, the Philistines had rescued Jonathan. Jesse rolled his shoulders and he released a tense breath. At least that was one less person to concern himself over. Now if only he could ascertain what it was Abigail had gotten herself into and then get her out of it.

She'd done her best to avoid him. She'd avoided looking at him but for that once when she'd been seated next to Jonathan. That one small glance had gripped him by his innards and twisted him all around. There had been no hate, no dislike of him. If anything, it had been what he'd seen in

Mira's eyes when she'd looked upon his brother Ari with longing. With love.

With love? He stumbled over his feet and near fell to his knees. Reuel, his assigned guard, righted him. "My apologies."

Reuel eyed him before giving Jesse a clipped nod in response. However, it was not the guard's increasing amiability that left Jesse stupefied. It was the idea that Abigail might have some sort of affection for him. Even love him. If that was possible, if she loved him, would he ever be able to let her go? Would he have a choice?

Jesse tilted his head and considered his guard. "Why is it you have remained loyal to your captain?"

The guard eyed him once again, and then glanced around at those who traveled with them. "I am a warrior. It is what I do." Reuel shrugged. "I have stood outside the princess's door for the last few years. I watched her mother enter and exit on occasion. When her mother requested her presence, I was her escort. I know she is the princess. I know she is the former king's sister."

"I do not contest who she is."

Reuel shrugged again. "No. You do not, but you would harm her if she posed a threat to this child you claim is the rightful heir. I would protect Abigail."

"Yet you would see her married to your captain after you've witnessed his cruelty?"

"It is the lot of a woman, no? To do as she is told."

Jesse bit back the words that crept onto his tongue. "Did you know her brother? King Ahaziah?"

The man's jaw hardened to stone. His pulse ticked at the side of his jaw. "I was with him when Jehu's men killed him. There was nothing I could have done to save him."

Jesse noticed the scars marring his body. How had he survived Jehu's ambush? "We trained together for a time."

Reuel flicked his gaze to Jesse. "I as well. He was like his father. And his mother."

Jesse understood the unspoken words. Ahaziah had worshipped the false gods. He also had a cruel streak. "The child, Joash. He has the look of his father."

They walked in silence for long seconds before the guard spoke. "The princess, she is not like them. I would not see her harmed. Her goodness is a rarity and I would see it protected. I would give my life to do so."

"As would I, my friend."

Suph raised his hand from his perch on his horse. "We will stop and rest."

Jesse scanned each direction, looking for any sign of Ianatos and Isa, as Reuel motioned him to sit. "There is water nearby. I will refill our earthenware jar while we wait for the captain's orders. Take care with those whom you speak. Loyalties are divided. Many see our captain as a way to advance their status, and to keep their families alive."

Jesse nodded, knowing the man risked his life and that of his wife and child if anyone overheard such a warning. "Before you go, what does Suph intend to do with the man from the cave?"

Reuel shrugged. "My orders were to leave him."

Jesse watched as he walked away. The weight of his burden was evident in the way his shoulders sagged.

"Here." Nathan knelt before him, holding a piece of bread in his hand. "I noticed you did not break your fast when we stopped earlier."

The corners of Jesse's mouth curved. "I was not given the option, my friend."

"'Tis glad I am you still consider me as such." He pushed a piece of the cake into Jesse's mouth and then helped him drink water from a jug.

Jesse swallowed and then glanced around, hoping for a glimpse of Abigail.

"Your guard has taken her to see to her needs. She would not like it if she saw me speaking to you."

Jesse's gaze settled on Suph.

"The captain would think something amiss if I did not pretend to be your friend."

Sharp talons gripped his insides. "Pretend?"

Nathan sat beside him and draped his arms over his knees. "I do not know what our Abigail has gotten herself into."

Twisting his lips, Jesse waited for him to continue.

"She has tried to convince me she is going to marry Suph."

The pulse in Jesse's temple picked up its cadence. He clenched his jaw, grinding his teeth together.

Nathan's gaze pierced his. "Before I tell you more, I must know, do you trust Abigail's heart?"

"I have stared evil in the face. Abigail is not capable of such things."

His friend nodded. "I believe she is trying to save you and Jonathan. Somehow she has convinced Suph to allow her to accompany you to Jerusalem."

"This I know, although I do not understand it."

"He has threatened to torment my brother if she does not carry out his wishes while she is there."

Jesse rocked back until his bound fists touched the ground. He ached for Abigail. "Jonathan was in a bad way. He would not survive any more torture Suph would dole out. Abigail knows this for she has seen him with her own eyes. However, I have it on good authority your brother has been left in a cave to die on his own."

Closing his eyes, Nathan nodded. "I told her as much, but she had hoped…she did not wish to be responsible for another's death. She believes the death of Shema, my real mother, is her doing. I told her she was just but a child. Then Bilhah."

Jesse shook his head. His arms ached with the need to hold Abigail close to his heart and comfort her. "Bilhah was alive with Dara tending her wounds when I left camp. I have no doubt my brother and Ianatos have scoured the area where Suph held us. I am certain Jonathan has been found."

"That is a relief." Nathan glanced toward the direction Reuel and Abigail had gone. "We do not have much time. No matter what Abigail might say against you, she does not believe it. Her words are a ruse for the captain." Nathan dropped his palm to Jesse's shoulder. "You made a vow to protect Abigail. I also know you have vowed to protect our young king."

"Aye. I have vowed to do both before God."

"What if I told you Suph believes she intends to kill King Joash when she attends him?"

He narrowed his eyes as bile rose from his stomach but he choked it down knowing she was incapable of such a thing. He recalled the way she sought to protect the child

Suph had used only the day before. Nothing had changed her compassion for the weak and the broken. Why, she had faced a griffon to protect a cub. She would have done the same even if the bird had held a rodent in its talons. She would not see Joash harmed. And even if she hated Jesse and could never forgive him for killing her mother, she would not see him harmed, either. It was not in her character.

Shrugging, he tried to raise his hands. "If I were not bound I would whisk her away from this place."

He gazed across the horizon. Although the land rose and dipped, there were very few places to hide.

"It seems our odds are good. The captain's men have dwindled and are succumbing to exhaustion. They have been coddled by palace life. Even if they were hale, you and I could take them."

Jesse caught Suph's stare of hatred and smiled. He should not goad the man, but the need to keep up their pretense prodded him. Let the man's thoughts run amok. Perhaps he would become more unstable and lose the loyalty of all his men. Then again, if he pushed Suph too far, Abigail could become a target for his anger. "I would rather not have Abigail close by. I would not risk her safety."

"Then what shall we do?"

He was not certain, but he felt God leading him to wait, to bide his time and not rush into action. Knowing he had allies made it easier. "We wait."

Nathan's eyes widened as if surprised. "Forgive me, but you are not one known for patience."

Jesse laughed. "You sound like my brothers. It is time I learned, is it not?"

Nathan grinned.

"Keep close to Abigail. Protect her above all else. And pray God's favor falls upon us."

Prickly thorns raced down Jesse's arm when Nathan clamped his hand on Jesse's shoulder. The inability to move his arms was causing his arms to sleep. Suph's glare at the two of them did not go unnoticed by Jesse. He only prayed Abigail would not suffer for the friendship between him and Nathan.

Chapter Twenty-Two

"My thanks for attending me," she said to Reuel as they returned to camp. His only response was to nod. He left her and returned back to Jesse, who sat alone. His legs were crossed, his eyes closed, and she knew he prayed. A pang of jealousy stole through her. She wished she could openly pray, but unless her prayers were answered and they were rescued from Suph's madness, she'd never be able to pray at will again.

It was strange to her that a few days ago she did not even know who this Creator of the heavens and earth was and now she could not imagine life without Him. How had the people of Judah turned their backs on the one true God? She supposed, just like she had rebelled against Suph, so had the people of Judah rebelled against God. She prayed that one day God would once again reign across the land.

A hand smacked against her arm and she cried out. She focused her gaze on her attacker. Suph's fingers dug into her flesh as he dragged her away. "What are you doing?"

She blinked her eyes, unsure of how to answer. "I have returned from seeing to my private needs. Certainly you would not deny me."

"You gaze upon the Levite as if he were the rarest of gems."

The mention of gems caused the jewel tucked beneath her tunic to warm against her skin. "I do not know of what it is you speak. I have not had the occasion to adorn myself with such things."

His fingers dug further. "You know well what it is I speak. You are to be my wife." His words seethed, sending chills over her skin. He had never once shown an obsession with her, only the kingdom he believed was hers.

"I know this, Suph, and have agreed. How am I to convince that murderous Levite to take me to the imposter if I do not show my affections?"

The captain released her and shoved his fingers through his hair as he paced. Abigail fought the urge to rub at the bruising of her flesh. Suph halted and pressed his mouth hard against hers. Abigail remained still uncertain of what it was she was to do. Just as quickly as the assault had begun, it ended. The corners of Suph's mouth curved upward and she wanted to scrub her hand over her lips. "I had to be certain you have not played me false. I can tell you have never before been kissed. Can tell the Levite has not tainted you."

The captain looked over his shoulder, his chest expanding out like a bird ruffling his feathers. His smile was like that of cat with a mouse. Abigail followed his gaze. Nausea slammed against her midsection and boiled upward. She sucked in a sharp breath. Even from where she stood, she could see Jesse's nostrils flare in anger, see the banded cords beneath the skin on his shoulders and arms ripple.

Abigail swallowed back the words threatening to spew from her mouth and released the tension curled in her fingers. Straightening her spine, she stared down her nose at Suph, commanding his attention. "Of course, I am not tainted. The Levite may have murdered my mother but he always treated me with courtesy. Whether or not he wished to kiss me is beyond my knowing."

In that she did not lie, for she did not know Jesse's reasons for kissing her. Suph firmed his lips into a hard line at her slight chastisement. The old Abigail would have cowered, but she pushed past him. Knees quaking, she kept her regal pose until she seated herself on the hard ground next to Nathan.

His comforting presence lured her to collapse against him, but she dared not. Instead, she smiled at her friend and ignored the fact that every man encamped watched her. Including Suph. And most assuredly Jesse. "I see you did not abandon me while I was gone."

Nathan stared at her. "Of course not, Abigail." He twisted a small twig between his fingers. "How long will you keep up this farce?"

Drawing in air, she blinked. "I do not know what you speak—"

"Do not lie to me, Abigail. Not if you hold dear our friendship. It is plain to see you cannot suffer the captain's attentions. Aye, he may be blinded, but it is written in the paleness of your cheeks." He reached out and clasped her fingers in his hand. "The way you shiver."

She sought out Jesse and willed the thunderous ache in her chest to go away. How long could she pretend to be who she was not? She shook her head. If Jesse was to return to his family alive, she had to continue. In this there was no choice.

Bowing her head, she dug the toe of her sandal into the hard ground. Dust lifted and carried on a breeze. If only it was as easy for her to disappear. "There may be no hope to save your brother, but if we can convince Suph to keep with my plan, if we can get Jesse to Jerusalem, then we can save him from the death the good captain intends to give him."

"You carry a heavy burden, Abigail, but there is no need."

If only it was true. If only she could deliver her burden elsewhere.

"Jesse has great affection for you. It shows when he looks upon you, in his fierce protectiveness over you."

She glanced across the camp toward Jesse. He stared at her, his eyes never wavering.

"If it had not been for the guard staying Jesse, he would have attacked Suph when he dragged you away." Nathan paused, and she turned her eyes upon him, waiting for him to continue. "Perhaps your cruel treatment was my fault. I visited with Jesse while you were gone."

"Why...why would you do such a thing?"

Nathan tossed the twisted twig he'd been mutilating away from him. "I trust Jesse. I do not trust Suph. And, although I trust you, I do not understand your misguided sense of responsibility. Jesse is a honed warrior, a genius at forming battle tactics. If anyone can save us, it is him."

"I don't know, Nathan. I don't want to risk..."

"Abigail, he has vowed to protect you before God and his family. He has greater affection for you than I have seen many a man for his own wife—all you must do is trust him. He's more than capable. He is not the babe you treat him as."

Nathan's words stung. Aye, of course Jesse was capable. She did not mean to imply otherwise. The more he healed, the more evidence she'd seen. But she could not remove the image of his battered body from her mind. The deep gashes, the pain he'd endured while she and Dara set the sutures. The wound on his head, an injury that had kept him unstable on his feet.

"He tells me Jonathan has been left alone in the cave."

"Left to die?"

"He is certain his brother and the Philistines have checked the area. He is confident Jonathan has been rescued."

Releasing the breath she held, some of her worries rolled off her shoulders.

"He also tells me Bilhah is alive." A grin split his face. "Dara was caring for her when Jesse left the camp."

She glanced back toward Jesse and allowed the love in her heart to spill across the space between them. Nathan believed Jesse held great affection for her, but he had not said he loved her. It did not matter, for she loved him. The tension in Jesse's jaw relaxed. The creases around his eyes softened and he smiled at her.

"What is it we do?" she asked.

Nathan winked at her. "Jesse says we wait. And of course pray."

The waiting would be hard, but she could pray.

~

Jesse leaned his head back. Even though his back was toward the setting of the sun, he still took pleasure in watching the lighter blues give way to the darker shades. He flicked his gaze toward Abigail sitting across the camp. Her arms wrapped around her legs, with her chin resting atop her knees.

For a moment he thought she watched the colorful artistry, but then the corners of her lips curved upward. His pulse kicked against his chest. Air lodged in his throat, burning his lungs. The suffocation was not like that when he found himself flat on his back during a sparring match with his brothers. This was much different, like basking in the warmth of the sun on a cool day. A feeling he wanted to hold on to for the rest of his days.

Her lids slid closed and remained so for several long seconds. When she reopened them, her silent apology and deep affection sought to embrace him. He clenched his jaw, strengthening his defenses against the love she conveyed. The emotion could not be returned, no matter how much he wished it.

She was a princess, he a warrior who had taken her mother's life. Their hearts could never meet as one.

Knowing it might cause her pain, he glanced at the sky and ignored the ache in his chest. The brightest star of the night had yet to meet its fullness, but Jesse knew exactly how close they were to Jerusalem. How far away they were from where his people camped. Whatever plans Abigail had made with the captain, he had changed them. The man was consumed with madness if he thought to enter Jerusalem's gates.

Whatever he intended, Jesse could not allow it.

Rolling his neck, he dropped his chin and risked a glance toward Abigail just as Suph pulled her to her feet. Jesse had wanted to rage when the captain had dared to take what she had not freely given. If it had not been for his guard halting him…who knows what Suph would have done, especially with his arms tied behind his back. Of course, that had never stopped him before.

His guard crouched beside him, a wooden cup in his hand. "There is something you should know."

Jesse raised an eyebrow and waited.

"When I took the princess to see to her needs earlier, there were signs of your people."

Surprise flowed through his blood. Not that his people were near, but that this guard, even after showing kindness, would risk treason in the eyes of his captain. The muscles in Jesse's neck twitched, but he didn't dare look for the giant Philistine and his brother, lest Suph notice and become suspicious. Instead, Jesse nodded. The guard pressed the cup to his lips.

"I do not know what it is he has planned, but it cannot be good for either you or the princess."

Jesse pulled his head back and scanned the occupants. Suph had not sent a single man to scout the area, which Jesse found odd and foolish, especially for a captain. There were ten men, not including himself and Nathan. One of those men seemed to be an ally. Would that change when it came to battle? If not, the odds were not terrible.

The *princess*...the word was like bitter herbs on his tongue. She was Abigail. His Abigail, but he should not, could not think of her in such a way. The more barriers he erected around his heart, the easier it would be to leave her when the time came.

"What is it you suggest?"

The instinct that often warned Jesse of deception did not prick his nape; however, he was not certain this man could be trusted with Abi—the princess. "I would see her away from here. We should not risk the captain using her as a shield again."

"I could take her to see to personal matters once again, but that would leave you to fight alone."

Jesse smiled at the guard. He would not tell him Nathan would have his back, especially since he was not certain if the guard was a true ally or a spy. "I have faced worse odds in my time and come out the victor."

The guard rested his arms against his bent knees. He toyed with the cup in his hand. "I suppose one does not gain a fierce reputation without earning it. The stories told among the guards are often exaggerated. The stories told about you rival those feats passed down through the ages of David's elite."

Lowering his voice, Jesse bent closer. "That is because we've had the same training as King David's elite. However, my brothers and I have spent much time training with the Philistines as well."

The guard firmed his lips into a thin line. The tip of his beard twitched as he hardened his jaw, and then he bent behind Jesse's back. "I will escort the princess now before the sun slips completely beyond the horizon."

The ropes tugged against Jesse's wrists as the guard cut them. The binding gave way, releasing his arms. Jesse was thankful for the waning light, yet he did nothing to begin working the feeling back into his limbs. The guard slipped his dagger beneath Jesse's thigh. "I would wait until it becomes darker, but not too long. Suph will wonder about the princess and send men out to search for us." The guard scratched his jaw. "However, that might not be a bad thing. It would lessen the numbers you have to deal with."

And increase the numbers seeking the princess. No, he would not tarry too long.

A muscle at the top of Jesse's jaw began to twitch as that instinct that not all was as it seemed roared to life. Perhaps he should refuse the guard's offer to whisk Abigail away. What if Ianatos and Isa weren't nearby? What if this man remained loyal to the captain?

He drew in a long breath. He knew this land better than most, knew how to track his enemies even in this barren area. Besides, even if this guard had lied about Ianatos, Jesse was certain he and his brother were watching. Waiting. "Even if the numbers were lessened, it would be a difficult feat for me to gain the upper hand."

The guard shook his head. "You said—"

"Aye, I know what I said. You forget I have been recovering from being the captain's sticking board." Leaving his hands behind his back, he rolled his shoulders. The guard flinched at the movement. "My muscles are weakened, strained from their bindings. I may be useless. However, if you take Abigail and hide among the brush near the creek..."

"If something goes awry, that is the first place he will look for us."

"Even if we outnumbered them, there would still be the possibility of a bad outcome. If my brother is near, as you say, he will see to Ab—the princess's safety."

The guard unfolded from his crouch. He scrubbed his hand over his bearded chin. "I will pray we find favor with God Almighty."

Craning his neck, Jesse considered the man. Perhaps he was a friend. Only time would tell.

Chapter Twenty-Three

Another tear leaked from her eyes. By now the sleeve of Jesse's tunic, which still carried a hint of sandalwood, was damp with her sorrow. Suph had witnessed another instance of what he called "a foolish desire for a Levite with no brawn." In his fit of jealousy, he had threatened Nathan with his dagger. Images of Jesse's wounds sickened her, and she was somehow able to convince the captain to spare her friend.

And then he sent him to sit with the other soldiers, leaving her alone with her thoughts. She had tried to pray. Pray for their freedom, pray for Jesse to glance her way. But he had avoided her, brushed away her affection like a bit of dust, leaving her confused and consumed by her erratic thoughts.

Did Jesse love her, or did he not? Would he abandon her or stay with her?

She had hoped... Suph had told her she was not going to Jerusalem. Which meant he had other plans for Jesse. Plans that would no doubt end his life.

That was a burden too heavy for her heart to bear.

A dark shadow fell over Abigail. "Princess?"

Recognizing Reuel's affectionate tone, she swiped the wetness from her cheeks. The smile she tried to force refused to show itself as another pair of tears fell.

"I've come to escort you to see to your needs." He held out his hand and pulled her to her feet.

"My thanks," she said in a whisper as she released his hand. The sooner she prepared for sleep the sooner tomorrow would come. She sniffed. The sooner the captain would abolish Jesse from her life. But then it seemed as if Jesse wanted nothing to do with her. She had hoped, prayed even, that Jesse would come to care for her as a man did a wife. Nathan's earlier words had caused that hope to soar like that of the giant bird. It did not take long for it to crash into the forbidding face of a mountain.

Perhaps Bilhah had been right. Maybe men did not give their affections as easily as women. Maybe not even at all.

"Princess?"

Blinking, she focused on Reuel. His eyebrows dipped in concern. "Are you ready?"

She folded her hands in front of her, tucking them into the arms of her tunic, and nodded. Before they took one step, Suph stayed Reuel with his sword. "Where do you think you are going?"

"The princess needs some privacy." Reuel glanced her way. Her cheeks caught fire with embarrassment. "I would escort her. It would not do for her to be ravaged by a lion."

Stepping to the side, Suph lowered his sword. "You will make haste."

Reuel dipped his head. "Of course, my Captain."

It wasn't until they stepped outside the reaches of the fire in the middle of the camp that she was able to breathe. Suph's madness seemed to be flourishing. Not even the peace of God's colorful display had been able to set her nerves at ease.

They walked for several minutes until they reached an area with shrubs. Reuel stepped in the midst, piercing the tip of his sword into the foliage. If her heart was not so heavy with sorrow she would have laughed at the staid guard warring with the little branches.

"I believe it is safe from lions."

She could not help but smile at his teasing, especially when it was unexpected.

"I will step away. Call out when you are finished."

Slipping behind the shrubs, she tipped her head back and looked at the darkening sky. Was it too early to spy the ladle Bilhah and Jesse had spoken of? If she had knowledge of the stars, she could find her own way to the safety of Jerusalem. Of course, she would have nobody to protect her from griffons.

"God of the heavens and the earth, will You bend your ear toward me? Will You hear my plea?"

~

Jesse's fingers itched to bully the captain the way he pushed Abigail and his men around. Patience had never been a virtue he was fond of, but Abigail's life depended on it. So, he had waited, even as Suph sent three of his men to follow Abigail and Reuel. What had been ordered, Jesse had not discerned, but given the captain's increasing agitation over the past few hours, his demands could not be good.

Unsure of how much time he had before Suph's minions caught up with the princess, he risked a glance over his shoulder. His timing had to be perfect. The men had to be far enough away in order to give him time to dispatch those remaining, yet not too close to dole out Suph's orders. From a battle stance he was grateful for the diminished threat, but his vow to protect Abigail roared in his head. He did not like sending her out into the night. Alone, with a possible enemy. He disliked it even more with the three vultures preying behind her.

The remaining soldiers sat near a small fire. Nathan between two of them chattering as if they were old friends, and perhaps they were. One of the men's hands twitched near his blade. Another looked like he was a great cat about to pounce.

What was Suph about?

Rolling his shoulders, Jesse worked his fingers, forcing blood to flow into his limbs. Fortunately, Nathan had caught his movements and gave a slight nod. Nathan claimed he wasn't a fighter, but Jesse prayed he would be ready.

He glanced over his shoulder once again. Abigail and Reuel had disappeared. The three minions remained visible.

His jaw clamped down. There wasn't much time. Jesse's patience had about reached the end of its tether. If he was to gain his freedom and go after Abigail, the time was now. *God in heaven grant me strength to do what I must and save Abigail.*

Before he was finished with the silent prayer the captain growled and snatched one of his men up by the neck of his tunic. "You dare to look at me?"

All the soldiers stood, and then froze with their hands near their hips. It took Jesse a moment to realize the captain had completely lost his wits. The spittle bubbling at the side of his mouth reminded Jesse of a rabid dog. Lifting his face toward the darkening sky, he gave his thanks to God for this small blessing. He drew in a fortifying breath that seemed to renew his strength. Jesse signaled to Nathan as he jumped to his feet, the small dagger in his hand.

One of the soldiers swung around. In two long strides, Jesse met the man face-to-face. Before the man blinked, he swept his foot to the back of the soldier's leg. The man fell to his back and stared blankly toward the sky. Nathan had two soldiers disarmed and his arms around their necks. Suph darted his gaze around, his knuckles white from holding on to his prey. He threw back his head and laughed. The sound was much like that of the sea when angered by the wind.

Suph cut down his own man and jumped toward Jesse. "You think to defeat me?"

Jesse shifted his weight, right foot forward, blade in his left hand. He kept silent and concentrated on Suph's slightest movement.

"I will rule this land. Athaliah promised Judah to me once we married." The captain's eyes narrowed to mere slits. "You took her from me, but you will not take Judah. It is mine." Suph darted forward. Jesse jumped back. The length of the captain's sword compared to Jesse's eating knife put him at a disadvantage. However, Jesse had his faculties.

"Just as Abigail is mine, Levite." He stabbed the tip of his sword into the air between them. Arching his back, Jessed sucked in his stomach.

"You are mad, Suph. You cannot rule when you pace like a coward."

The captain growled and rushed forward, his sword arced high. Jesse stepped to the side as he twisted around. He grabbed the captain's arm and, ducking, rammed his shoulder into his chest. Jesse rose to his full height, lifting Suph off the ground and flipping him over his shoulder. The sword clanked to the ground as Jesse twisted Suph's arm and bent his wrist, his foot on the captain's chest. "You should not act with haste, Suph. It'll only get you killed."

The captain fought against Jesse's hold, but Jesse clamped further down on his wrist until Suph's fingers near touched his forearm. The sound of horses' hooves beating the ground brought Jesse's head up. He shook the hair from his eyes and smiled. "Isa, Ianatos, it is about time you showed your faces."

"We had full confidence in you, little brother." Isa jumped to the ground.

"That we did." Ianatos swung his leg over the back of his horse and stepped down.

Suph laughed. "You have not won, Levite."

Jesse jerked his arm upward and forced more weight into the foot pressed against the captain's chest. "You are no longer a threat."

An evil glint sparked in his black eyes as he narrowed them. "You may have captured me, but you will not save your princess."

Chapter Twenty-Four

"Princess, we've not much time before the captain comes looking for us."

"A minute if you will." She squeezed her eyes closed and warred against the sobs filling her chest. "God, Jesse says You'll rescue those who call on Your name. I am calling, God. Please rescue us. I will go with Suph and become his bride, if only You save Jesse from the captain's wickedness."

"Princess!" Reuel's shout was followed by thumps like Dara pounding her herbs into powder.

"Reuel, whatever is the matter?" She pushed apart some of the branches and began to walk toward her guard.

Just as she was about to break free from the secluded area, an arm shot into the shrubbery and yanked her toward the creek. She dug her heels into the ground with no effect. She swatted at this hand. "Reuel, explain yourself."

He jerked her forward and tossed her over his shoulder.

"Reuel!" She pounded on his back. "What are you doing? Put me down."

"Not now, Princess." His voice was strained as if he wanted to shout but did not want to be heard. He jumped into the water and trudged through it. Her hair caught in the swirls and twisted, pulling her from his shoulder. She smacked the palm of her hand against his back as he climbed the other side of the bank.

"Please, put me down."

His chest heaved as he gulped in air. "I cannot do that, Princess."

The hiss of refined iron slicing through the air sang above her thundering pulse. "Put the princess down."

Abigail froze as her mouth fell open. She waited for several heartbeats, waited to hear the deadly tone, but not even the night creatures stirred. Reuel's grip fell slack and she slid to the ground. She twisted around and pushed her hair from her eyes. Before she could catch her breath, Reuel shoved her behind his back and unsheathed his sword.

Clinging to the back of Reuel's tunic, she shivered in fear. What was going on? She recognized their attackers as two of Suph's men. Why were they here?

Reuel widened his stance and raised his sword. She lost hold on him and her footing on the edge of the bank. She fell right into the water. The coldness seeped into her tunic, swirled around her neck as she tried to claw her way to the other side. Her fingers dug into the muddy bank as she started to climb. She was met by a pair of sandals and hairy legs. She craned her neck but could see little through the drape of her soaked hair.

Strong hands gripped her upper arms and pulled her out of the water. She brought up her hands and once again pushed her hair from her face. She sucked in a sharp breath as she looked into the cold eyes of Suph's second in command.

"Hello, Princess."

She wriggled and kicked at his shins, but he turned her so her back was against his chest and pressed a blade against her throat, cutting off her scream.

"Toss your sword aside, Reuel." The hardness of his voice vibrated through her. She clutched at his arm, trying to loosen his hold. His hot breath fanned her ear. "Halt right now or I will kill the princess."

Reuel's gaze filled with apologies as he tossed his sword to the ground. None of this was his fault. That could be laid at the madness plaguing Suph. If they were here, had something happened at camp? Had something happened to Jesse? She renewed her struggle and the blade bit deeper into her neck. A tear slipped from her eye as a warm rivulet of blood slid down her neck. Reuel jumped into the creek; the other two guards jumped on top of him.

"Halt! I warned you, Princess. I will not do so another time. The captain no longer has need of you." He loosened his hold and she gasped for air. "Bind his hands and feet, then leave him in the water."

"No!" She twisted around, swinging her arms wide and hard. The guard's hold slackened and she fell into the water next to Reuel, who was being held by the other two guards.

"Grab her."

She fought against the water and tried scrambling away. One of the soldiers grabbed the back of her tunic. His arm caught around her midsection, forcing the air from her lungs. He straightened and pulled her out of the water.

"Leave her be."

Abigail blinked and tried to peer through the wayward strands of hair once again dangling in her face. "Jesse?"

"Aye, Princess." There was a bit of commotion, which she could not see through her hair and the near dark night, before the man released her. Her body rocked forward and she fell back into the creek, pebbles poked her knees. She shoved the hair from her eyes. Jesse stood on the edge of the bank, a sword raised high. She sucked in a breath at the magnificent sight. He truly looked like the fierce warrior Jonathan and Nathan had warned her about. However, he was not frightening as she'd suspected. Or perhaps he was to the men standing around her, but to her he was gloriously beautiful.

But then she knew the man beneath the corded brawn. She knew the curve of his lips when he smiled and his compassionate heart for his people. She knew his honor and his kindness. The touch of his lips. Any woman would be fortunate to call him husband. Especially her, a discarded princess with no future to speak of. No alliance with kings and kingdoms, very little family…

Would that be enough for Jesse, or would he be like Suph and use her to gain Judah? Aye, she knew the answer. Jesse was more likely to disappear into the sunset rather than suffer palace life.

Suph's second in command lurched forward. A large arrow struck the ground between his feet. Abigail rose and the moving water rushed around her hips, rocking her with the force. Her tunic clung to her like a newborn kitten. For the first time she noticed Jesse was not alone. Isa and Ianatos, as well as several large shadows, surrounded them.

"Let Reuel go." Jesse's tone gave no quarter. The guard confining Reuel released him and then moved out of the water. Reuel grabbed hold of her hand and helped her onto the bank. She had hoped to fall into Jesse's comforting arms, to hear the sound of his pulse beat beneath her ear, to feel his heart with her palm. But even in the waning light she could see Jesse's gaze travel from her feet to her head. His lip curled and his eye twitched in what seemed like irritation.

Releasing a sigh, she pushed past him.

~

The red trail of blood sliding down Abigail's neck filled him with a rage he'd never known. The hurt and anger in Abigail's eyes pulled his nerves taut. As much as he longed to gather her in his arms, he could not. Not yet. Mayhap never.

Suph's second in command glared at Abigail's back as she moved between them. His nostrils flared, his hands clenched at his side. Just as she was almost out of reach, the man grabbed hold of her arm, twisting it behind her back. With his other hand he clutched her to his chest. "The captain will pay a nice ransom for her."

Jesse narrowed his eyes and forced his pulse to calm. "Your captain is no longer an issue."

A hint of surprise flickered in his eyes.

Shaking his head, Jesse took one stride forward, his gaze focused on Abigail's and the pain radiating there. "Did you think your captain allowed me to go free? I think not."

The guard trembled and turned to the side. "There are others. Faithful followers of Athaliah who will rise up and conquer your false king."

"Then they, too, will be dealt with." Jesse took another step. Holding Abigail in front of him, the guard twisted further. An arrow hissed through the air, piercing the guard's shoulder. The man jerked with a howl and Abigail screamed as he released her. She stumbled back. Jesse reached out and grasped her arm, pulling her from another attack. He handed her off to Isa and wrapped his hand around the man's upper arm. Ianatos and his men gathered the other two prisoners.

"Hold still, and I'll remove the arrow." Jesse guided him to a place where the water was not so deep. "Sit."

Jesse held on to him as he plopped to the ground with a moan. Cupping his hands, he scooped some frigid water and poured it over the front of the wound, and then the back. "I may not like you, but even so, I don't relish what I'm about to do."

The man glared and then shrugged. Jesse motioned for one of the Philistines to hold him still as he broke off the back of the arrow. The man helped. Jesse inspected the exit wound. "It is fortunate for you the head pierced through, else I'd have to dig it out."

Fortunate, too, Abigail had not been injured by the arrow. A hand's width of the tip of the arrow poked through the front of the man's tunic. Even just the tip could have caused grave injury. Death, if it pierced the right spot.

He pressed down on the man's shoulder, grasped the shaft and pulled. The man grunted and growled, but he kept his wits about him. After cleansing the wound with more water, Jesse helped the man to his feet. He gripped his arm to keep him from escaping.

He was glad to be done with Suph. Glad that, soon, all would be right in Judah. His only regret was that his time with Abigail would end. He would take her to Jerusalem as he promised, and then he'd go back to taking care of Ma-Maw and protecting Judah when the need arose. Of course, some of his duties included attending Jehoiada, which meant a possibility of seeing Abigail. Perhaps he could finally convince Ma-Maw to move to Manna. Save himself the ache of wanting to talk to Abigail. To hold her hand. To kiss her while watching the sun rise. The sun set.

He glanced toward the western sky. The last of the pink hues clung to the night. It was as if the sun wished to hold on to the day. Much like Jesse wished to hold on to Abigail.

Reuel paced back to Jesse, his hands hanging at his side, his eyes darting around. Thorns pricked the back of Jesse's neck. What had this man nervous? "You did well, Reuel. My thanks for protecting Abi—the princess."

He shook his head. "I did not do so well, else we would not have been captured."

"A traitor and a coward," Suph's second in command cried.

Jesse burrowed his fingers around the man's arm to still his voice. "She was not killed."

"Another moment and I would have killed her. Next time I will not hesitate."

"You will hush. It is fortunate for you she was not injured beyond a few scratches."

Reuel hung his head. The thorns pricking Jesse's neck raced down his spine and clawed through to his stomach. "What has happened to Abigail? Is she well?"

"The princess, she, uh…" He shook his head before looking Jesse in the eye. "She's fainted."

Air expelled from Jesse's lungs as he peered through the dark. Abigail hung limply in Isa's arms. Jesse curled his fingers against the jealousy boiling in his blood, which was ridiculous considering Isa loved his young wife more than his own life. He forced his body to calm, his muscles to relax. "She has been through quite an ordeal."

Reuel reached up and scratched his bearded chin. "There's a chill in the air and the cold water…"

"Aye, that is enough to make one faint." Although, Jesse had never heard of such a thing, unless their body had been weakened by sickness. Had the nick to her throat been deeper than he expected? He dug his fingers into his prisoner's muscles. "If anything happens to her, I will personally see you suffer," Jesse growled.

"It was nothing he did. The arrow—"

Jesse jerked his prisoner around and probed the wound on his back and then the front. He'd already discarded the pieces, but he knew a good portion had protruded from the man's chest. He pushed the man toward Reuel and strode the distance to where Isa cradled Abigail.

"Isa!"

His brother stopped and turned. In two long strides, Jesse tore her from his brother's arms. Her tunic was soaked, but she did not shiver with cold. "Your cloak."

Isa removed his cloak and draped it on the ground. Jesse laid her down and turned her to the side. Crimson seeped from the wound on her shoulder. Isa knelt beside him. "It looks to have hit the bone."

Jesse gently rolled her onto her back and smoothed the hair from her face. He drew his finger over her eyebrows, along the curve of her cheek until he met the nick on her throat. He gave in to his longing and pressed his lips to hers. The clammy skin beneath his touch worried him. Her lack of shivers left him chilled. He wrapped Isa's cloak around her and lifted her into his arms.

"She is strong, Jesse. She will be fine."

Jesse prayed his brother was right. Although her wounds seemed to be minor, he'd seen men die of lesser inflictions. He unfolded his length and stood, cradling her next to his heart. He needed to get her to Jerusalem, to Jehoiada, where she'd be far from harm and receive the truth she longed for. He needed to get her to Jerusalem before he decided he didn't care if she was a princess and never let her go.

"Isa, we are not far from the city gates. I would see her to her home this night."

His brother shifted his weight as he glanced toward Jerusalem. Ianatos approached, his arms crossed over his chest. "I will be at rest once these scoundrels are locked away."

"I am not certain, the sun has disappeared," Isa said.

Ianatos tipped his head back. "There is little to light our way."

"Then we will follow the stars."

Chapter Twenty-Five

Abigail snuggled deeper into the soft cushion. It seemed like weeks since she had slept on something other than the hard ground with nothing to cushion her head but simple sheepskin. She stretched her arms and halted at the pain in her shoulder. Flashing her eyes open, she tried to recall how she'd come to be hurt.

She scooted back against the fluffy pillows until she sat upright. Her arm hung loose at her side. Reaching across her body, she probed the area of pain and wrinkled her nose at the familiar scent of honey. Memories bombarded her. Reuel in the water. Jesse free, standing on the bank. Suph's second in command twisting her arm behind her back. The jarring impact of an arrow as it hit.

Relaxing, she leaned back against the pillows. Her eyes focused on the fine purple cloth draped over the bed. Walls of rich fabric surrounded her. Although she recognized many of the palace noises out in the court, she was certainly not in her own chambers, for her bedding had not been so luxurious.

How had she come to arrive here? Where was Jesse?

A light sound of sandals hitting the marble floor approached. The fabric parted and the most beautiful woman she had ever seen sat on the edge of the bed, a chalice in her hand.

"I see you are awake."

Abigail grasped the cup the woman offered her and gave her a slight smile. Who was she? Was she here to harm her? A friend of Suph's or Jesse's?

The woman's tinted lips curved upward. "I see you are cautious, as you should be. I am Jehosheba."

Blinking, Abigail tried to recall if she'd ever heard that name.

"Your father was my father. Your brother, my brother."

"My sister?"

"I see you do not know me. I am not surprised. Your mother whisked you away from our shared chambers when you were young."

"Are there others?"

"Sisters, you mean?" At Abigail's nod she continued. "There is one other but she was given in marriage to a man in Israel. I have not seen her since before our brother's death."

"I believed I had nobody left but Bilhah."

Jehosheba patted Abigail's hand. "I know it may seem as such. There has been much dissension amongst our family. Jesse tells me you long for the truth, and you shall have it." Jehosheba rose and pulled the curtains back, tying them to the carved wooden posts. "If you are well enough, a bath is ready. You must be tired from your days in the wilderness. Once you are revived, we will go to my house and attend my husband and your nephew. Then you will have the answers you seek."

Abigail knotted her fingers in the folds of her tunic as her sister neared the door. "Jesse, where is he?"

The corners of Jehosheba's mouth curved upward. "He has gone home." Abigail's heart thudded to a halt. "But he will return when it is time for our evening meal."

"He will?"

"Yes, dear sister. His home is not far from mine."

A renewed sense of hope filled Abigail. She swung her legs over the edge of the bed. "I believe I am ready for that bath now."

"Of course. I will send someone in to assist you."

Abigail planted her feet onto the cool marble and rose.

"My, I heard you were a graceful creature and now I see for myself the truth."

Heat crept up Abigail's neck, into her cheeks, burning her ears. "My thanks."

Jehosheba glided back toward her and embraced her for a long moment and then pulled back. "It is good to meet you,

Abigail. I had prayed often for God to protect you. When Shema died—"

"You knew of Shema?"

"Aye, she had been my nurse, too. When your mother had you removed from our chambers, Shema volunteered to care for you." Jehosheba glanced out the open widow. A solemn look flashed in her brown eyes. "She was the only one willing to bear...to leave the rest of us."

Abigail worried her lip. She'd often heard the whispers behind her back about the color of her eyes. Some believed she would cast a curse if she was crossed. Was that what Jehosheba meant? "Bear what?"

Jehosheba squeezed her fingers. "Soon you will have your answers. Do not fret, Abigail. God's ways are always higher than our own, even in the midst of tragedy.

"Now, how would you like to see some familiar faces?"

Abigail felt her brow crease in confusion. Before she could ask who that would be, Bilhah glided into the room, Micah beside her.

"Cousin!"

"Princess, you are well? I took care of the cub like you asked." Micah leaned closer and lowered his voice. "I'll sneak him in later for you to see."

"Ach, do not crowd the child, let me see what she's gotten herself into." Dara pushed between them, a toothless grin beaming at Abigail.

Abigail's heart filled near to bursting with love for these people. The only person missing was Jesse.

~

Jesse tugged on his outer tunic for the third time since he had arrived at Jehoiada's. The white stone seemed to close in on him as he paced the walled courtyard and waited for the high priest. Waiting to make his intentions clear where Abigail was concerned.

The fear he experienced as she lay unconscious and bleeding made him realize how much he cared for her. Aye, loved her deeply even. The fear of losing her was kin to racing into battle unarmed.

"Ah, I see you have returned. You look much improved, my friend." Jehoiada limped into the closed courtyard, leaning heavily on a staff. "I must thank you again for seeing my wife's sister safely returned. She was quite upset when we realized Abigail was no longer at the palace."

Jesse thought of his sister Lydia and how sorrowful he would have been if anything happened to her. "I am grateful to have been of service."

"My wife has seen Abigail. They will arrive to break our fast together."

Jesse's blood thundered with anticipation. She was his sun to his morning sky. "Then she is well?"

Jehoiada smiled. "Aye, that she is. Sore, from what my wife tells me, but well considering her ordeal." His hand clenched around the polished wood of his staff; a serious expression lined his eyes. "We have spoken of her future. My wife and I have considered suitable husbands."

Jesse's teeth ground together. "Do you not think it is too soon? She has escaped a scoundrel who would use her for her royal position."

"And that is the reason I must secure her a husband. The sooner she is married, the better for Judah. We cannot risk another man zealous for power to use her."

Emotions he was uncomfortable with warred within Jesse's thoughts. Years of training for difficult tasks had not prepared him for this. He knew how to serve his people. Knew how to fight for what seemed right by God. But how did a man fight for the woman he loved, especially when he had no rights to her future? A muscle in his jaw ticked. He crossed his arms and pretended to inspect one of the many rare plants hanging from an upper balcony.

"Of course we will consider Abigail's wishes."

"Of course," Jesse said through gritted teeth.

Jehoiada tilted his head as he drew his fingers down his gray beard. "Jesse, do you have something to say in this matter?"

Jesse dropped his gaze to the high priest. How was he to tell this man he loved his wife's sister? To many, love held no consequence within the bounds of marriage. Even though the high priest seemed fond of his wife, Jesse had no idea where he stood on the thoughts of love. What if Jehoiada rejected Jesse's suit?

It did not matter. Now was not the time for reservations. His heart told him as much. "It is not my place. However—"

"You have arrived early, Jesse, son of Isaiah."

An ache filled his chest until it restricted the air in his lungs. His confession lodged in his throat. Why could he not just say the words? Was he doomed to hold his love for Abigail in secret?

Releasing a sigh, he pasted on a smile and turned to greet Jehoiada's wife. What he saw stole his breath and thundered his pulse. Abigail stood beside her sister, outshining the priest's wife. Fine purple linen draped over her shoulders, hugging her curves unlike her borrowed tunic had. The gold belt cinched around her waist accentuated the flare of her hips. A thin veil hid her tresses, from his view. It did not matter, however, for each glint had been branded into his mind's eye. The purple-and-gold material framing her face only made her eyes more prominent. The greens, now more gold, seemed to catch fire. Much like his signet stone.

His gaze fell to the base of her neck, to the rounded protrusion beneath her tunic where he was quite certain his signet rested. The corner of his mouth twitched as he fought against the joy bubbling up and curving his lips. Did she wear it as a sign of hope between them, or did she wear it only because she liked the gem?

Moisture grew on his palms as his need for the answer expanded in his heart. The feeling was like the surge of excited nervousness as he prepped for battle, only now so much more was at stake. It was not a matter of life or death, or loss of limb—it was a matter of purpose, of existing on this earth solely to serve the Almighty and to love her.

Twin spots blushed her cheeks as she bowed her head. Jesse gathered his wits. "Jehosheba, Abigail."

Jehosheba, in her gold and purple tunics, glided toward him and embraced him. "I cannot thank you enough for returning my sister to me." She released him, moved toward Jehoiada and tucked her arm around his elbow. Although she was much younger than her husband, a genuine smile graced her mouth. "My husband will see to it that you are well compensated."

Jesse shook his head. "There is no need. I would not receive payment for serving God and Judah."

Abigail sucked in a breath. It was barely discernible; however, Jesse caught it, felt it strike against his tender heart. He snapped his gaze to her. She shielded her eyes as she dipped her head. Her shoulders trembled. What was it he had said to upset her?

"We thank you anyway, Jesse, son of Isaiah."

Jesse tore his gaze from Abigail

"That we do, Jesse. You have done your family proud." Jehoiada patted his wife's hand. "Of course, I would have expected no less from Ari's brother. You are much like him, you know? I was not pleased to lose him. We are in need of good men like you to guard the royal house. Perhaps you would consider being a part of Abigail's personal guard until we can decide on a husband for her." A strangled noise mumbled from Abigail, drawing Jehoiada's discerning eye. "Unless, of course, you are not prepared to marry, my dear sister. You have had quite the ordeal."

Straightening her spine, Abigail held her head high. Fire sparked in her eyes as she glared at Jesse. "I would be honored to serve God and Judah, even if I must leave my home and my newly found family."

Her words were like a jab into his healing wounds. His hope for a future with her as his wife plummeted to the marble beneath his feet. The white stone forming the walls of the courtyard seemed to press against him. He clenched his fists before folding them behind his back. He forced calm into his blood, even as he drank in one last look at her to forge her into his thoughts, to keep her with him in the days and years of solitude to come. He glanced at the high priest. "I am humbled by your request, Jehoiada. However, I am afraid I cannot accept your offer."

Jesse bowed. "Jehoiada, Jehosheba." He paused, unfolded his length and strode toward Abigail. He grasped her clammy, trembling fingers in his. He gazed into her eyes. "Abigail, it has been an honor. May the one true God guide your path and if you shall ever waver in your faith in Him, watch the night sky as the sun slips past the horizon." Tears brimmed on the edge of her lashes. If she had not been a princess...he bowed over her hand, pressing his lips to the softness. Rising, his eyes halted on the gem nestled beneath her tunic. Everything that he was, a Levite, his very identity was corded around her neck. With one snap of the cord he could retrieve it, but it did not matter. Without her, his existence would be hollow. Nothing.

He squeezed her hand. "God be with you, Princess."

Her hand fell to her side when he released it. He stepped back and began to turn on his heel.

"Jesse, will you not stay to break our fast?" A hint of wonder and confusion colored the usually serene Jehosheba's voice.

He shook his head. "I fear I have duties to attend. Preparations for my journey home."

"You speak of Manna?" Jehoiada released his wife and braced a shaky hand against Jesse's shoulder.

"Aye, it is time."

"Then you must share one last meal with us before your travels."

The brush of soft linen as Abigail moved to gaze upon a plant captured his heart. "This time is for your family. I will not intrude on what little time the princess has with her sister and King Joash."

Jehoiada pressed his lips into a firm line and nodded. "Then I bid you well and safe journeys."

"My thanks, Jehoiada. May God hold you tightly to His bosom as you seek to restore Judah back to Him."

Chapter Twenty-Six

Abigail sniffed in a shuddering breath as Jesse slipped out of the courtyard. She had been so hurt at his mention of God and duty to Judah. Had he only returned her to save the kingdom? Had he not felt anything for her? Not even friendship?

A comforting arm embraced her. Abigail laid her head against Jehosheba's shoulder as unwanted tears slid from her eyes.

"You have been through quite the ordeal. You do not have to marry, dear sister. Not as yet, if you do not choose."

Pulling back, Abigail swiped her fists beneath her eyes. "I do not mean to weep. It is a weakness my mother was never fond of."

Jehosheba lifted Abigail's chin with her fingers. "Tears are not always bad. There is time to mourn."

"You are mistaken." Abigail stepped away and crossed her arms over her midsection. "I do not mourn the loss of my mother."

"We can mourn many things, Abigail. People who have passed from this earth, a wounded bird." The corners of her mouth curved upward at Abigail's disbelief. "Yes, I know of your compassionate heart for broken vessels. The twins often informed me of your escapades, and of your mother's cruelty. I am sorry I was unable to protect you. Will you forgive me?"

Abigail flung herself into her sister's arms. "There is nothing to forgive. You cared. Even if I did not know of your existence, you cared."

"As I do now. Your heart weeps for lost love, does it not?"

Pulling back, Abigail shook her head.

"I see the pain in your beautiful eyes, dear sister."

She dropped her gaze toward the marble beneath her sandaled feet. Her eyes had forever been a curse to her. Unusual, some would say. Evil. Jehosheba brushed her hand down Abigail's cheek, once again lifting her face. "You are beautiful. Do not let anyone tell you different. Your mother feared you, feared your beauty would overrule the power she held over men like Suph."

Abigail shook her head.

"This I know. She often ranted her fears to her personal servants. It is why she kept you hidden. You must not allow her behavior and jealousies to rule your future, Abigail. Do not allow her rejections to cause misunderstandings in the matters of your heart. If you love—"

"King Joash, may I introduce you to your aunt, Princess Abigail." Jehoiada stood beside a child in kingly attire. She'd known him to be no more than a child, but he was nothing more than a mite with a head full of dark curls. She had not cared whether this child was, in truth, the rightful heir. She had never wanted to rule Judah, had never been groomed for such an honor; all she had wanted was the truth of the part Jehoiada had played in her family's demise. But even that had lost its desire in her heart as she'd come to love Jesse. However, now that she looked into reflections of her brother's eyes, she knew with no doubt this was her brother's son, a child Jesse had sought to protect, one in the care of the high priest.

This young child, her own flesh and blood, was the rightful King of Judah, which meant Jehoiada had not killed her cousins. Her mother had, which meant Jesse…had doled out justice. And rightfully so.

Jesse was a man of honor, a man who took his vows to God and Judah seriously. A man who took all of his vows seriously. Including the one he'd made to protect her, even though she could have been a threat to the good of Judah.

She recalled the somber farewell. The sadness in his eyes. Was it possible he thought of her beyond duty? Did he feel in his heart the same as she did? The stone beneath her tunic began to warm. She pressed her palm to her chest.

"It is a pleasure to meet you, Abigail."

Startled, Abigail focused on her king and smiled. She dropped to her knees and bowed.

"Please, rise. It is only to the great Almighty that anyone should bestow such an honor."

Lifting her head, she gazed on this child innocent of the suffering her mother had caused. Before she could halt herself, she pulled him into her arms and hugged him. "It is a pleasure to meet you as well, Joash."

Jehoiada laughed. "Shall we eat?"

She unfolded her length and rose. "Jehoiada, Jesse nearly died to protect Joash. I believe the House of Judah should honor him with a meal before his departure."

"As you know, Abigail, he refused my offer."

"He will not refuse me." Joash's soft childlike tone washed over her.

"No, he will not." Abigail smiled, her heart much improved, knowing she'd get one last chance to discern his feelings for her.

Jehoiada tapped his staff against the marble floors. A servant rushed forward. "Send four temple guards and four palace guards to retrieve Jesse, son of Isaiah."

The thin man bowed and left to do Jehoiada's bidding. Abigail pulled her eyebrows together. "Why the guards? Jesse is no threat."

"No, but it is obvious his attendance is of some importance to you, and so to our king." Jehoiada pulled on his beard, and then smiled. "I did not wish risking his refusal. The temple and palace guards will make it clear his refusal is not an option."

"My thanks, Jehoiada."

Jehosheba tucked her arm through her husband's and smiled. "You may thank my husband once he completes the negotiations for the bride contract with Jesse."

Abigail stepped back, her hand to her throat as her courage began to wane. "I do not even know if Jesse—"

"Aye, he loves you, Abigail. There is no doubt. Now if only he will allow his pride to be pushed to the side long enough to accept that he is a proper husband for you."

~

Jesse hunched his shoulders as he walked back toward the home he shared with Ma-maw. He did not respond to the peddlers selling their wares as he usually did. There was no joy in him to jest. Only sadness. Aye, he wasn't sad to be leaving Jerusalem so much as he was that he'd never see Abigail's glittering eyes or the alluring smile too big for her cheekbones.

He recalled the chill of her hand beneath the press of his lips. His farewell had been like losing his sword arm, only worse. Placing one foot in front of the other seemed difficult now, and he did not perceive the action getting easier. Inhaling a painful breath, he sniffed. Never one to shed tears, he clenched his jaw and fought the sadness trying to consume him.

Feet pounded the cobblestones behind him. He glanced over his shoulder at the scuffling commotion. Four temple guards, followed by four palace guards, pushed their way through the throng. Jesse looked around and then toward the city walls. What had caused these men to become alarmed? Was the city being attacked?

Abigail.

His heart pounded as he started back toward Jehoiada's home. The guards surrounded him, their hands on the hilts of their swords. One of the palace guards stepped forward. "Jesse, son of Isaiah?"

Jesse crossed his arms over his chest. "Aye. What is this about? Is all well?"

"You are to come with us."

He drew his eyebrows together. "Why?"

Uriel, a temple guard he had trained and fought with, stepped forward. "Jesse, King Joash has ordered it."

Every muscle in his body tensed, prepared to fight. He forced himself to relax and allowed the guard to escort him. He wasn't surprised when they led him toward Jehoiada's home, since that is where they were to break fast. What did surprise him was that Jehoiada met him in the courtyard instead of King Joash.

"You may leave," Jehoiada addressed the guard, and then waited until they each filed out of the courtyard.

The high priest, no longer toting his staff, folded his hands in front of him. Where the man had looked old and frail only moments before, he now looked imposing. Almost frightening.

"It has come to my attention that we have some unfinished business concerning Abigail."

Jesse searched the shadows to see if she was hidden amongst them.

"As her kin, she is my responsibility."

Jesse did not wish to take part in the discussion of Abigail's future husband. His heart could not take it. "What is this about, Jehoiada?"

Jehoiada tilted his head as he drew his hand down his beard. "I am certain I do not need to ask, however, for formality's sake, I will. Do you love Abigail?"

Jesse's heart lurched, hitting hard against his chest.

Jehoiada smiled. "I see that you do."

Shaking his head, Jesse tried to make sense of the conversation.

"You are not a king, nor do you have vast amounts of land." Jehoiada paced with an unsteady gait in front of him. "However, I fear she loves you and she—"

"She what?" He shook his head again. "How do you know this?"

"Jehoiada is a very discerning man, Jesse."

He swung around. His heart thundering in his ears, he held his breath, afraid she'd disappear if he moved. Afraid he had misheard Jehoiada's words. She was as beautiful as she was only moments earlier, perhaps even more so.

"Your tears—"

"You cried, Abigail?" Jesse rushed forward, cupping her hands in his. He searched her eyes for the truth. "Why? Does your wound pain you?"

She shook her head. "You...your farewell seemed so final. I could not bear the thought of never seeing you again, Jesse."

He dropped her hands. "And I could not bear watching another court you." A man could only face so much temptation before he broke, and he feared seeing the woman he loved marry another would push him over the edge. "That is why I must..."

Swiveling around, he rushed toward the archway.

"Jesse, please."

He continued, ignoring the tug on his heart and the way his palms burned from holding her hands. Two steps more and he would be free to suck air into his lungs. Free to release the anguish building inside.

"Guards! Halt that man!" Jehoiada's command was like a disabling blow.

Two guards blocked the only exit. Widening his stance, Jesse brought up his fists. The guards drew their swords.

"No!" The sound of Abigail's sandaled feet on the marble as she ran the distance had him clenching his fists further. She grabbed hold of his tunic and flung herself in front of him. His chest swelled with pride. If only he had the right to feel such an emotion.

Jehoiada stepped between the guards and Abigail with his hand raised. "Stand down."

The blood pulsing through Jesse's body refused to calm, especially since Abigail's palm now rested against his chest, her eyes pleading. "Please, Jesse, do not go."

He pressed his lips together, afraid if he spoke the tears pressing against the back of his eyes would flow.

Her head fell against his shoulder. The warmth of her palm burned through his tunic. "Please."

He closed his eyes. His arms wrapped around her, holding her to him. "Do not ask this of me. If you have any compassion for me, Abigail, do not ask me to watch you marry another."

"Jesse, it is obvious you misunderstand the reason you were called here."

Jesse glared at Jehoiada over Abigail's head and blew out a ragged breath. "Have mercy and do not tarry with your explanations."

Jehoiada waved the guards away. "I have asked you here to negotiate a bridal contract between you and Abigail."

Jesse's knees threatened to buckle, but he leaned back and lifted Abigail's gaze to his. "You would marry me?"

The corners of her mouth lifted. "Of course, Jesse, son of Isaiah. I love you and would have none other."

He pulled her back into his arms and pressed his lips against her forehead. "And I love you, my beloved, but I have no lands, no home to call my own."

Jehoiada chuckled. "I know this, but it does not seem to matter. Perhaps, you would consider living in the palace with your bride for a time. At least until the uprisings against

Judah have quieted. I do not doubt your abilities to protect her—however, I would not wish to take any chances either."

Jesse crooked his finger beneath Abigail's chin. "Is this your choice?"

"Aye, Jesse, my beloved, it is my choice."

He didn't need any more reassurance. Her eyes illuminated all the love he felt encompassing his being. "Abigail, Princess of Judah, will you share the rising of the morning sun and its setting with me for the rest of your days?"

She rose up on her toes, a mere breath between them. "I will, Jesse, son of Isaiah."

He closed the space between them and touched his lips to hers.

Epilogue

Thin gray clouds hovered near the eastern horizon as Jesse leaned against one of the pillars forming the roof of the portico. With Abigail nestled against him, and God at the center of their hearts, his purpose in life seemed complete. He smoothed her tresses behind the cup of her ear before dropping a kiss to the curve of her neck.

"Are you happy with your choice, Jesse?"

He tightened his arms around her midsection. What caused such a question? He rested his chin atop her head and smiled. "Have you doubts?"

She turned in his arms and gazed into his eyes. "Not about us. I wonder if you would not rather roam freely. To be out in the open. To watch the sun rise wherever you wish."

Lifting her chin, he pressed his lips to hers and then pulled back. "It is with you I wish to be, wherever that is, Abigail. What better way to watch God's gift as it crests the horizon than with the woman I love?" He kissed her again, this time deepening the caress until she melded against him with a sigh. He drew his lips along the side of her jaw and then nipped at her ear.

She tapped him on the shoulder. "We are not watching, Jesse."

He pecked her cheek, before turning her back in his arms. Together, they watched as the gray clouds gave way to the brilliant hues of the morning sun.

"I love you, Jesse. Thank you for showing me the one true God."

"I love you as well, Abigail. It was my great joy."

"Do you think we can share these spectacles God creates with others?"

An image of tiny girls with cedar-colored tresses and green eyes filled his heart. Only for a seed from her womb would he be willing to share these moments with her. "How about we compromise? We will tell others of God's mercies and how they are new each morning."

Her hand went to the curve of her stomach, covering his. "Dara tells me I am with child."

He twirled her in his arms and kissed her again. Pulling back, he knew a grin overwhelmed his face. "You and God have granted me the greatest of gifts, Abigail. I would be joyous to share these moments I have alone with you with our children.

"I love you, Abigail." He covered her mouth with his.

Don't miss His Master's Daughter. Read the first chapter here.

Chapter One

Near En Gedi, Judah
835 BC

Ari's heart hammered in his chest as the horses thundered toward the groves. Instinct had him reaching for where his sword should have been, a sword he had discarded years ago when he'd traded his life of a warrior for that of a bond servant. He'd been a fool to leave his weapons hidden away when danger lurked close at hand, but he could not very well play the servant dressed as a soldier.

It would do no good to dwell on this lack of foresight, even if it had almost got him killed years ago. Instead, he picked up a curved lava stone and prepared for battle.

He peered around the corner. The queen's soldiers brought their mounts to a halt on the dusty pathway, their eyes trained in the distance. Ari followed their line of sight and inhaled a sharp breath.

Sh'mira, his master's daughter, stood at the edge of the grove. She cradled a white flower in her palm, her nose mere inches from the petals with her eyes closed. He knew she was lost in the fragrance as she was wont to do and completely unaware of her audience.

Hefting an empty pot onto his shoulders, he straightened to his full height. With the lava stone firm in his palm, he stepped out of the shadows and made as if he were about his everyday chores.

Perhaps his presence would discourage the warriors from their wicked intent, for their arrival could result in nothing but evil. Ever since Queen Athaliah had killed most of the royal family near seven years ago—her sons, daughters and grandchildren—the royal guards had terrorized all of Judah. Stories of their infamous conquests had reached even this remote village, putting a fear into the hearts and minds of all. A fear that rivaled the fear of the fabled Leviathan and other sea monsters.

A horse snorted. Ari's feet wobbled on the pebbles as he worked his way toward the grove. He'd never feared a battle before and although his warrior instincts thrummed through his veins, his years out of service shook his confidence. Perhaps, it was the crude scar on his thigh, a reminder of his last encounter with the queen's men.

"You should not be here alone."

Mira turned, her lips tight, gaze guarded. "Who are you to tell me such?"

He sat the clay pot to the ground and broke off a dying branch. "A servant looking after his master's interest."

"I am a grown woman, able to care for myself." She jerked a withered limb from its mooring. "Just because I am *maimed*," she bit, "does not mean I'm helpless."

He dropped his hands to his sides. Her gaze a pool of desert water after a heavy rain. "I did not mean—"

This woman was far from helpless, he knew that.

"Did you not?" She tossed the branch into the pot. "You are forever following me around tending *my* duties. You would think Father bonded you to be my nurse."

"I only think to repay your kindness for tending my wounds when I first arrived."

"For seven years?" She let out a disgruntled sigh and walked further down the lane.

Ari grabbed her arm, turning her back to him. Her cheeks flushed and his warmed at the contact. He released her. Crossing his arms over his chest, he stepped back. "If not for you, I would have died. I would not have you meet the same fate." He tilted his head toward the guards high on their mounts.

She leaned forward, peering around one of the trees and then straightened. The length of her tresses brushed over his forearm like a feather. The flowery fragrance of henna blossoms tickled his nose. How had he not noticed this about her? Odd, one touch after all these years, and he was suddenly aware of how she smelled.

A whinny from the horse brought his head back to reality. He glanced over his shoulder and bit down on his tongue. The devastation left in the guards' wake, remained fresh in his mind even after all these years. The young king's mother had been badly used before they slit her throat. Fortunately, Jehosheba, the boy's aunt and Tama, Mira's cousin, who had been serving as a nurse in the palace, had the wits about them to take the babe from his dying mother, giving Judah hope for the future. A truth Mira did not know. "In their eyes, all women, young and old, are helpless."

Mira's gaze shifted toward the riders once again. "I will not cower before them."

Her lack of cowardice was worthy of any warrior. However, it was not courage that fueled her attitude. "Would your pride see your father brokenhearted?"

She sucked in a sharp breath. "I wonder how a man of your wisdom became destitute enough to become a servant."

The horses' hooves came closer. "As you know, I repay a debt of kindness. Your father offered me refuge when I was wounded. Come," he extended his hand toward the small village. "We must get you back within the walls of your home."

The sound of the muffled clops halted, replaced by the creaking of leather as the men dismounted. Ari's muscles tensed. He faced the pair of guards and forced his life's blood to an even rhythm. The men standing before him were the queen's own personal guards which meant they were on a mission much higher than destroying altars to God and keeping peace. Had they discovered the child survived?

"Looks like we've interrupted two lovers."

She squeaked. "You dare—"

Ari pierced her with a dark look and shoved her behind his back. He bowed his head. "Forgive my mistress."

*

Words clung to the tip of her tongue. Self-control had never been one of her gifts. The blame could be tossed at Ari's feet for causing her lack of speech. His humility had been replaced with an uncharacteristic bold protectiveness leaving her confused. Not to mention the touch on her arm had caused her knees to turn to honey and her toes to curl. Something Esha, the man seeking her hand in marriage, had never caused.

Who was this man who often offended her with his kindness? This man who insisted she was weak and helpless by his actions?

"She's distraught over the immature crop." Ari picked a budding green fruit from the tree as if to prove his statement.

"Your mistress, you say?" The taller of the two soldiers stepped forward and pushed Ari aside. He lifted his fingers and touched her hair.

Bile churned in her stomach. It was squashed when Ari grasped the guard's wrist and stepped back in front of her. Protecting her like a shield. The shorter of the two soldiers placed his hand on the hilt of his sword even as he took a step back.

The man laughed. "You are bold, slave."

"Servant. I am a servant." He dropped the soldier's wrist. "It is my duty to protect my master's property. Including his daughter's virtue." Ari seemed to grow ten feet taller and two feet wider. His bronzed skin gleamed in the hot sun. His stance and bearing caused both guards to shrink. How had she not noticed how strong and handsome he was? *Because he treats you like a crippled beggar.*

"If this woman's virtue is a matter of importance to her father, why does he allow her to venture away from her home alone and without covering her head?"

Mira bit down on her tongue. Her virtue was hers alone, not her father's. Not any man's. However, the law said otherwise. A law the guard did not recognize. She arched onto her toes and tried to peer over Ari's shoulder. His silky black hair lifted on a breeze, tickling her nose and forcing her back to her feet.

Ari shifted, blocking more of her view. "Forgive me, we were under the belief God's Law no longer mattered."

Laughter erupted from both the guards. "You are correct, slave. God is dead. The queen's law rules this land, along with the wooden idols she worships."

Hidden behind his back she couldn't see much, but she could see the tick in Ari's jaw, feel the heat emanating from his skin, the controlled anger exuding with each of his measured breaths. She knew he did not approve of Queen Athaliah's worship of idols made by men, knew he continued to worship God and keep His commands.

A low rumble vibrated from Ari. "Her—"

She fisted Ari's tunic in her hands, halting his words.

"Her father, my master is expecting us."

Mira relaxed her hold on his garment but kept her fingers pressed against his back. His solid presence brought her comfort in the midst of danger, and for once she was thankful for his interference.

"Your master can wait." The guard reached around Ari and grabbed a hold of her wrist.

www.ingramcontent.com/pod-product-compliance
Lightning Source LLC
LaVergne TN
LVHW012015060526
838201LV00061B/4322